<u>**Message to the reader**</u>
Welcome to Octairion, a land of faith, hope, and love. May your mind be open and your heart free. Allow the spirit of this book to speak to you generously. May any and all feelings that arise be shown love, care, and acceptance. I hope this tale will comfort any pain and destroy all fear. Might this story forever change our world for the better. Thank you for your time. Enjoy the journey.

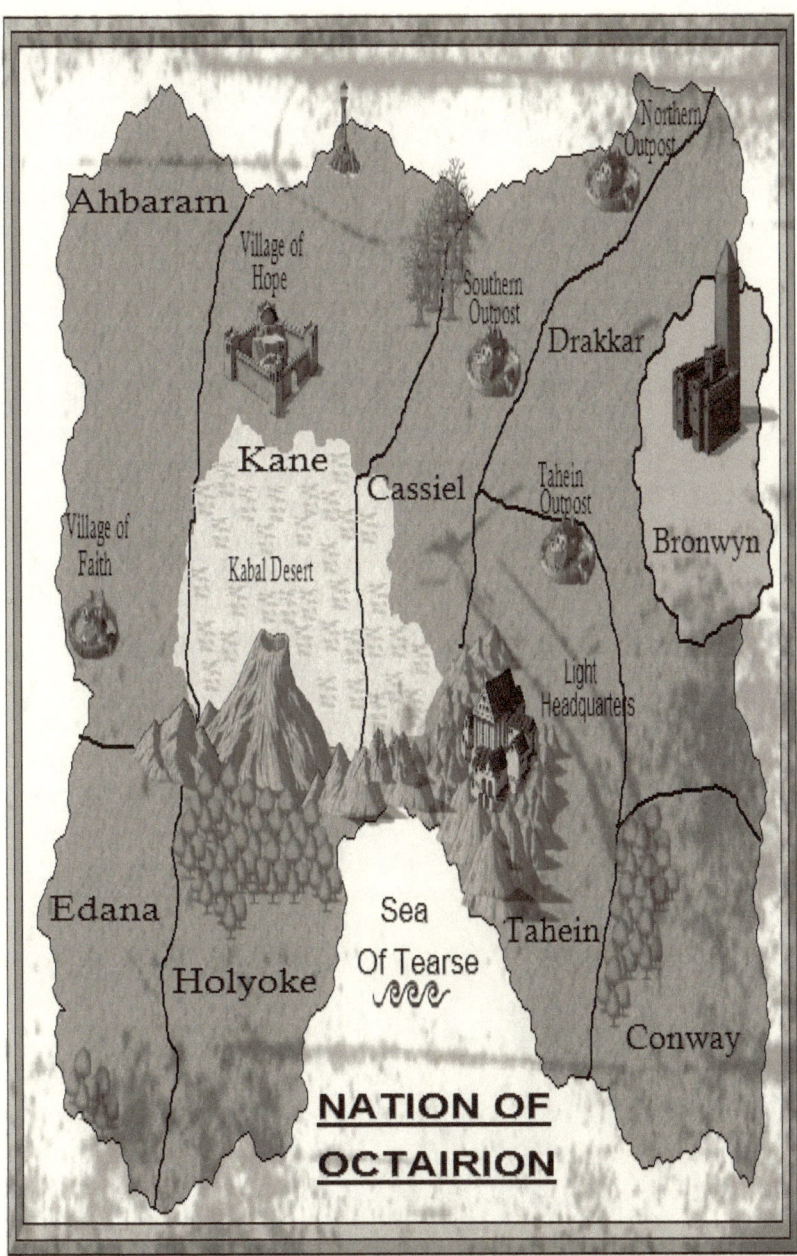

NATION OF OCTAIRION

BEAUTIFUL ROSE

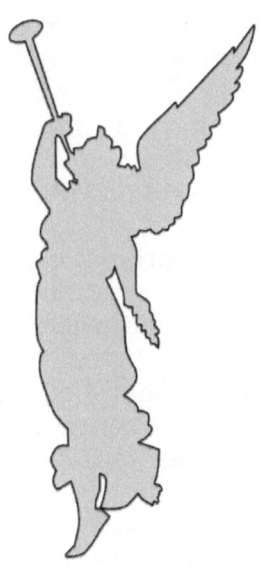

By Aaron Falagan

Aurea Publishing

Published by Aurea Publishing

This is a work of fiction.
Edited by Michaela Chane and Phil Wyman.
Any and all mistakes are mine.
Cover image created by Gracjana "vinegaria" Zielinska.
http://vinegaria.com/
Map of Octairion made with Campaign Cartographer 3.
Photos used in the book were taken from free clipart sites
around the web.

© 2015 Aaron Falagan

Aurea Publishing
196 Lafayette St.
Salem Ma. 01970
www.Aurea-Publishing.com

ISBN-13:978-0692417447

ISBN-10: 0692417443

Printed in the United States of America

First Edition

Dedicated to
Ayana, for inspiring me with your precious
heart,
to my mother Jodi, for giving me the
opportunity to chase my dreams,
and to Michaela, who has supported me
every step of the way.

Contents

<u>Acknowledgements</u>

I would like to acknowledge the countless individuals who have impacted my life. Dave Reece, Tim Brown, Bronwen Moyer-Newcott, and Melanie Bruechert, you helped me survive the wilderness.

David Hernandez and Ken Weekes, thank you for bringing me into the fold.

Kazuma Harima, you were closer to me than any other. Thank you for your beautiful soul.

Introduction:

Welcome Home

*S*taring deep into a dark chasm, silent and empty, she can't grasp the eerie feelings that are flooding her. She steps back and tries to shake off the confusion, but it won't budge. She stares deeper into this darkness and questions if she dares enter into the void. What, or who, could be inside this creepy cavern?

Long jagged spikes hang grimly around the mouth of the rocky cave, like the savage jaws of a shark waiting to swallow her whole. Trickling streams of water drool over the shiny metal deposits embedded in the cavern walls, like a starving predator ready to pounce. Scattered about are piles of busted boulders rearing knife like edges that should make her passage quite difficult to maneuver.

As she hesitates before the entrance an ice cold breeze bellows from the depths. Chilling jitters rumble inside her stomach like a quaking snow cap. She knows that one step is all that is needed. One step to change her life. A tension so powerful pulses through her body as her nerves tremble like a rattling skeleton. What is there to be afraid of? Possible danger, threatening spirits, or is it just fear itself? The same fear that has held her back her whole life?

Staring into the blackness she finally builds up the nerve to take the first step, and just as she does, BOOM! A white light shines from the opposite end of the cave. A shimmering beam of light that is so brilliant and enticing. Tiny gold orbs rocket throughout the cylinder shaped shaft. The zipping spheres move so quickly that she can barely lock onto the incredible little flecks. Mesmerized, she gazes into this amazing ray and can feel her spirit come alive.

Oddly enough, the puzzling beam does not illuminate the dark cave. It seems to be merely a guide. What could be the source of this light that is penetrating right through the thick darkness like sunlight through blackened storm clouds?

She raises her head into the stream and the warmth of the light on her face calms her as she approaches the unknown. She begins to slowly edge her way deeper into the mysterious cave, following the light beam as if it were a golden tether leading her to safety.

Is it a guiding light from her Angels? The hairs rise on the back of her neck as she feels the presence of the majestic beings hovering above her. Her confidence kicks in as she remembers the love of Great Spirit and how he has always protected her from day one. Although she has taken her bumps and bruises, he has never allowed her to be swallowed up by death.

Now walking faster and more focused on finding the source of this light, all fear fades away. Walking tall and determined, she continues to quicken her pace. Dodging sharp stones and sudden holes, she strides like a moth to a flame.

As she travels further into the dark tunnel a spooky curiosity twists her mind. *How deep is this cave?* she wonders. She quickly glances back and can no longer see the entrance, just the solitary beam of light disappearing into the endless blackness. Fear bubbles up and she is tempted to retreat, but she fights the distracting urge. *I have already come so far. I can't turn around now. I must continue,* she thinks filling herself with confidence. But how far has she really come?

Turning her head forward and fixating on the light, more determined than before she runs faster and faster. Her heart is racing like a wolf chasing its prey through the moonlit night. Her eyes widen as she targets her destination. Even faster, she continues to run until, BAM! She tumbles onto a staircase.

Dusting herself off, she looks up the bulky staircase to a door. The sparkling white light is shining from its keyhole. Without any hesitation she climbs up the creaky stairs to the door. Feeling her way around the cold wooden frame with her hands, she can feel all kinds of gems embedded in the massive door. She leans in close to the marvelous quarts and sapphire crystals that can barely be made out in the dim light. She peaks through the keyhole and a cool breeze caresses her face as she peers into a crowded classroom. At the back of the room sits a little blonde girl. It is her! Alone and cast out. All the other students glare and point their fingers at her. They can smell the weakness on her skin.

"You are not like us," the students taunt. "You dress different. Why are you so quiet?" The little girl, so fragile, just endures the barrage of insults like a delicate rose in a hail storm.

In shock, she cannot even function. The room now shifts into her family's kitchen, where her father and mother are arguing, "You stupid whore! Why do you always have to push me over the edge?" her father yells at her frightened mother. Raising his hand, he slaps her mother across the face and she drops to the ground. Her mother's coffee cup falls and smashes at her feet as she witnesses the abuse.

Her father kneels before her with an intimidating presence and whispers, "Now Rose honey, daddy had to teach mommy a little lesson. I am sorry you had to see that dear, but daddy can't have momma getting outta control. You understand don't you?"

Rose can sense the darkness surrounding her father. Years of regret fester in his soul from the risks he never allowed himself to take, along with the pain of the wounds caused by his abusive father, who did not know how to love. As she stares into his depressed eyes, she can see the demons dwelling within. Pitch black ghouls beckon her deeper into his manipulations.

The demons release from his eyes and slither all around him like a tornado of death and ensnare his soul in their power. The demons retreat into her father's being and a dark aura now surrounds his body, shrouding him in a black mist. Rose is aware that something is not right here, but her father is already lost. The demons entrapped him as a youth and have built a mighty stronghold within John. He was oppressed by his father and forced into the darkness. He had no choice but to succumb to the overbearing oppression from the evil that haunted the family.

Blind to the power that was overtaking his soul; he lived as if nothing was wrong. But Rose can see the disparity inside of her father, and sadly there is not a glimmer of hope left in his eyes. He has been completely overtaken by the demented spirits. For too long he has dwelled in his obscure pit of misery, tormented by the echoing voice of his abusive father who would yell at him constantly from a drunken stupor. "You will never amount to anything, you coward," he would scream, unintentionally killing his son's spirit and marking him for doom.

Jan, Rose's mother, so beautiful and fragile, lays on the floor watching as her husband tries to fool Rose with his sharp tongue. The same way he has fooled Jan for far too many years. Jan's eyes flare as John attempts to twist little Rose's mind and taint her innocence with the dark energy he so easily slurs. But Jan will not have it. Neither will the legion of Angels who have descended into the house, and are now watching over young Rose and her mother.

The light in her mother's eyes begin to blaze like flaring torches, as she picks herself up with the help of the magnificent Angels now surrounding her and Rose. Darkness has reigned in this house long enough. Rising to her feet Jan screams at John to back away from her daughter. Her voice blasts through the room like supersonic waves, startling John as he moves away from young Rose.

Jan runs over to Rose and embraces her in her arms. John comes to and screams, "Woman, this is my house!" He raises his hands again to strike Jan but is frozen stiff. Standing before him is Michael, Rose's guardian angel. Young Rose has been exposed to enough trauma and Michael will not stand for it anymore. Fate has dealt Rose her wounds and now Michael steps in. Glaring into John's eyes, Michael opens his mouth wide, releasing a bellowing roar! Light bursts from his mouth at the same time, consuming John whole. Just as the entire room fills with brilliant white light, Rose awakens!

Part One: Rite of Passage

"One of the pitfalls of childhood is that one doesn't have to understand something to feel it. By the time the mind is able to comprehend what has happened, the wounds of the heart are already too deep."
— Carlos Ruiz Zafon

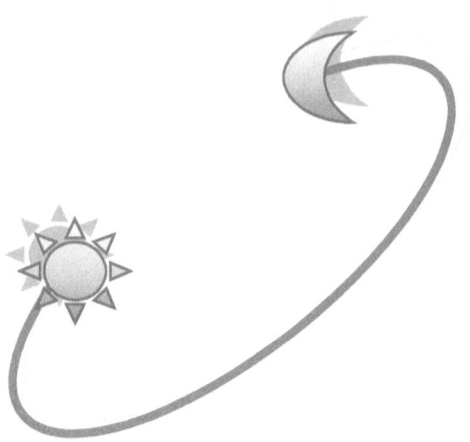

1) <u>Family Issues</u>

ℛose had been dreaming! She had fallen asleep in one of her favorite nature escapes; so peaceful, so serene. The comfort of Mother Nature had whisked her away into a deep slumber.

She rolls over and wipes the sleep from her crystal blue eyes. Large arching oaks line the road like soldiers, creating a tunnel effect before her. The giant trees possess a guardian's presence that is rumored to protect all souls that come to find peace here in the Holyoke Forest, located on the southern edge of the nation of Octairion.

Rose stretches in the small patch of grass and continues to relax while she observes the forest come to life before her. Butterflies flutter through the many beautiful paths that trail through the wooded area. Red Cardinals and Blue jays soar from branch to branch completely free, just like Rose longs to be. The sound of a big fat buzzing beetle irks her, and she shews it away, but the insect is merely doing what it was created to do.

Today, Rose has ventured out to the Holyoke Forest to think about her life after a heated argument with her foster parents. Her family in Holyoke is a nice family. They're well educated people who come from wealth and pride themselves on intelligence. They put a lot of pressure on Rose to perform academically, but she had a hard time focusing on the curriculum since it bored her to death.

Morel, her foster father, has strong convictions and thinks money and an education can solve any problem there can be, but Rose does not agree. She believes all the answers we seek can only be found within. She is a free spirit and does not want to be told what to think by her controlling foster parents.

Just graduating High School, Rose, had a heavy burden placed on her from Olivia, her foster mom. She was pressing Rose to figure out what job she wanted, what college she wanted to attend, and what major she wanted to dedicate her young life to. But none of this seemed to interest Rose. Although all of society tells her that financial and material gain is success, her heart tells her otherwise. In a world full of greed where people climb over one another to get to the top of an imaginary ladder, Rose has a deep hunger for something more.

The common man in today's society is preoccupied with consuming and buying, buying, buying! Prone to escape through television, substance abuse, overeating, vanity, and the list goes on. Finding their self-worth in how much money they make, or what kind of luxuries they obtain. They distract themselves with video games and celebrity gossip. Poor people, if only they knew the beauty of their divine nature and their relationship to Great Spirit.

It seems as though we all go through life collecting baggage and wounds to our souls from the damage handed to us through time. But if we choose not to escape the pain, and rather dig deep into our hearts, we can transform the weakness into true power. We must listen to the subtle promptings of our hearts and the guidance of Great Spirit as we are led in this re-birth. Trusting ourselves, knowing that there is something more planned for us here on this earth. More than just being another cog in the machine of the economy and becoming a slave to our distractions.

Some would rather numb themselves or hide from the pain instead of walking the path of awakening, which will lead us to our true royal nature as kings and queens of our lives. We can become perfected and whole, knowing the love and abundance of the universe we live in and that there is no need for fear. No need to strive and struggle against the unfolding of life but simply to be, who we were created to be, and let life reveal our true purpose in its perfect time... or so they say.

As Rose sits up from the patch of grass, an emerald calcite rolls off her lap and falls onto the ground. It was a gift from her uncle Layne. The crystal represents the passing away of old negative energy patterns and the new creation of positive patterns of love and family bond. She bends down to pick up the precious green gem in the olive colored grass and reminisces about her uncle as she stares into the crystal.

Layne was a major influence on her. He gave her this crystal when she was taken away from the family. No one was able to provide a stable environment for young Rose at the time, so she was taken into foster care. To prepare her, her uncle Layne told her that she was going on her first adventure, and that he was proud of her for being so brave.

Her uncle Layne was born into a prison of darkness and fought his way out. He did not make it out unscathed though. He survived and bears scars like badges of honor.

Layne was plagued with fear. He had no confidence in himself, although he too possessed great spiritual abilities. They were just hidden under all the damage inside. Layne's father abandoned the family when he was young, leaving Layne with his younger brother and sister to depend on their struggling mother.

Many demons haunted their whole family; demons of perversion and abuse. Addiction and prostitution riddled Layne's family and left mighty strongholds inside of him. Jan, Layne's sister, and Rose's mom was a product of this environment as well. As Layne grew older he found success financially in the world, but this only became a bigger pit for him to wallow in.

Layne's prison was in his mind. The demons inside him distorted his vision and haunted him with false images that kept his true potential locked deep inside. They told him he was worthless and should be ashamed of the man he had become, but they were all lies. Having no father to approve of him, Layne was looking to sell his soul to the devil for approval. Darkness began to surround him. Layne used drugs, women, and fantasy to try and escape the hell inside, but there was no escaping. He was slowly killing himself and diving deeper into the darkness while the demons slathered and licked their lips.

His light was close to being extinguished, but the warrior within would not give up. Layne cried out to Great Spirit in the night, and he was led to leave the land and all the riches he had acquired. Nearly dead and contemplating suicide, Layne had no problem making the choice. Great Spirit presented Layne with a journey to liberate his soul. He gladly accepted and set out immediately.

Layne was led to the land of Kane, one of the most desolate lands of Octairion, where he lived in the wilderness with other lost souls. There he was stripped of the false identity he had created to protect his ego. His false identity consisted of pride and vanity to make him feel that he was better than everyone else. It was the only way Layne could function with the constant lies of the darkness screaming in his head, making him feel like a discarded piece of rubbish.

Over time Layne was humbled and purified by the fires of Kane. Living outdoors, stripped of all wealth and luxury, Layne was acquainted with who he truly was on the inside. With nothing to distract him from the pain he preferred to run from, he was forced to deal with all of his pent up emotions and confront the falsities his demons whispered. But he was not alone in this battle. The Elders of Kane fathered young Layne and taught him the ways of the Inner Realm.

The Inner Realm is the dimension of Spirit where Great Spirit sits upon the throne. True knowledge of the Inner Realm is gained through life experiences. One can be told about our special relationship with Great Spirit, but if one does not realize it personally they can never fully awaken to the miracle of this life. They will simply miss His hand moving in their lives. The Inner Realm is constantly speaking to us. Can you feel them? Some call their language coincidences, or synchronicities, but that is merely one way the Spirits interact with us.

The elders informed Layne that we can sense guides with our hearts and be directed by many different spirits, both good and evil. Depending on his choice he could do more damage with evil, or spread love by following the good. Although some blindly follow the Spirits, unaware of their automatic patterns of behavior, this was not the case with Layne. He was awake.

He chose the good. Together Layne and the Elders slayed many demons inside of him, and also in countless others exiled to the wilderness of Kane. Layne suffered greatly from being cut off from life as he knew it, but in the end he was transformed through this journey, and he discovered the transcendent love of Great Spirit.

Passing all his tests and trials and illuminating the darkness within, Layne established a new identity. He had earned the title of Light

Warrior. Great Spirit advanced him to the Village of Hope where he was trained in the ways of Faith, Hope, and Love. Spiritually maturing, and evolving his soul with other Light Warriors on the same path. Layne continued to strive forward and he quickly rose to become one of the leaders of the Village due to his persistence and determination to rid his soul of all darkness.

After three years of being exiled in Kane, Layne was found worthy in Great Spirit's eyes and was led to come home. Upon his return, he faced his past self at every corner and quickly defeated his old demons. The darkness told him he was pathetic, but Great Spirit said he was powerful. The demons said he would never amount to anything, but Great Spirit said with Me, you can do all things.

Now Layne was more aggressive and assertive. He also possessed self-love. No longer was this an immature boy afraid of taking risks, or unsure of his own skill and character. This journey had matured Layne into a man, a man tried and true.

Rose is distracted from her memories as something rustles in the leaves overhead. She takes her eyes from the emerald calcite and glances up into the canopy of sun blocking foliage and spots an orange bobcat. The fat kitty watches Rose from up above, curious to what the girl is holding. "Hello there handsome boy," Rose yells up to the nosy bobcat. She holds up the gem, "This is just a stone that holds the good memories of my childhood. You don't want to eat this."

The finicky kitty keenly observes the stone from the treetop. He rolls around on the thick limb momentarily, licks his paws and cleans his face, then dashes off along the intersecting highway of branches. *What a strange little intruder,* she thinks looking back at the stone. Gazing at the soft edges of the emerald calcite, her mind drifts back to the memories of when her uncle came home from his journey.

Arriving at the family house in Conway, a poverty stricken area in the southwest coast of Octairion, Layne found his young niece Rose thirsty for knowledge and ripe for her uncle's attention. She was also blessed to discover her uncle Layne came bearing many gifts, but not gifts of silver or gold, nor toys or games. He came with gifts of the spirit, and gems of wisdom. He came into young Rose's life to teach her all she could absorb. It was obvious to him that Rose was a special girl, quick witted and a fast learner, but not only did she have a lot to absorb from her uncle, he had a lot to learn from her.

She was the first person that Layne could love strongly. Layne felt it safe to love her with all his heart, and she could do the same. Except the love that young Rose had inside her was something uncommon to this family. Her love was unconditional.

Layne and Rose spent several months together, and in that time he took her on many fun adventures. Climbing rocks and trees, running and hurtling obstacles, and playing games of all sorts were her favorite. She was full of energy and a natural athlete. She brought the child out of Layne, and in return he showed her the sacred beauty of life.

He spoke to her about the soul, our own personal journeys, and of Great Spirit and the Inner Realm. Yet these things were no mystery to young Rose. Layne also showed her how to focus her energy and use it creatively. He instructed her in how to draw, play musical instruments, and meditate. Uncle Layne would expand her mind and expose her to all kinds of new ideas, and young Rose absorbed it all.

Looming clouds shift high in the sky and cover the sun as Rose continues to reminisce. They block out the already little light that is shining into the Holyoke Forest. Gloomy shadows consume the once peaceful escape, and Rose's mind drifts off into the darker memories of her uncle's return.

Her mother Jan was now abandoned by John, her father. Jan had become bitter from all the abuse she had suffered at the hands of John, so she took her anger out on Rose. Jan would blame Rose for being such a burden in her life and robbing her of her freedom. She would belittle her and call her stupid for not being able to care for herself.

Jan constantly screamed at young Rose and would bully the poor girl when she was bored and lonely. Layne would step in and defend Rose when it got too far. He would try to awaken Jan to the damage she was cursing Rose with, but some things are out of our control no matter how hard we try. Layne would do his best to inform his niece that this was caused by her mother's demons and not because of Rose.

Due to the neglect Rose received from her mother, she was removed from the household, but before she was taken away, Layne prepped her with a story about the hero's journey. The hero receives her wounds and plaguing demons. The healing of those wounds and the conquering of the demons become the mission. Through the completion of this challenge, your true power will be revealed.

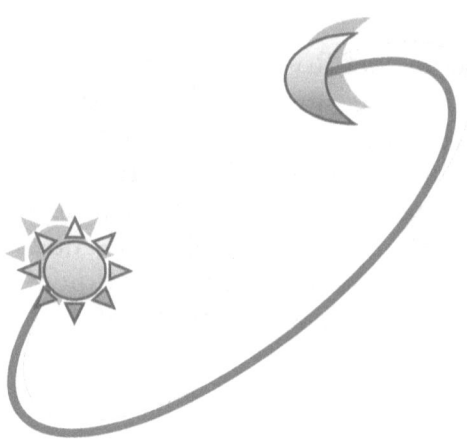

2) <u>The Adventure Begins</u>

*R*ose snaps out of the daydream and rises to her feet. To her surprise the emerald crystal in her hand starts to sparkle. A pulsing glow like the beating of a heart shines from the smooth stone. She quiets her mind, slows her breathing, and begins to listen as if stretching an antenna to the Inner Realm. She pays close attention to the sensations in her heart and tries to receive what the Spirit is communicating. After a moment she feels a subtle nudge in her core to go to the lake nearby.

Walking through a family of large cedars and down a rocky dirt path, Rose comes to a tranquil lake. The water is still. Not a single wave ripples through the placid lake. She bends down and stares at her reflection in the turquoise colored water. Her beautiful flowing blonde hair rests on her shoulders and her enchanting blue eyes glimmer.

She sits down at the lake and begins to meditate. Sitting ever so quietly, she lets the world slip away. A brisk breeze gusts across her body, also kicking up leaves and flower petals. The wind continues to swirl faster and the leaves and petals turn into a cyclone, spinning and picking up speed. Out of the eye of the spiraling wind funnel a figure suddenly appears. Rose opens her eyes and to her amazement the lake water is shooting up like a geyser and slowly compounding together to form a liquefied body.

The mysterious deity has long wavy turquoise hair and plump sapphire lips. "Hello my dear Rose," she says with a subtle wispiness in her voice.

A little stunned, Rose tries to make sense of what she is seeing. The spirit has a beautiful translucent body and a flowing gown of purples and blues waves in the air behind her. Rose marvels at the shimmering light sparkles that twinkle throughout her curvy feminine frame as she floats above the lake.

"Rose my dear, do not be startled. I am Isis, Spirit of the Waters." Ripples of light flow through her body gracefully as she bows her head, "I am here to inform you of the devastation that is occurring in the world," she proclaims.

Rose squints her eyes and fixes her gaze on Isis, "You mean there is more than I have already witnessed? More pain and destruction than I have experienced?" Rose replies. She raises her voice as she becomes filled with more emotion, "Isis, it seems as though as far back as I can remember, all there has ever been in this world is pain and darkness running rampant. It's as if the demons have always just had their way with the people of Octairion and no one can do anything about it."

Rose becomes more passionate as she speaks, the years of pent up emotion are just pouring out of her. "Isis, I have endured so much, I have had so much taken from me, I have seen my friends hurt and family destroyed by this darkness, and you want to tell me now that there is more? Of course! Of course there is!" She falls to the ground and weeps into her hands. Young Rose has been so strong for so long, and it is too much for her to bear in this moment.

Isis watches as Rose breaks down in front of her, but she knows this is for the best. Rose has been such a warrior, and now she is venting and releasing all the old energy stored inside her. Thus making room for the healing love of Great Spirit to consume her and ease her aching soul.

Isis approaches Rose lying on the ground. Her shimmering gown leaves a trail of speckling glitter as she hovers closer. She reaches out her hand and caresses Rose's youthful face, wiping away her tears. "Believe me Rose, I know what you have been through," responds Isis with an endearing look of compassion upon her face, "We of the Inner Realm know all about you Rose, and consider you worthy in our eyes. You have done well."

Rose wipes her eyes and looks up at Isis. Her nurturing presence comforts her like that of a mother cradling her baby. Something Rose has not felt for quite some time now.

"We are proud of you, and would like to ask for your assistance in battling this great darkness Rose."

"Why me, what do I have to offer?" responds Rose as she gets back up to her feet. Her pale cheeks are now puffy and red from the emotional release.

Isis waves her hand before her and a slew of water droplets plop rhythmically into the lake below. "You have many powerful gifts that lie dormant inside your spirit. You have a potential of which few humans possess on this earth. It is no coincidence we are speaking today. It is time to awaken your true nature as a Light Warrior, and join forces with us against the growing darkness spreading through Octairion.

You are well aware of all the attempts by the Dark Forces to stamp out the light inside of you Rose. This was not for nothing. They know of the great fire inside of you dear, and if they could extinguish it there would be little to stop them. You see, there is only so much that the beings of the Inner Realm can accomplish on our own. We need humans like you, enlightened people who are sensitive to our promptings, who are in tune with their souls, and believe in the power of love over fear. Without good souls like you, we have surely lost."

With the nightmares of how the darkness has haunted her family all these years still fresh in her head, Isis's words spur a powerful surge of inspiration inside Rose. She locks eyes with Isis in a serious manner, "I am ready. I am more than ready!" she yells, raising and clenching her fists in the air. Just then, an owl swoops in between them and startles Rose. Stumbling backward she yelps, "What in the world!"

The owl perches himself up on a mighty oak tree above them and watches. Oh, what an amazing creature. The owl is snow white and mysterious.

"You see, Rose," continues Isis as if the bird doesn't exist, "there are greater powers of darkness being awakened as well. Just as there are many light beings that have been sleeping for so long now, there too have been powerful dark souls waiting to enter into the war of light and darkness, and that time is now. There are violent hordes of demons gathering in towns and villages all around our nation of Octairion. Anyone who is damaged enough is susceptible to the curses of darkness. Those who are blind to the light have no chance, and that is what we are calling upon you for."

Rose's eyes widen as she recognizes the seriousness of this calling.

"You are to be amongst the warriors of the Army of Light. Conquering the Dark Forces and recovering the lost souls of the people of Octairion is your mission, but first you must journey to the Village of Hope where your uncle was trained."

Isis thrusts her hands out by her sides and pulsing pillars of water explode skyward from the lake. Rose stands in awe of the beauty as Isis gazes deeply into her soul with her swirling cobalt eyes.

"As we speak, your human race is evolving and new powers are arising from the spirits of those who feel the call," says Isis. "These are powers that your uncle Layne has laid an amazing foundation for inside of you, a mighty foundation of love and spiritual wisdom. He planted the seeds that will bring forth the fruit of your superior spiritual abilities.

Before humans had to merely cope with the pain of their wounds and transmute the darkness inside. Many did, but many also chose to succumb to the darkness and devolve into demons. The time has come to fight for your lives, as the darkness has formed an army and is preparing for an onslaught."

The seriousness in Isis's voice is unmistakable. This is a definite turning point in the history of the universe. Rose is filled with a sense of honor and also a bit unnerved by the great responsibility that has been presented to her. But she is willing to take on the challenge. Oh what glory to be a part of such a period as this!

"Time to get moving," commands Isis. "There is no time to waste. You must travel through Holyoke Forest and over the Mountain of Strength. Just over the mountain is the land of Kane. There you will find the Village of Hope."

"Isis, I have never been out of Holyoke," nervously replies Rose. "How will I find my way?"

Isis staring lovingly into Rose's eyes replies, "We of the Inner Realm are always available to you my dear. Whenever you are in need, focus on your heart and listen for our faint whispers. We will never abandon you sweet Rose. Do you see the angelic owl waiting for you in the trees?"

"Yes," she replies raising her gaze up to the powerful bird.

"He is August. He will guide you where you need to go. Now my dear, take heed of the dangers. Move and act swiftly. These are urgent matters at hand."

August spreads his wings and begins to fly towards Kane.

"Goodbye," concludes Isis.

"Farewell," yells Rose as she runs after August who is setting a brisk pace.

Dashing through the Holyoke Forest, she jumps over fat stumps and climbs up giant rocks like the natural born adventurer she is. Determined to keep up with August, Rose pushes on through the heavy collection of trees. He leads her over beautiful stone bridges that span the many lakes of Holyoke, and rushes by the cascading waterfalls that bless the sacred forest.

Squirrels scurry and chipmunks charge, as all the little animals start to find their way home to their holes. All the birds make their way to their nests as the sun starts to go down. A somber silence falls over the forest as day fades and night comes alive. Crickets begin to serenade the moon's rising, meanwhile bats begin to fly. Foxes and coyotes emerge to prowl and play in the shadows of the forest. Cougars claim the night as their own, and stinky skunks stalk.

Rose and August enter into the Holyoke burial grounds. She skids to a stop, as her eyes fall upon the cryptic graveyard. Glorious flaring fireflies light the desolate burial ground like festive Christmas lights, such a beauty to behold. Scattered flares of exploding sparks burst in the air. They glisten above the old green stained tombstones of the many honored Holyoke folks who have come and gone.

Rose makes her way through the aisles of moss covered headstones. Glancing at the faded names of the deceased she spots the Nova family and the Aurea family. Names she recalls hearing around town. Then she comes across a tinged cast iron statue of a tall man draped in flowing robes. He holds a double-edged sword to the sky with his adoring eyes staring heavenward. The smooth markings on the giant gray stone base reads "Be the Light." The insignia on the bronze grave plaque says "Masters" in elegant letters. Rose recalls her uncle Layne speaking about a man named Ken Masters, but everyone just called him "Masters".

Masters was a Leader at the Village of Hope who had impacted Layne more than any other. He was not a fancy man by any means, and did not possess any outrageous abilities. Layne said that the love this man possessed was what was so special about him. He was so humble and knew how to care for people in a delicate, yet empowering way. Layne loved Mr. Masters dearly. He had referred to him as his spiritual father once before.

Rose pauses in the dark night and thinks about the fallen Light Warriors and all the people being affected by the darkness that is attempting to consume Octairion. She remembers her uncle Layne, and wonders where he could be and if he is alright. She lost contact with all of her family when she was taken into foster care and brought to Holyoke. Last she knew her family was still in Conway, her hometown, far away from Holyoke. Her memories fill her with fervor and she shouts, "I will do this for them!" thrusting her fist into the midnight sky.

August loudly screeches along with her.

"I will be the LIGHT!" yells Rose.

Just then a roaring howl comes from the nearby shrubbery. Seems Rose and August are not the only ones lurking in the graveyard tonight. The bushes rustle behind her and Rose whips around. She prepares herself for the worst and August clenches onto a thick branch up above and does the same. They fix their eyes on the rattling bushes and watch as something starts to appear.

Rose quickly jumps behind a tree to avoid being seen. Her heart pounds heavily like the rhythm of a war drum. She waits a moment and listens to the pattering of what sounds like weighty paws. She then sticks her head out slightly and spots a giant gray wolf. With his nose down to the ground he sniffs as he investigates the area. He has got a slight limp to him. Maybe he has been cast out of his pack, or could he not keep up any longer and came here to die? He limps towards Masters large gravestone and plops down lazily before it. This old boy is worn out.

Rose reveals herself from behind the tree as August flies down to a lower branch for a better view. "Hello Mr. Wolf. Are you a good boy?" she asks.

He looks over at her and lets out a great big yawn. His long pink tongue stretches way out of his big mouth, and he sluggishly drops his head down onto the ground. This pup looks like he's had enough for the night.

Rose slowly approaches him. Her curiosity may be getting the best of her, but the resting wolf is paying her no mind. He seems fine with the fact that young Rose is approaching. She sits down across from him, about three feet away, and examines the beautiful beast. His coat is weathered and body heavily scarred from past battles.

She boldly leans in with her hand out for the wolf to smell. He opens his tapered eyes wide and growls at Rose as he rears his sharp decaying teeth. Rose backs away for a moment startled, and then leans in once again. Is she daring or stupid? Something inside her is telling her that this wild animal is harmless, but can she really afford to be wrong?

The wolf moves his snout close to Rose's hand and gives her a sniff, and then submissively licks her finger. Rose moves in a bit closer and lifts her hand onto the wolf's head to pat him. He receives her love. "Good boy," says Rose as the wolf surrenders and lets Rose scratch his old tired body. "I'm going to call you Sirius," growls Rose.

The wolf's stoic demeanor and slender build reminds her of her uncle Andrew who had a Siberian Husky named Sirius. He moved away to a faraway land and lost contact with her years ago. He always adored wolves.

Rose lets out a mighty yawn, and the wolf follows right behind her. "Yawns are contagious, you know," says sleepy Rose to Sirius. It has certainly been a long and emotional day. She has had her whole life change in one day before, but today was intense as well. She was called into her life's purpose. Something so many are searching for. Chosen, Rose was chosen for this journey. Her unique attributes are what give her the right to walk this path. No other person could do it the way she will. No other person is fit for such a journey as this.

Rose snuggles into Sirius as they both attempt to fall asleep. How comforting is the love of Great Spirit. He has provided a warm furry partner to comfort Rose on her first night alone in the wilderness. Great Spirit knew his little girl would be nervous and cold, so he provided some support. Sirius sleeps beside her, and August rests in the tree above, but both are certainly on guard. Rose stares up into the bright glowing moon and drifts off into dreamland.

A red rose bud breaks through the hard concrete. The little persistent flower pushes its way through the thick cold stone. The persistent rose then blossoms in the starlit night sky, and detaches from its stem and hovers into space. Dodging clusters of comets and massive asteroids it speeds through the expanse and comes to a new unknown planet and glides down into its atmosphere. The red rose then lands in a luscious garden full of all kinds of exotic flowers: splendid water lilies, tons of toppling tulips, and many magnificent magnolias.

A large stone fountain with a divine male and female pair pouring water from large jugs is centered in the middle of the garden. The divine king and queen are donned with crowns and stand in full glory. Their nude bodies are cut and chiseled to perfection. The water crashes in the pool at the bottom of the fountain and sprits up into the air. The mist fills the garden, nourishing all the beautiful flowers so fortunate to be planted in this wonderful plot. The soil in this special place is packed with nutrients. Satisfying the plants and allowing them to grow to their full potential.

The sun rises on Rose, still asleep in the graveyard. August lets out an alarming screech alerting her to awaken. It's time to journey on. Rose awakens and looks around. Sirius has vanished! He has completely disappeared, other than a fang that must have fallen from his mouth.

"That poor old boy is falling apart," sadly says Rose as she picks up the tarnished fang. She wraps a ribbon around the tooth and secures it round her neck. Holding the fang in her hand Rose lovingly says, "I won't forget you friend. Thank you for keeping me safe through the night."

She then peers off into the distance and can see the Mountain of Strength in view. What an intimidating sight. The discouraging peak stretches high up into the sky! The black stone cliffs will certainly be no easy task to maneuver, but she has too. Rose looks up at August who also glances at the mountain and then darts into flight. She settles herself, remembers why she is doing this, and then rushes ahead towards her destiny.

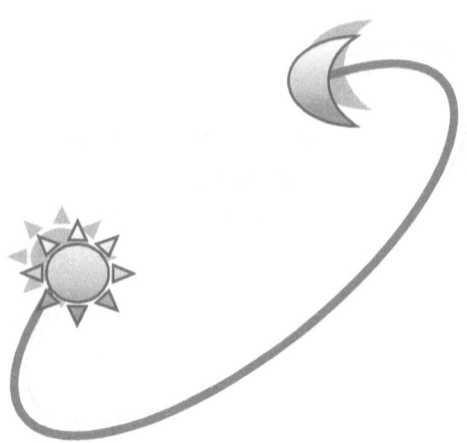

3) <u>Unsettling Insights</u>

$\mathcal{R}$ose and August zip through the mammoth trees of the northern region of the Holyoke Forest. She watches in awe as August glides around their massively wide trunks. His flight is so magnificent. He soars with such a royal temperament, like the skies belong to him. She notices a few of his beautiful white feathers release into the wind as he moves out of sight up ahead.

She sprints faster and nearly stumbles over a thick root protruding from the ground. She regains her footing and spies August resting atop the roof of a decrepit old shack. He shakes his tail feathers and makes himself comfortable in the straw like materials that abound on the ridge.

"What are you up to?" she yells to the wild bird.

"I am enjoying my home," answers an unexpected voice around the corner from the front of the shack.

Rose grabs her mouth in shock. She had no idea that there was anyone else around.

"Well are you just going to hide from me? Or are you going to come say hello?" says the low raspy voice. She listens closely to his words and he does not give off any need for caution, so she watchfully makes her way around the collapsing corner of the shack.

A slender old man in all white robes sits on a rocking chair and steadily sways back and forth. His eyes are closed and he looks like he is in a trance. Rose moves a little closer and notices his strange necklace made out of red beads and what looks like small animal bones.

"Have a seat my friend," suggests the solitary man.

Rose is not so sure about this guy and his nasty necklace, "I am kind of in a rush. I am on a special journey and don't have much time to waste," she replies.

The man slowly opens his ghoulish gray eyes and locks onto Rose. He raises his thin hand and the long sleeve of his tattered robe drops down as he points towards the giant mountain just beyond the next bunch of trees. "Are you traveling up there?" he asks.

"I am," replies Rose a bit thrown off by how big the mountain has grown now that she is closer.

"Then you might want to hear a few of the many legends about the Mountain of Strength before you continue," advises the old man. "But it is up to you honestly. If you must rush off that is."

Rose leans down and brushes off the dead leaves that coat the bench across from the old man and she has a seat.

"I am Arian, welcome to my home."

"My name is Rose, nice to meet you,"

Arian nods and adjusts in his chair. His ancient bones ring out a crackling serenade as he moves. "So it is said that all of those who desire to cross over the Mountain of Strength must be called or you will certainly fail, and even those who are chosen still may fall short."

Rose keeps her mouth closed and continues to listen to Arian's not so pleasant story.

He strokes his bare face and adjusts once again, "You see it is said that only the weak can approach the mountain. Only those who can humble themselves and admit their faults and flaws are worthy. If you cannot rise above your weakness, then surely you will never rise up the Mountain of Strength."

Rose rubs her finger across her narrow lips as she thinks about Arian's words, "How can I do that?" she asks.

A smile breaks onto Arian's wrinkled face and his necklace of bones jangles as he rocks, "You don't have to do anything Rose, the mountain will be sure to pull it out of you."

Rose's curious blue eyes narrow as she studies this strange old man. "The Mountain is going to bring it out of me, huh?" she repeats.

"Oh yes. You know, I don't want to say too much but life has a mystical way of tearing apart who we think we are and revealing our true selves."

Rose takes a moment and silently stews on the wisdom the old man shares. Then all of a sudden, up above them, little bits of straw start to rain down from the rooftop. They both look up and see August perched proudly and peering at the mountains.

"I think it's time for me to go," says Rose.

"Certainly," replies Arian with a bow, "be well young lady."

"I'll try, thank you," replies Rose as August blasts up off the roof and rapidly flaps his mighty wings. *Here goes nothing,* she thinks and dashes off the porch.

Rose sprints from the site of the old shack and hustles towards the massive mountain with Arian's wisdom still fresh in her mind. *Who am I?* she contemplates as she hurdles over a boulder. *Am I humble enough to admit my weaknesses and make it over the mountain? Or will I be a failure in the shadow of the great task?*

Rose slows down to an even paced stroll and reflects on her life, but August doesn't wait up. He keeps soaring forward until he disappears over a grassy hill.

She pauses for a moment. Rose doesn't seem too concerned about the vanishing owl, but instead, some difficult questions come to mind. *What makes me think that I am capable of all that is asked of me? What have I accomplished in my life? Nothing really.*

Rose glances up to the sky and can see the mountain standing proudly above the trees. Its strong presence almost seems to be taunting her as she questions herself. She exhales deeply and runs her hands through her long blonde hair. *Relax Rose,* she tells herself, *breathe and remember what Isis had told you. The Inner Realm has found you worthy.* She quiets her mind and prays, *Great Spirit am I truly worthy to cross over this mountain? I am just a girl who has come from nothing, yet I am supposed to believe that I can accomplish such an incredible feat? Can this be so?*

She continues to walk and pray. Then the sudden sound of crashing water can be heard up ahead. The heavy splashing soothes her anxious spirit and she can hear the voice of Isis, "We believe in you Rose. With the power of Great Spirit, you can do all things. Keep going." The message from Isis knocks Rose out of her funk. *That's right, it's not about who I think I am, it's about what Great Spirit can accomplish through me,* she thinks and hurries towards the crashing water.

Whizzing through a giant collection of red pine trees, she comes to the edge of a river. Across the watery expanse August rests on a large boulder. He taps his talon against the stone surface as if he is angrily keeping time. *What an impatient bird,* she thinks shaking her head.

Rose follows the winding river with her eyes until she meets a mighty waterfall pouring from the Mountain of Strength. The giant cascade flows down from a cliff half way up the mountain and crashes down to the base. The roar of the colossal torrent reminds her of a ferocious lion warning all who are not welcome to stay away. But she has essentially arrived. All she has to do now is cross over the river and she will be at the foot of the mountain. Rose can't back down now.

As she examines the seven small stepping stones that lead across the river, she realizes this is a task that is much easier said than done. The row of wet stones are set a few feet apart from each other and form a make shift bridge. *Should I run and try to skip across in a single shot, or should I jump one by one?* she wonders while watching the powerful river break around a few of the fat rocks. The fast moving water washes over some of the smaller stones though, raising some caution in Rose as she plans her approach.

"Eeaarrrrrrrccchtt," cries August demanding a snappy decision. He's got to keep Rose on her toes.

She stops thinking about it and acts. "Alright, Great Spirit with this first leap, I forget my judgment and I depend on yours," she speaks and jumps to the first stone. Along the sides of the stone are slimy brown roots that slither like a nest of snakes swaying in the water. *Gross,* she thinks and looks to the second stone.

"Great Spirit, I believe you will give me the strength to complete my journey," she whispers. Rose swings her arms back and then springs forward and lands on the wet stone. She plants her left foot and as she brings the right one down she slips on the slick green moss. Rose quickly throws her arms out to the sides and regains her balance. *Phew, that was close,* she thinks as she looks down to her feet and the clear water is running over her black boots. *I better hurry to the next.*

She spots the third rock and it looks a little further than the others. "Great Spirit, if you say I can, then I trust You," she yells. She throws her arms down by her sides and thrusts forward with a mighty leap of faith. She lands on the bumpy stone but she has used too much power. Her momentum keeps her moving forward rapidly and she is forced to jump off kilter to the next stone. August throws his wings up over his eyes expecting the worst, but Rose successfully settles onto the fourth stone. He drops his wings and lets out a sigh of relief, as does Rose, who can't believe she is still dry.

Now in the middle of the river, she takes a moment to inspect the water. All around her she can see exotic Koi fish swimming against the current. Some fiercely whip their orange and white tail fins and try to make it up river, while other black and gold Koi's rest behind the large stone. She kneels down and watches as the persistent fish keep trying to move forward. No matter how hard the river is raging they will not give up. They will fight until the end.

That's right, thinks Rose, inspired by the determined Koi's. "I won't stop until I make it to the Village," she yells and lines up with the remaining stones. She grits her teeth and clenches her fists. Huffing and puffing she builds up some anger. "Nothing's going to stop me," she yells, and hurls herself onto the fifth stone. She swings her arms forward and immediately catapults herself to the sixth stone, then uses her powerful momentum to launch herself to the seventh. "Whoo hoo," Rose yells with her hands in the air. She steps onto the shore and celebrates before August who doesn't seem too impressed. "C'mon you stubborn bird, be happy for me," she says. But August ignores her celebration and directs his gaze up above to the Mountain of Strength.

The haunting presence of the rocky giant is quite menacing. Rose gulps deeply and swallows her pride as she steps forward to the base. She halts in the shadows of the incredible elevation and shudders under the intimidating wonder.

August is not fazed. He flaps his bulky white wings and flies towards a jagged ridge overhead. Rose watches the brave bird rise higher and her eyes bulge in shock as she notices the tip of the huge mountain is hidden inside the clouds! She drops her head in dismay. *What a daunting task*, she thinks. Rose examines the rocky incline in front of her but finds no marked paths or easy routes that can be seen. *Oh boy just my luck. One step at a time I must forge my own trail to the top.*

Rose recalls the many times her classmates had spoken about the Mountain of Strength. She recalls a young boy named Wyatt ranting about the many dangers on the way over: mountain lions, the numerous possible falls, and dare I mention the sizzling volcano at the top. He had told her that a magical black-scaled dragon with big red horns lived at the core too. Who knows what to expect though, her teacher Mr. Shultz said they were all just rumors.

Anyway, enough of the mumbo jumbo, now the challenge of ascending and descending the Mountain of Strength stands before her; the largest mountain in all of Octairion. Surely this will be one of the greatest challenges of her life, but Rose knows if she cannot conquer this mountain and make it to the Village of Hope, there is no way she can defeat the darkness spreading throughout Octairion. There is no way she can fulfill her destiny.

4) <u>The Mountain of Strength</u>

𝓡ose boldly steps onto the mountain's base and initiates her ascent. Adrenaline pulses through her body as she starts to climb. Hand overhand she pulls herself higher using her upper body strength, and drives downward with her powerful legs.

Grateful for the training her uncle Layne had given her in rock climbing, she builds a fierce momentum. Grasping onto the sharp edges of the rocky incline she lifts herself to greater heights, and lunges across the small gaps in the jagged rocks. Keeping her face forward she focuses on the task at hand and tries to maintain a balanced pace.

Clutching spikey corners she hangs and shimmies across long ledges. She plants her boots in tiny cracks, boosts herself up to a rocky slope, and sprints like the natural athlete she is. The fresh mountain air fills her lungs and brings a special joy to this wild girl's heart. What did she have to worry about? Nothing can be more thrilling to her in this moment.

Enjoying the challenge, Rose boldly scales a great length of the mountain side and makes her way to a spooky passage. August flies above the dark entrance of the cave up ahead. He lets out an echoing cry signaling that this is the way she must go, and he will meet her on the other side.

Staring deep into the dark chasm, silent and empty, she can't grasp the eerie feelings she is being flooded with. She steps back and tries to shake off the confusion, but it won't budge. Has she been here before? Something seems strangely familiar about this place.

Despite her cautions, Rose knows she must enter into this cave. She slowly creeps her way into the dark damp tunnel and the cool air greets her with a kiss upon her face. The dripping of water droplets can be heard plopping all around her. The rhythmic pattering of the liquid soothes her as she is led into an enormous crystal chamber.

A beam of light is blasting into the chamber from the top of the cavern. Shining through the cracks, the glorious light illuminates the beauty of the elegant crystals. Giant quartz stalagmites and stalactites fill the marvelous cavern. Such power radiates from the alluring gems. Rose is overjoyed at the amazing sight. She has never seen anything like it!

Inching her way through the chamber, she crawls along the incredible crystals like bridges through the room. Heat can be felt emanating from the large mineral stones. She presses her cheek against the smooth surface. The warmth comforts her and brings a shining smile to her face.

She looks ahead and can see a circle of seven crystal pillars in the middle of the chamber. The mysterious pointed pillars create a ring around the outer edge of the circle. All seven equally spaced around the border.

Rose slowly makes her way to the center of the unusual circle. She looks around trying to figure out exactly what the purpose of this crystal structure could be. Suddenly a chorus of screaming voices fills her head! She quickly becomes overwhelmed! The screams painfully echo through her mind and chant indecipherable speech. There is nothing she can do other than fall to the ground and block her ears.

The voices continue to grow louder, piercing her air drums and torturing her mentally. She is powerless against the wailing. Rose stares up at the top of the cave and tries to gather herself. She begins to intensely focus. Concentrating deeply, she attempts to hone in on the voices. She can hear words forming from the shattered shards they were before but can't maintain her focus. Rose forcefully shakes and bucks on the ground and releases a spine-chilling scream.

She suffers greatly and tries to fight through the agonizing pain. She continues to center her mind on deciphering the echoes and tries again to concentrate. Little bits of words start to form like a vase being reconstructed. She must continue to hold it through the excruciating pain. Focusing intently she hears, "Every fragment is related to the whole. Every fragment is related to the whole."

Rose yells it out at the top of her lungs, "Every fragment is related to the whole," and the voices go silent. She lets out a great sigh of relief, thankful that the intense situation is over, and lies there breathing heavily on the cold ground as she tries to recover from the ordeal.

The crystal pillars surrounding her begin to glow. Shimmering golden light flows from the base of the crystals and up into the tips. The light energy becomes contained in the points of the seven pillars as if being charged. As the vibrant light continues to build and surge through the pillars, they start to rumble.

An amazing explosion of light bursts from the pillars and connects high above the center. Right in front of Rose's eyes a spirit body is etched in the air by the moving light.

"Hello Rose, I am Ahzhaire, Spirit of Light," announces the miraculous being.

Rose is so drained by the whole experience she can barely speak. She sits up, "Hi," she responds and then collapses back onto the ground.

Ahzhaire hovers above her exhausted body, "I do apologize for such an extreme test, but Rose, you precious girl, we need to be sure you know how powerful you are," he reveals.

She rolls over and curls into a ball, "Uh huh," she utters. Rose can't even think let alone form full sentences at the moment. Her head still aches tremendously from the hazardous noise.

She slowly looks up at Ahzhaire. His electrified body is just an outline of sparkling light. The light is dull other than the pulsating yellow beams shining from his giant smile.

"What's so funny?" she whispers.

"Nothing, I always carry this smile on my face, for I know how good this life is," declares Ahzhaire. "We all just have to wake up to the power within." He floats down to Rose still on the ground. "You did an exceptional job focusing your mind, blocking out all else, and listening for that still small voice coming from inside. In spite of the pain you felt, you did well under the pressure. I applaud you, dear." Ahzhaire claps his hands together and sparks fly all around them.

Rose twitches as she recuperates from the overstimulation, "Wow, that surely was severe Ahzhaire," says Rose. "Next time spare me."

Ahzhaire lets out a deep laugh as sparks bolt from his face. Drifting higher towards the cavern's ceiling he yells, "I hope you can see the value in your testing Rose. Being exposed to such stimuli is the only way to reveal your capabilities. Picture yourself in the middle of a raging battle." Ahzhaire shoots sparks from his hands like bursting bombs in the sky. "There are frantic people screaming on all sides and distraught men and women falling on your left and on your right." He paints pictures of faces screaming with glowing trails of light. "Remember what you survived here Rose, and how you had to regain your composure and focus. You had to persevere in order to complete the challenge my dear, and you did."

"I did!" she exclaims with great joy.

"Believe in yourself dear," shouts Ahzhaire.

"I do!" excitedly yells Rose raising her fist in the air victoriously. She can feel the spiritual power inside of her soul expanding. She lifts herself up off the ground and brushes off the strain of the event. She understands the value of the lessons she has learned here today and not only does Rose believe in herself more, but she can see the way the Inner Realm works with her to reveal her increasing power. Her faith is now greater than ever.

Just then a screech can be heard booming through the large cave. It is August signaling that it is time to carry on. Boy he can be demanding.

"Thank you for the lesson Ahzhaire," yells Rose sluggishly running through the cavern.

"It has been my honor precious Rose. Good luck on the rest of your journey," replies Ahzhaire.

Rose waves goodbye and exits the cave.

Staggering from the exit of the cavern, Rose's eyes are met with the grand vision of the gorgeous blue sky. The clouds pop like popcorn from Mr. Terenzi's snack shop back in Holyoke. Her mouth waters as she remembers the tasty treats: delectable jelly filled doughnuts, creamy cheese danishes, and fancy frosted cakes of all kinds.

Rose can see her whole town from up here. There is the high school where she spent so many boring days, and the library where she truly learned from her favorite books. A flash of thoughts strike her mind, *just how serious can this invasion of darkness be?* Rose wonders what could be going on in the rest of Octairion. What kind of powers were developing in the dark souls that had succumb to the demons inside them, and what kind of power is ready to come out of her?

Right before Rose gets lost in her imagination, the mountain rumbles mightily under her feet, knocking her back into reality and off balance. She stumbles about as the earth quakes and she manages to grab onto a jagged rock in the mountain wall for stability.

After a few moments the quake subsides. Rose looks at August, "Jeez, do I even get a break?" August squawks and shakes his beak no. She drops her head in submission and continues to run. Rose comes to a round cliff with a small ledge that she must shimmy around. "Oh boy, here we go," yelps Rose as she prepares herself.

She places one foot on the small ledge as the mountain quakes again. Rose instantly freezes in a panic. "Oh, no way," she yells. "This is too much!" She looks back to the cave. She knows there is no going back. She looks down to see how far the fall would be. Peeking into the gorge below, she jumps back. "Bad idea," cries Rose as her heart drops into her stomach.

August is mounted on a rock just after the ledge and gazing down at her. There is no question in August, and no doubt that she has to make it across. He stares at Rose as if to say, "Let's go. Time is wasting." She steps on the thin ledge again and begins to shimmy along. Sweating profusely and breathing deeply, she scoots with her back against the rumbling mountain, inching her feet sideways.

Rose is almost half way when the mountain rumbles aggressively. She searches frantically for anything she can grab. One hand latches onto a pointed stone, and the other onto some weeds sticking out of a crevasse. Big rocks and pebbles fall on both sides of her. Rose hangs on for dear life while she waits for the mountain to quit rumbling.

Then finally the mountain calms down. About a minute has gone by but it has felt like a lifetime. She takes another step sideways and the ledge beneath her crumbles. Rose quickly jumps and just barely grabs the opposite ledge before she falls. Her fingertips struggle to clasp onto the jagged edge as she dangerously dangles from the cliff! She swings side to side hanging from one arm! The weight of her body puts a tremendous amount of pressure on her shoulder and it feels like it might rip out of the socket. Her nimble fingers start to slip away but miraculously she finds a foothold, and pulls herself up.

She has made it across. Letting out a giant sigh of relief she falls to the ground, "I can't believe this. Arian was not joking!" Rose is continually being pushed to her limits over and over again. The stress starts to weigh on her. Pushing her to the brink of mental breakdown, she cracks.

She sits and sulks for a brief couple of seconds, and a dark Shadow slithers out from under a boulder. The creepy demon is formless and pitch black like a puddle of sludge. He sneaks up her body and onto Rose's shoulder.

The demonic Shadow whispers in her ear, "I don't know if I can do this. You're not good enough." The evil Shadow is tempting Rose to doubt herself. A dark purple energy oozes from his mouth and wraps around Rose's head, attacking her mind and infecting her thoughts with darkness. "You should have stayed in Holyoke. All the other kids were right, you're pathetic. Give up!"

Rose is being beaten down by the insults of the demon. Already weakened from the stressful journey and the many difficult challenges, she seems to be defenseless against the curses of the taunting Shadow. He digs his claws deep into the weak spots in Rose's mind, and attempts to bind her in a prison of fear.

Right before he can consume her in total darkness she becomes aware of her thoughts, *this is not who I am*, she thinks to herself. *I have come so far. I know I can make it to the Village of Hope.* She remembers all that Isis and Ahzhaire have shared with her, and all that she has accomplished since setting out on her journey. *I know the love of the Inner Realm and this is not it.* Then all of a sudden the taunting demon becomes visible to Rose. She jumps up and lashes at the demon, and he races away back into the shadows.

Rose is astonished at what has just occurred. "Spiritual attack," she utters to herself as she comes back to her senses. She has seen the demons in her father's eyes, and witnessed them on other people before, but never has she experienced a direct attack so powerful.

She reflects on the situation and realizes how she became vulnerable to the attack. The demon went right for her childhood wounds the second she let her guard down. Then he hit her with the criticisms that affect her the most. *Whoa,* Rose thinks to herself as she gets a grip on how serious this is all becoming. *As soon as I became aware of the poisonous lies and battled them off with the truth, the demon became visible and ran away like the cowardly rat he is.*

"Eeeaaaarrrrrcccctttt!" there is August again, signaling that it is time to move on. He flies up over her head towards the peak of the Mountain of Strength.

Rose quickly follows behind, racing up the rocky plateau, jumping from stone to stone, and dashing around big boulders. What an intense pace August is keeping. He leaves little time to dwell on any of the events from the insightful journey. He keeps her moving to increase her stamina, and to prevent any backsliding.

Rose is quite the young warrior. She is not only demolishing the challenges, she is thriving. She is learning so much about herself, and absorbing all the spiritual knowledge available for her to mature her evolving soul.

Arriving at the peak of the mountain, she can feel the heat from the volcano that lies at the summit. She peers over the edge of the giant crater, and into the vast pool of molten lava.

Bubbling spurts explode into one another. Waves of hot magma crash up against the sides of the incredible crater. Bright burning blazes flare up all over the opening of this astonishing volcano.

Fiery reds, combusting oranges, and inferno yellows burst out. Ignited flames burn like the sun and scorch lava rocks that smolder on the ashy shore of the charred pit. Oh! How beautiful are the sounds of the crackling embers and the colliding ripples of molten rock. Rose feels honored to witness the super power of Mother Nature. Such devastating destruction is contained in the Mountain of Strength. How brutal it would be if Mother Nature chose to purify Octairion with a fiery eruption?

Rose becomes mesmerized by the stunning view. What a gift for successfully trekking to the top of the Mountain of Strength. She travels from the southern side of the peak, around to the northern side where she will begin her descent.

She walks slowly while staring into the volcano. Taking advantage of this time to reflect on all that has occurred. She watches the flowing lava as she contemplates the unfolding of her life so far; the family she was born into, the damage she endured as a child, and how the demon targeted the wounds while attacking her. She recalls how her uncle Layne had been taken out and brought back into her life at such critical times, and the skills that he passed on to her. How crucial have they been to her journey so far? She is starting to see meaning behind all of it. Rose becomes more aware of the magical flow of life, and the mystical love of Great Spirit.

She reaches the northern peak of the Mountain of Strength. She stands in awe of the immense land of Kane, stretching as far as her eyes can see. She spots a walled-in settlement far off in the distance. *That must be the Village of Hope*, she thinks. Excitement shoots through her body, "Almost there," she shouts.

It seems as though after she descends the mountain there is only a desert in between her and the Village. *Judging from how the first half of this journey has unraveled I don't expect it to be so easy*, thinks Rose.

August lets out a loud screech and begins to fly away. Rose watches August as he leaves her behind, and soars all the way down to the Village of

Hope. "Well, I guess I'll have to find my own way down," says Rose realizing she has to rely on herself to get to the Village from here.

5) <u>The Kabal Desert</u>

*R*ose sizes up the Mountain of Strength and makes her descent. She advances down the tedious mountain rather quickly. Hustling down a dried up water track that once led into the land below before it was a desert, she makes her way to the bottom. It takes her less than half the time it took her to climb to the peak to trek down. Sliding on rocky slopes and rushing through well-worn paths, she arrives at the base and plants her feet onto the desert sands.

Her boots sink in slightly to the warm sand as she ventures inwards. A sudden gust of wind kicks up a flurry of sand that rudely welcomes Rose into the Kabal desert. She ducks her face behind her hands to block the flying particles. Holding her hands in front of her eyes, she continues to walk a few more paces and, BANG! She smashes into something solid that knocks her on the desert floor.

Cringing on the ground, Rose opens her eyes and before her is a man who has set up a chair and a tent out here in the middle of nowhere. He wears long brown robes similar to the one's old man Arian was wearing. Except this man is young and has a long curly beard that hangs halfway down his scrawny frame. He wears a strange animal bone medallion on his neck with a Sapphire stone tied in the middle with wire. How strange.

"Excuse me my dear, I am so sorry," says the man as he reaches out his boney hand and assists Rose off the ground.

She rubs at her eyes to clear away the specs of sand, and as her vision clears the man is standing directly in her face. His oily skin and scraggly hairs make her cringe. Surprised by the man's uncomfortable closeness she jolts back slightly, "Who are you? What are you doing out here?" she asks.

"Oh, forgive me for being in your way. My name is Soratu and I am just taking in the beauty of this marvelous desert," responds the man. He speaks with a peculiar accent that Rose has never heard before. She backs away to a comfortable distance and studies the strange man. Her first impression is that he is up to no good. Maybe he is a thief waiting for unsuspecting travelers.

"You like it out here?" she asks trying to wrap her head around his response.

"Yes, very much so," he replies then turns his back to Rose and walks into the white powdery sand, "You see there is nothing that compares to the harshness of the desert. Only the truly determined can survive out here."

Rose stares out into the heaps of sand and resists the temptation to be fearful. That is the last thing she wants to feel before she has to make her trek, "I have to cross this desert mister. Your words are not really helping much," she replies.

The strange man turns around and his brown robes whip up sand as he moves. He looks Rose dead in the eyes with a savage stare and says, "I shouldn't hold back then, for your sake of course. As much as we would want to deny the harsh realities of our world young girl, they remain true."

Rose becomes alarmed by the man's aggressive spirit. Her sensors begin to go off causing her to become defensive, "There's no need for you to act this way. You're just wasting my time with your negativity. I have a journey to complete," she responds to the devilish man and cautiously walks past him into the desert.

"Don't say I didn't warn you sweetheart. You will be deprived out there," he warns as she passes.

Rose turns around angrily and glares at the man. She can see a dark aura pulsing all around his body that hangs on him like a glowing black cape. She can feel her heart telling her that he is not worth it. Turn around and focus on your mission. Now is not the time, and she does just that. Rose turns away from the evil man and keeps moving forward.

She travels further into the desert until Soratu is no longer in sight and then inspects the borderless wasteland that lies in front of her. She can see some mysterious patches of purple flowers that have actually bloomed out here in this harsh environment. Beautiful tall rows of lupines, and desert lavender. Rose kneels down and smells the flowers. She inhales their precious fragrance, and then looks back into the desert. There seems to be less life further in. Well, there doesn't seem to be anything but endless sand ahead. Miles of desolate dusty dunes blowing grit in the wind, and yet she still walks forward into the lonely land.

She must be careful and keep her bearings about her, or she may end up deprived of her life like that jerk Soratu had warned her. Rose takes a deep breath and keeps walking before doubt can start to creep in. *As long as I keep the Mountain of Strength to my back, I should be able to walk right into the Village of Hope,* she thinks to herself, trying to keep a positive outlook.

Step by painstaking step, Rose treks further into the empty desert. The shifting sand is difficult to walk in; it is so soft and deep. Each step she takes requires a high amount of energy, yet she journeys on.

After about a mile Rose is starting to walk a bit slow and sluggish. She is feeling increasingly drained from struggling through the tough terrain. Her steps become more like stomps and she brings up pounds of warm white sand every time she raises her boots to stomp again.

She comes to a hilly collection of dunes and attempts to climb up a small bank and it collapses underneath her. She slides back down the avalanching dune and becomes frustrated, but she won't give up that easy. Rose digs her feet into the supple sand and tries to propel her way up, but the small dune is not stable and the sand streams from underneath her and she falls down into the burning hot sand. She quickly jolts back up and growls angrily! Her blood is beginning to boil as she gets annoyed with the difficult obstacles of the desert. She glances up at the blinding sun and droplets of cool sweat pour down her face. Rose lets out a great big exhale and calms herself. *I must keep my composure and save my energy,* she thinks, *becoming frustrated and angry will only waste time.*

She searches around the empty desert and finds a larger dune that looks more secure. She climbs up the large sandbank and walks along the giant parallel ridges. To the untrained eye there is nothing to this empty desert but endless sand, but the barren land certainly has a language of its own. The way the wind whips across the ranges is reminiscent to a cooling kiss upon the scorched earth, and the mighty mounds that have grown tall and sturdy from years of compounding speak of a desire to survive.

Rose looks back to see if the Mountain of Strength is still at her backside. Almost fading out of sight, the peak is barely visible. Rose shakes her head, *No, don't disappear on me,* she thinks to herself. She is beginning to become a little irritable from the hot sun beating down on her. *Ok, ok, when the Mountain of Strength is out of view I can still carry on. I will find my way. I am almost there and getting closer with every step.*

She continues to push on, forcing herself to walk although her body and mind want to stop. "Just keep going, just keep going," Rose says to herself. "Please give me the strength Great Spirit," she prays. "Please let me get through this."

The desert journey is beginning to weigh on Rose. Her stress limits are really being stretched. She staggers forward another couple hundred yards and anxiously looks back only to see that the Mountain of Strength is now out of sight! Rose becomes a bit desperate and panicky thoughts about her stranded situation flutter into her mind, "Oh no, it's gone. What am I going to do?!" she yells raising her hands up in the air. She is becoming intimidated by the boundless desert but then remembers what she learned in the crystal cavern. *Focus and regain your composure. You must persevere.* She concentrates on her breathing, trying to cope with her rambling mind, and calm herself down like Ahzhaire had shown her.

The heat is so thick around her, like she is in a sweltering oven. She wipes the sweat from her forehead and BAM, she gets an idea. *My footprints! My footprints are coming straight from the Mountain of Strength. Ok, I just carry on in this direction and my footprints will be my marker,* she thinks and a hopeful smile cracks onto her face. Rose turns back towards the Village and excitedly rushes on. She has got her second wind!

Rose has really covered some ground and she is determined to get to her destination. A breeze begins to gently blow across her face, refreshing her as she walks. The stream of air blows through her waving blonde hair and soothes her momentarily. "Oh thank heavens," she responds, but then the gust picks up speed. The wind fiercely whips sand around and consumes her in a whirl of debris. She covers her face with her arms, defending herself against the hazardous sand. The airstream pushes her around as it becomes more and more fierce. Sand is now thrashing all around her as the wind howls viciously like banshees on the prowl. It becomes too much and Rose has to kneel down and curl into a ball to protect herself. The stirring wind continues to roar around her like a tornado as piles of sand build up along her sides. She must bunker down to weather the devastating sandstorm.

After a few moments of wading out the storm the sand rises up to her knees and threatens to cover her, so Rose has no choice but to get moving again. She looks behind her to see that all of her footprints have vanished in the sandstorm, buried by the piling sand. She nervously spins around searching for any sign of her footprints. Nothing! *Oh no, Oh no*, Rose thinks. She panics while the merciless sand continues to beat against her. She tucks her head into her arms and continues to press on. "Please Great Spirit, guide me through this desert. Do not let me waste away in here." She battles against the severe elements, not knowing if she is even heading in the right direction, but still she prayerfully journeys forward.

Miles in, poor Rose is becoming exhausted. Blindly, she continues to walk in the severe sandstorm. It's the only thing that makes any sense to her. *Just keep going, just keep going,* she encourages herself. Rose is doing all she can to not collapse in defeat to the mighty stretch of desert. Mentally, physically, and spiritually she is being pushed to her limits again, but young Rose is somehow continuing.

As all hope fades, she spots something in the sand. It is a Desert Rose. She picks it up and studies the gem. It is a selenite stone that has been etched by the whipping sand. Her blue eyes narrow as she examines the beautiful white grooves worn into the gem that cause it to resemble a rose. How wonderful.

She continues to kneel down, grasping the precious stone in her hand. Thoughts of her purpose begin to flood her mind, *you carry the light Rose. The people need you. You must survive this!* She lifts her head and to her surprise she sees a damaged stone structure becoming visible. The blowing sand rapidly flying away reveals more and more of the tanned stone blocks. She dashes as fast as she can over to the old ruins and spots an entrance becoming unburied.

Rose enters through a doorway and takes cover. Sounds of the storming wind drawl outside. She is eternally grateful to be out of the fierce desert climate, and finally safe indoors. Disoriented, she gathers herself on the dusty slate floor. Breathing deeply, she tries to bring herself back from the distress of the harsh conditions she just endured.

She looks around the room and spots some old clay pots of fluid. Rose rushes over to the pots and without even inspecting the liquid she scoops what she hopes is water into her mouth with her hands, and splashes it all over her face. Rose feeling exhausted, sits back down onto the cool ground. *My goodness that was tough,* she thinks. She begins to feel light-headed and leans her head up against the carved stone-wall and blacks out.

6) <u>Baptized in Suffering</u>

𝓡ose is awakened by the flickering light of a dimly burning torch fastened to the cracking stone-wall. She attempts to shield her sensitive eyes but her hands won't budge. She groggily twists around for a moment. Rustling back and forth, she realizes she is restrained. Rose looks down at her body, and she is bound by heavy hemp ropes. The dirty tan ropes are wrapped around her legs and constrict her arms to her torso. Frightened, she jolts wildly like a trapped horse, trying to free herself from the ropes.

Out of the shadows a soft and elegant voice speaks, "Dear girl, I wouldn't waste all your strength. If I were you, I would relax." Rose looks up and emerging from a dim corner is a beautiful woman. She is dressed in elegant dark robes with long black ribbons that hang to the ground. Her straight black hair and dark tanned skin give her a deviant look. The mysterious woman stares at Rose with enchanting eyes that resemble two precious stones.

"Why did you tie me up? Let me go!" yells Rose.

"You are an intruder in my house. Why would I not take you captive?" responds the woman. "What would you have done if someone barged into your home and began to partake of your goods without permission?"

"I have traveled miles through the desert, I was so dehydrated and beaten down from the sun-," responds Rose while being interrupted by the woman.

"I care not for your story! As far as I know you have ill intentions and are equipped with all kinds of falsities. Would you trust a random stranger in your home girl?" The woman gazes deep into Rose's eyes as if she was staring into her soul. She smiles wide and her piercing eyes turn an abysmal black. "Do you understand my reasoning? I must hold you captive. It's the only way to ensure my own safety. Wouldn't you agree?"

Rose, becoming mesmerized blinks her eyes and shakes her head to resist. "But, but I'm not trying to hurt you," she replies.

The woman stalks closer to her. She now stands above her and looks down on defenseless Rose. Her presence is threatening. "I would sure hope not," warns the woman.

She kneels down in Rose's face, and the woman's eyes are pitch black. Rose can see demonic spirits trapped inside. There looks to be a whole world of tortured souls swirling around inside the dark orbs. Their faces portray agony as they scream and circle in an endless effort to escape. They are the captured souls of all the victims she has consumed in the years past, now having turned into hopeless demons.

"Rose!" yells the woman. Rose shocked that she knows her name becomes alert. "I know exactly who you are." The woman, now directly in Rose's face, sticks out her large snake like tongue and slithers it up and down. Wiggling it through the air she tastes her scent. "I am Kaylark, Queen of the Kabal Desert. Welcome to my home."

The torch on the wall burns brighter revealing more of the room. Rose lays tied up in Kaylark's demented torture chamber. There are multiple skeletons lined up against the adjacent stone wall. Rusted chains hang from the ceiling, and are wrapped around the hands of the deceased. She looks to her left and can see a bloated man hanging from the ceiling by a noose. He looks as if he has been dead for days now; the pool of blood by his feet has dried. Piles of aged bones are stacked in the far corner. Skulls line the shelves along with the tools she used to torment her victims before robbing them of their souls.

Dark Shadows begin to swarm in and out of the torture chamber. They scream and howl as they cast upon the ground next to rose, creeping in on her ever so slowly. Rose trembles as the reality of the situation sets in. This young girl has been exposed to so much as of late; her nerves cannot handle all this trauma, and she faints from the grueling anguish.

Rose awakens in complete darkness. Her arms are hoisted above her head by heavy chains and locked into a shackle. Her feet dangle, barely touching the ground. The pressure from her bodyweight pulls her hands down into the metal shackles. Her only relief is to step on her tippy toes to relieve the tension wrenching her wrists.

Rose investigates the area around her by swinging throughout the room as far as the small chain permits, but there is nothing in reach on either side. She listens for any hint of sound, but there is only silence. Rose accepts her fate for the moment and waits. She hangs there helpless in the cold dark dungeon.

What seems like a few hours has gone by and Rose questions her life and all she has been through. Her mind is stressed right now due to the devastating trials she has endured. She has traveled through the Holyoke Forest, climbed the Mountain of Strength, dealt with the tests from Ahzhaire, had her first direct encounter with a demon, and then survived the severe conditions of the desert.

The journey alone has taxed her, but now she must deal with being tortured in this desolate room. This young girl has been through a lot, but still she stands in one piece. She is held captive, but she has persisted so far. The burden of all that has occurred becomes too much, and Rose begins to weep.

All alone she sobs in this room in the middle of a desert, where no one knows where she is. "No one," cries Rose. "Where are you? Why hasn't anyone helped me?" Shaking and jerking back and forth she thrashes herself about, trying to break free of the shackles. "Isis, Ahzhaire? Where are you? You said you will always be there to help me. Where are you now?" she screams!

What seems like a few more hours drags by. The feeling of abandonment swells up inside Rose as she hangs there deserted in the room. The darkness has swallowed her whole. She is isolated from the world. All hope is being ripped from her, and her faith is fading fast.

She remembers the wolf fang that Sirius had dropped is tied around her neck. Rose pushes herself up and down with her feet and bounces the necklace. She scoops it up with her chin and licks it into her mouth. She then pulls herself up by her wrists. She lets out a horrific scream as the shackle digs into her skin. The sharp metal edge slices into her wrists, but she manages to get the fang into her hands. As she lowers herself, the ribbon from the necklace snaps, and falls to the ground, but the fang remains in her hands.

Rose desperately attempts to pick the lock on the shackle with the fang. She scrapes the jagged tooth along the metal clasps, but it is no use, she cannot reach the lock on the shackle. Her hands are forced straight up into the air, and the lock is on the bottom. Her small hands just can't reach.

Rose raises herself up again. The sharp metal shackle carves into her wrists once more and cuts her skin deeper. She winces from the pain but manages to place the fang back in her mouth. Thick warm blood now flows down Rose's arms and drips to the floor.

She pulls herself up another time and tries to pick the lock with the fang using her mouth. The metal shackle continues to puncture her tender wrists as she places the fang in the tiny keyhole and tries to move it around with her teeth and tongue.

But again she fails!

Rose spits out the fang onto the ground below her and lets out an agonizing cry. Her bleeding wrists now throb in pain. How much misery can this young girl withstand?

Rose feeling hopeless, shrieks at the top of her lungs, "HELP! GET ME OUT OF HERE. GET ME OUT OF H-H-HERE!" Rose hysterically screams as she loses control, "SOMEBODY PLEASE HELP, HELP, HELP!" She thrashes her hands from side to side trying to break free, but has no luck. Rose has exhausted herself. She stares into the darkness as she becomes light headed, and fades in and out of consciousness.

Waving slowly to all sides as she hangs from her wrists and leans on her toes, Rose is nearing death. Blood is dripping down her body and pooling at her feet. She holds onto life with the last bit of energy she has. She has fought hard to survive. She has truly given her all.

An extreme silence falls, and a sudden peace settles over Rose. A state of bliss descends upon her, as all pain is relieved, and all is now okay. She reflects on her family: the beauty of her mother, Jan, and the strength and stature of her uncle Layne. Rose recalls a day when she felt most alive; running through a field free, the fresh air filling her lungs. She felt at one with life, weaved into nature. She drifts back into the pitch black room and sees a light forming in front of her, growing in intensity.

The amorphous orb of light is hovering before Rose. Methodically it shifts shape as it gathers energy. She opens her eyes wider and is entranced by the radiant sphere. Her heart tells her to be one with the energy, don't resist. She feels the warm comfort of the lights presence as they begin to bond. It seems this baptism of pain and suffering has led Rose to a spiritual evolution. The darkness and turmoil has brought death, but this angelic light brings life. Her soul has reached a new level of maturity, and a transformation ensues.

The orb of light splits into two equal spheres and they enter Rose's body through her feet, illuminating her being. She can feel the warmth of the lights rise up her spinal column, intertwining with her chakras and blasting their essence throughout her body. White light shoots from head to toe in multiple flashing strikes, illuminating Rose's whole body over and over again.

She squirms in ecstasy as the two orbs spiral and coil around her spine and up to her crown chakra, where they intertwine and blast another storm of energy through her body, energizing and amplifying her spiritual capabilities.

The orbs continue up and down Rose's spine, expanding all of her chakras, and then combine into a beam of light that hoops around Rose's head like a halo. Light surges all throughout her body. The pressure of the energy builds inside her chest and rips through the skin of her back. The light beam slices through the tender skin of Rose's shoulder blades, and out bursts a pair of luminous wings!

She rips her arms down from the hanging chains, and shatters the shackle. Finally free, Rose takes a moment to examine her new self. Her translucent blue wings extend just above her head and down to her knees. Waves of pulsating white light shoot from her back like electric explosions and ripple into the bright tips of her wings. She unfolds her bioluminescent extensions and sparkles of light detonate in the air like dazzling fireworks and sizzle to the ground. What a beautiful and shocking transformation.

She can feel the heavenly power pulsing through her veins, so warm and majestic. She doesn't quite understand exactly what happened, but she will have time to ask questions when she arrives at the Village of Hope. Right now she needs to finish some unsettled business.

She spreads her wings and storms out of the dark cell. She flies through an underground tunnel and smashes through the shabby wooden door to Kaylark's chamber. Kaylark is startled as Rose rushes over to her and slams into her with great force. She crashes up against a wall and falls to the ground. Two frightened men are bound and gagged on their knees in the room. The whimpering men wear soiled tan clothing and look to be treasure hunters.

Kaylark and Rose lock eyes. "Thanks for the support," says Rose.

Kaylark's eyes widen as she takes in the sight of angelic Rose. "Anything for you my dear," replies Kaylark as she shoots a blazing beam of Dark energy from her hand that soars straight at Rose. She ducks and charges across the room towards Kaylark! The women exchange a flurry of devastating punches. Kaylark, feeling a bit overwhelmed, grabs hold of Rose tightly. They grapple furiously. Rose overpowers her and tosses Kaylark to the ground then jumps on top of her.

"Give up!" yells Rose screaming into her face.

"Never," replies Kaylark, forcing Rose off of her and quickly jumping to her feet.

Kaylark lunges at Rose, and Rose catches her by the neck. Gripping her throat tightly she suspends her in the air, and stares deeply into the darkness of Kaylark's eyes. She can see all the victims that have suffered in this woman's hands. They howl and wail in terror. They have been trapped inside this hell for who knows how long.

Rose squeezes tighter onto Kaylark's throat as her anger builds! Suddenly Kaylark's eyes widen greatly and she hisses wildly! Then right before Rose's eyes she transforms into a shadow and slithers away into the darkness.

Kaylark flees the chamber in a fearful rush and the horde of tormented souls that have been held captive, escape from their prisons. Ear-piercing cries fill the room, as the tortured souls fly away into the light. Rose walks over to the two men, cuts their restraints, and sets them free. They're gem hunters who got lost in the desert night. They thank her and then run off.

Rose freezes for a moment. Everything feels so different. How could she explain what has happened to her? How does she even begin to process what has occurred here? She just dusts herself off and flies out of the temple into the desert.

It's not time to worry, she thinks, *I must complete my journey to the Village of Hope.*

Part Two: Divine Communion

"Suffering is only suffering if it's done in silence, in
solitude. Pain experienced in public, in view of
loving millions, was no longer pain. It was
communion."
— Dave Eggers

7) <u>Village of Hope</u>

*A*rriving at the Village of Hope, Rose lands before its massive golden gates. My! How they sparkle with an enchanting glare. With eyes wide open, she gazes over the immense complex in a moment of awe. She has finally made it.

The Village of Hope is a giant walled in settlement in the middle of Kane, also known as the wilderness, where lost souls come to wander. The walls surrounding the Village are tall, thick, and completely encase the hidden community, keeping all who are not called from intruding.

She approaches the entrance to the Village and the giant golden gates begin to open wide for young Rose. She steps in cautiously, not knowing what to expect.

An explosion of loud voices greets her!

"Welcome!"

"Hooray!"

"You made it Rose."

The people of the Village have gathered in the courtyard and are celebrating her arrival. "We're so happy to have you here! We're so proud of you," yell the excited people.

Her face lights up with joy. She is completely surprised. Rose enters and walks down the bumpy cobble stone path leading through the crowded courtyard. There are people on both sides clapping and cheering for her accomplishment. Cheerful faces full of happiness. Young men and women wearing sleek suits of blue and white armor jump up and down, full of praise.

As she moves further in, the celebrating crowd splits and an excited man comes forth. It is her uncle Layne! He is reaching his arms out for her! "Welcome home Rose." he says as he embraces her in the world's greatest hug. Both of their faces stretch out the biggest smiles ever.

Layne takes a step back and looks at who his young niece has become.

"My goodness, I knew you were destined to be a Light Warrior, but who knew you were going to evolve into an Angel."

Rose looks up at her uncle Layne with tears in her eyes. It is so good to hear his joyous voice and feel the comfort of his calming presence.

"Is that a good thing, uncle?" she asks.

"Of course it is. There are many types of Light Warriors being birthed in this time. But no one has evolved into an Angel before."

"Yeah, well it has certainly been a difficult journey," she replies.

"I know it has been my dear. To be a true warrior, you must walk the warriors path every step of the way, and Rose, you have done just that."

Exhaling, she smiles, as the deep honor of the moment flows over her.

"Come now. Let me show you to your room so that you may rest. Tonight we will celebrate your arrival with a Pilgrim's Feast," says Layne placing his arm over her shoulder, and leading her to the dorms.

The Village of Hope is a training ground which houses the chosen Light Warriors. All who have been called to the Village have exceptional abilities, and are extra sensitive to the Inner Realm. They have been guided here to excel in the knowledge of their gifts, as well as learn about their relationship to Great Spirit and their true identities as Light Warriors.

Just as Rose had to persist in her arduous journey, all who inhabit the Village have also succeeded in a rite of passage. Their perseverance has earned them a place amongst the elite. Once training is complete they will be sent to outposts positioned around Octairion to battle off the spreading darkness, and save anyone who has not been consumed by the Dark Forces.

Rose awakens to the sound of the bell tower as it rings in dinner time. She hops out of bed remembering her newly altered body. Expanding her light wings from her shoulder blades, she begins to experiment. She fully extends them and small bursts of blue speckling light shoot from the ends.

She then disperses her wings and they disappear with a buzzing flash, making her look like a normal girl again.

Rose holds out her hand. She can feel the light energy flowing through the tips of her fingers. She extends them and little fizzling sparks zap out and crackle. *How awesome is that,* she thinks.

Rose is intrigued and grateful for her new gifts. She can't wait to discover the extent of her angelic abilities. She throws her arms up over her head, still a bit weary from her journey, and has a good stretch. *Alright, let's see what this place has in store for me,* she thinks, and heads out the door to the Pilgrim's Feast.

The students make their way to the dining hall where an elaborate celebration has been set up. A giant banquet has been prepared to commend Rose on completing her expedition, as is the custom for all who survive the journey to the Village of Hope.

Rose is seated at the center table next to her uncle Layne and the other leaders of the Village. Three long tables are set up adjacently and filled with many hungry warriors. The tables are set, loaded with fruits, vegetables, and loaves of bread. Tonight they feast on a savory pork roast.

Everyone sits comfortably and prepares for the celebration to commence. Layne arises dressed in a ceremonial suit of blue and white armor, looking especially well dressed for this occasion. He clears his throat and addresses the community.

"Alright, listen up everyone!" he says as the clamoring crowd quiets down. "I am proud to introduce the newest arrival to the Village, my beloved niece Rose." The students applaud and cheer for her. People she doesn't even know are proud and screaming her name. She is overwhelmed by the love. Rose begins to blush and hides her face.

"Tonight we praise your efforts and remarkable persistence. Not only are you my own flesh and blood, but now you are a part of our grand family here at the Village." The warriors raise their glasses and cheer. "Let's eat!" yells Layne as the warriors begin to dine.

Rose glances around the room at all the dining warriors. She spots Lucian Luzz, a pasty faced blonde boy, levitating his peas into his mouth one by one. *What in the world,* she thinks, watching the boy lifting the food with his mind. He misses his mouth and one flies back into Amber Durgens hair, who then looks around confused. Rose catches Sydney Blake, a tall girl with a long brown pony tail, teleporting Abigail Day's drink to the opposite side of her plate, and Abigail doesn't even notice. Molly Sue, a short girl with red hair, is not even using a chair as she confidently levitates at the table.

Rose cracks a smile as she takes in her new family full of gifted individuals. The dining hall is beautiful, the courtyard is cozy, and so far the people are, well, interesting to say the least. She looks down at her plate and begins to eat her food.

Layne chats with the other leaders, as Rose observes and eats quietly. Layne speaks with David, Headmaster at the Village, a large man known for his passion. David is the combat trainer. He laughs loudly with a great big grin on his bearded face, as he shares stories of the battlefield with Layne.

"Things have changed a lot since our days on the battlefield," chimes in Corporal Krystah. She is a mesmerizing blonde beauty, tall and thin. "Only in the last few months have humans evolved to possess greater powers. The new generations have an advanced ability to harness their powers and they grow at exceptional rates."

Rose overhears talk about the growing Dark Forces in Drakkar and their plans to send out troops. She waits for a moment of silence and questions her uncle. "Uncle, how did you get back to the Village and become a leader?"

"Well Rose, you see, my mentor Masters called me back to the Village shortly after you were taken away from our family. I came back here and continued my training, developing into a Sage."

"A Sage uncle?" questions Rose.

"Yes, a Sage is someone who has abounded much wisdom through their life's path, and my job now is to share it with all who are capable of absorbing it. That was Master's job here prior to me but sadly he passed away recently. Before he passed though he requested I be a part of the leadership here at the Village."

"Oh, I see." replies Rose.

"Any other questions?" asks Layne.

Rose shakes her head no.

Layne rises again, "Ok, listen up!" he yells. The warriors quiet down and give commander Layne their undivided attention. "Today we enjoy a nice feast Light Warriors, but tomorrow we get back to business. The Dark Forces are assembling in

Drakkar. Their numbers are increasing and growing more powerful. It won't be long until more and more demons head west. Demonic Shadows roam Octairion looking for people to possess, and when the Dark Forces march they will be looking to reap a harvest of souls. We must rescue these people Light Warriors. This is our mission, this is our purpose. Get some rest. Tomorrow we step it up."

The warriors exit out of the dining hall to enjoy the rest of the beautiful night. A group of people enjoy a fire in the courtyard, and some of the levitators toss light balls back and forth with their minds. Rose overhears another group talking about heading to the library to do some reading. What a peaceful and relaxing place.

A young man and woman walk up to her, "Hi Rose, I'm Kaz, and this is Larissa." Larissa curtsies to her.

Kaz is an eccentric looking person. He has tattoos up and down his arms with a tribal style haircut; long on top and shaved on the sides. Larissa is a proper and pure looking girl with curly black hair. She has a fair complexion and light aura.

"Nice to meet you Rose, I am so happy to inform you that we will be roommates," says Larissa.

Rose smiles at her. *A roommate,* she thinks. *I have never had a roommate before. This just keeps getting better.*

"Rose would you care to sit and meditate with us?" asks Kaz. He notices the cuts on her wrists but doesn't dare ask what happened. "I know when I arrived I really needed to settle," he says compassionately.

"I could definitely use that," says Rose, accepting the love.

The group walks into the courtyard and sits in a triangle together.

"Ok, deep breaths," says Kaz, as they begin the exercise. "Exhale all of the tension and all the stress that is inside of you. Let all the negativity fall away. Let all the worries and cares of the world fade quietly from your mind, and surrender to the flow of the universe. Let Great Spirit fill us with peace. Inhale the love and light of all things as we become one with life."

Rose slows her mind and listens to all that is going on around her. She hears the crackling of the fire and the whispers of people winding down. Wind chimes create beautiful melodies in the distance. She continues to take deep breaths and tries to release the crazy events that have just past. She surrenders all that has occurred for the present moment.

"Let go of all the questions about the journey, about life," continues Kaz, "and accept that it was meant to unfold as it did to make you the person you have become, and are becoming. Let go of the damage and the trauma. Let it all fall away and look forward to the beauty of now. Rest and relax in the loving embrace of Great Spirit. Think about all you are grateful for, and all that has blessed your life. Thank Great Spirit for your transformation, and for allowing us to advance in the Light."

Rose releases all the questions of why she had to suffer, and thoughts of why no one came to her rescue slip from her mind. She settles into a healing peace. Her nerves relax and she is slowly becoming grateful to finally be in a safe place surrounded by good people.

They sit in silence for a short period of time until the courtyard bell tolls signaling it's time for everyone to head to their bedrooms and call it a night.

"Thank you for joining us Rose," says Kaz.

"You're welcome and goodnight," replies Rose, as her and Larissa make their way to their bedroom.

Larissa and Rose converse as they walk slowly in the starry night. "How long have you been here?" quietly asks Rose.

"I was called here about six months ago," responds Larissa, as she moves her curly black hair from her face.

"Where did you travel from? What was your journey like?" asks Rose.

Larissa turns and faces her. She intimately gazes at Rose and doesn't hesitate to share her story with her new friend, "I came from a small town in Drakkar called Pentane, located on the northeast tip of Octairion. I had been a quiet and introverted girl. Never really mixing with other people, and always kind of fantasizing about a new life in a faraway magical place. I would sit in my room, and swear I could hear voices. At first they were scattered about, but years later I could eventually hone in on them and interpret what I was hearing.

"What were they saying?" asks Rose full of curiosity.

"They were people crying out for help. Distress calls from those being tortured by demons around Octairion."

"That is terrible! What did you do?"

"I didn't know what to do honestly, but in my heart grew a desire to help them and shortly after that, I could hear the Oracle of the Village calling me to leave my hometown and journey here for further training."

"That is incredible," replies Rose. She scratches at her head nervously as another question instantly pops into her mind. She doesn't want to seem too naïve, but she asks it anyway, "Who is the Oracle of the Village?"

Larissa thinks nothing of Rose's inquiries, "She stays in the sanctuary and is holy unto Great Spirit. She is our connection to all of the Light Warriors stationed around Octairion. A psychic like myself or other Oracles at other locations can communicate with her. Our leaders will consult her and form strategies against the Dark Forces when the time comes."

"What's the difference between you and an Oracle?" asks Rose.

"An oracle is a more advanced form of a psychic, and can communicate much longer distances. I hope to one day experience enough to evolve into an Oracle," says Larissa with stars in her hopeful eyes.

Rose and Larissa enter into their bedroom. A simple little room with two twin sized beds on each side. Larissa has trinkets and candles set atop her dresser, and some books and a journal spread open on her desk. Her inhabited side of the room reflects her studious personality, while Rose's bare half speaks of a blank canvas waiting to come to life.

Rose lies down in her comfy bed, as Larissa gets down on her knees and prays, "Great Spirit, I thank you for all of your love and goodness. Thank you for my new roommate Rose, and bringing her to the Village safely. Please bless us with a peaceful rest and beautiful dreams."

Rose smiles and snuggles into her bed. She is comforted by the customs of the people of the Village. Larissa gets up and enters into her bed, and turns out the lights. "Goodnight Rose," whispers Larissa.

"Goodnight," she softly replies, and both girls drift off into dreamland.

A deserted baby tiger roams the shore of a raging river. Waves surge down the rapids, exploding as they crash into the rocks. The baby tiger is petrified by the intensity of the stimulating torrents. Overbearing sounds like an avalanche thundering down beat onto his eardrums, and foamy white eruptions like lightening from the clouds crash onto the riverbed around him.

Paralyzed, he freezes in fear. All alone, he cries out in despair, but his youthful cries are drowned out by the wailing water, roaring so severe. He panics and frantically searches about for his father, until a splash softly sprays his face, wetting his little whiskers.

The cub is knocked out of his frenzy and looks to the jungle, and there stands papa tiger, full of pride. Baby tiger dashes to his father and nuzzles in the comfort of his nurturing presence. He feels safety, protection, and love return to his world. He trots along confidently next to him. There is no other place he would rather be than in the security of his father's shadow.

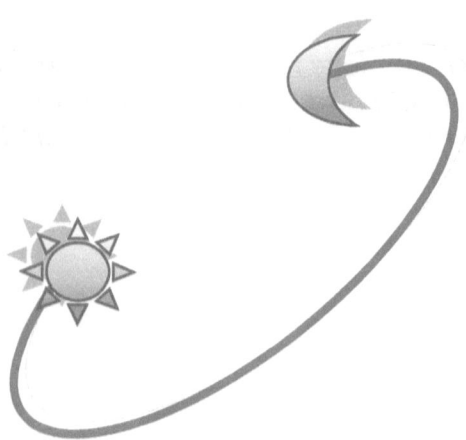

8) <u>Shocking Surprises</u>

*B*ung! Bung! Bung, tolls the clunky bell tower. Time to wake up! The sun has arisen and the new day is here. Rose awakes and rolls over. She spies Larissa down on her knees in prayer. So focused and so dedicated.

"Dear Great Spirit, I am grateful for this day. May our efforts please you, and may you give us the strength to overcome all the obstacles that stand before us."

She rises to her feet and turns to Rose, "Ready for your first day?" asks Larissa.

Rose sits up on the edge of her bed and looks out the window. Sunrays shine and gently caress her beautiful face.

"You bet I am," yells Rose as she springs out of bed.

"Good, you should be. After all, you slept through breakfast," replies Larissa tossing her a juicy red apple.

Rose catches the apple and is stunned by Larissa's comment, "I must have been really worn out from my journey," she replies and takes a bite.

"It's no big deal. You'll want to get suited up in your Light Warriors uniform," says Larissa as she points to the closet. "We're going straight to combat practice."

Rose heads over and opens up the large wooden doors of her very own closet. Inside, there are numerous blue and white uniforms. Rose takes one down and slips into the stretchy one-piece suit. Armor plating is sewn into the arms and legs of the protective outfit. Stitched into both shoulders are star tetrahedrons, the emblem of the Light Army.

"Are you sure you're ready to start training so soon?" asks Larissa concerned for Rose's wellbeing.

She stares at Larissa, *What a caring friend*, she thinks to herself. She isn't used to that. "We have a mission to prepare for. There is no time to waste. I'll be fine," says Rose. Then her mischievous side kicks in, "I'm as ready as I'll ever be," she yells as she darts out of the room laughing.

"Hey!" Larissa yells, following right behind her.

Rose shoots down the long hallway of the dormitory, dodging half sleeping warriors. Larissa zigs and zags trailing behind her closely. Rose fires down a spacious spiral staircase and rockets into the courtyard, and BAM! She runs right into Captain David's bulky belly and bounces to the ground.

"Whoa, whoa, whoa, I like the enthusiasm, but watch who you pick your battles with around here, ha!" says David as he extends his hand and helps Rose off the ground. Rose looks around embarrassed as all the other warriors gather nearby.

"Whoa, looks like the new girl thinks she can take out the captain already," snarks Lucian Luzz. Lucian is a blonde haired, blue eyed young man, well-built and proud of himself.

Rose glares at Lucian and shouts "I was not."

Kaz chimes in, "Lucian, I see you can't ever mind your own business, can you?"

Lucian snaps back, "Hey Kaz, why don't you take your own advice and buzz off, huh? No one was talking to you."

"Enough!" yells Captain David. He does not have much patience when it comes to nonsense. "Well I see we all have plenty of energy this morning, why don't we get to work, huh? Everybody fall in!"

The soldiers start to dash about the courtyard. Rose stands there watching a bit confused. The warriors' line up in multiple columns as the squad quickly gets into formation. Kaz catches Rose's wandering eyes and waves for her to line up next to him. She darts over and clumsily falls into position.

Captain David paces before the crowd with his hands behind his back, "Alright so let me break down the game for you new Light Warriors here. The battle of light vs. darkness was one that was fought in the mind. Great Spirit would guide and assist those who wanted to be supported in growing in love, and the dark spirits would tempt and possess those who were wounded or blind to the manipulations of the darkness.

As time passed, humans advanced in their abilities as spiritual beings, and began to evolve into actual beings of light or darkness. The battle has moved from the spiritual plane into the physical plane. Depending on your life calling, and if you chose to heed that call, you will evolve into a new being according to your spiritual gifts." Captain David pauses before the squad and moves his hand from left to right, "Just as all of you who have made it to the Village have done."

He turns back and continues to pace.

"Can anyone tell me the name and types of Light Warrior classes?"

Kaz quickly raises his hand, jumping up and down. "Me, I can Sir!" he yells eager to answer.

"Okay Mr. Kaz, I can see you might have a heart attack if I don't choose you. Come up front and tell us all about the different classes."

"Yes Sir!" replies Kaz as he jauntily walks to the front.

"First off, I am a Healer, or a Shaman," he yells out extremely excited to talk about his gifts. "My expertise is using my words or actions to help someone heal their mental and spiritual wounds that have been inflicted upon them through their life journey. I can also guide them in destroying negative thought patterns and behaviors that may result in sickness and disease physically. If someone is suffering from sickness and disease already, I may be able to assist them in releasing the negative energy and guide them in replacing it with positive light energy." He blurts out all this information without even taking a breath. "I can also use my Light powers to manually heal anyone who is not fully overcome by the darkness Sir."

"Alright, a Healer, our first example, well said," replies Captain David, "how about the next class?"

"Sir, next we have Kinetics. Kinetics can levitate objects or people with their minds. They can even learn to fly with their wonderful ability."

One of the pesky Kinetics from the ranks levitates Kaz's gold amulet on his neck. The group of warriors laugh as it moves up it hits him in the face.

"Hey! Alright enough of that! Kaz, continue please," says Captain David.

"Right, um, then there are PsyComs Sir. They are our psychic communicators. PsyComs are our means of long distance communication here in Octairion. Psychics can contact each other as well as the Oracles of different stations."

"PsyComs are extremely important during war. They can give and receive important details that could make a huge difference," adds Captain David.

"Then we have Flashes Sir. Flashes can teleport themselves or other objects from place to place. We also have Rangers who are expert marksmen and can nail a demon from a mile away."

"Very good Kaz, head back into the ranks," replies Captain David, and Kaz pride-fully struts back into his place. "Kaz has just given you the gist of what we know so far. More and more advancements are being found as time goes on. Now, the powers of the darkness are quite vague, as we have not witnessed much of their capabilities.

This shift is occurring right now as I speak, ladies and gentlemen. New data is coming in every day. The Dark Forces can travel as shadows, and can possess and steal the souls of humans. If we come across a human soul that has not been fully consumed by the darkness, we may be able to awaken or heal the person with our powers. When a person is consumed by the darkness, they too can evolve into numerous advanced dark beings. Unfortunately we do not have all the information we would like on these demons, but we do know that they can be killed.

When people transform into these demons, they are no longer humans. That's right; they are no longer your brothers, sisters, or even your parents. They are now a part of the darkness. If you do not kill them, they will kill you."

Captain David marches over to Rose and slams his feet down right in front of her. "Rose, do you know what abilities you possess?" asks David.

Rose shocked that she was called first, looks at David. "Well, I can do this," responds Rose as she bursts out her glistening light wings. Her fellow warriors flinch and jolt back as she blasts off and flies around the crowded courtyard. Rose circles through the air a few times and lands in front of her stunned classmates. None of these young warriors have seen an Angel before.

"Well now!" responds David. "Your uncle Layne didn't tell me we had an Angel on our hands."

The group of warriors stands in awe as they examine the majesty of Rose's angelic form. She stands so confident and beautiful, shimmering in the glory of all she has become. What a wonderful reward for all her hard work.

Lucian picks his jaw up off the ground and wipes his eyes. He cannot believe what he has just witnessed, and neither can majority of the camp. I don't think he will be mocking and picking on Rose much longer. She has shown her true identity here today and it is not something to take lightly.

"Wow, that was incredible," replies Kaz, "I'd like to see you move like that Lucian," he says elbowing Lucian in the side.

"Shut it, Kaz." Lucian snaps back. You see, Lucian can levitate himself and other objects, but levitating is nothing compared to the flight of an Angel.

"Alright, that is quite an amazing gift Rose," responds David, "Of course you've walked quite the path to receive it. I'm sure."

Rose nods her head yes.

"Well, I'm glad you're on our team darling."

Captain David glances across the group of warriors. Scratching his chin he contemplates who he will choose for the next challenge. "Okay, today's lesson will be target practice. Do we have any volunteers who would like to demonstrate the use of the light beam?

Roger Redcliff raises his hand. "Right here, Sir," he yells as he shoots his hand up in the air. He is a cocky young man but he doesn't intentionally look down on everyone, he's just tall, with short brown hair and narrow green eyes. He really prides himself on his shooting abilities.

"Okay Roger, step up and let's see what you got," challenges David. "All spiritually evolved beings can harness their energy and shoot a projectile beam of light from their hands, inflicting damage to their opponent. Both Light and Dark beings possess this ability. Depending upon your evolutionary traits, different results may occur. Some can paralyze their target, while others severely burn or stun their victim."

Rose looks down at her hand and remembers the sparks she shot out earlier. She extends her fingers and little lightening sparks shoot from the tips and fizzle out. She has not yet experimented with this ability, and has no idea what to do. She looks around nervously hoping no one has seen that she cannot shoot a light beam, but no one has noticed her misfire.

Captain David has four target boards set up across the courtyard. Blue discs with white bull's-eyes in the middle. "Okay Roger, let's see what you got. Hit all four bull's-eyes consecutively down the line, that is, if you can young warrior," says David pressing Rogers buttons.

"Piece of cake Sir," says Roger as he raises his open hand in front of his face. A beam of light energy forms in his palm. He clenches the energy in his fist as it continues to grow. Roger squints his glaring eyes as he intently focuses on his targets. Drawing back his hand and plunging it forward, Roger releases four super charged light beams. The rays of light spiral out of his hands and stream like rays from the sun straight into the four targets. Bam! Bam! Bam! Bam! Four bull's-eyes at once!

"Incredible! What a display of marksmanship," declares Captain David, slapping his hands on his knees in excitement.

Roger turns with a grin, "Humph, it's nothing," he says as he walks back into the crowd. The rest of the warriors stand there stunned.

"Thank you, Roger. Alright Light Warriors, everyone line up and face your targets across the courtyard. Let's practice your marksmanship abilities," yells Captain David.

The warriors line up and start blasting away at their targets. Rose lines up and attempts to focus the energy in her hand. Little sparks fizzle in her palm and the small flashes of light begin to grow into bigger bolts. Lucian Luzz catches sight of Rose struggling from the corner of his eye and yells out, "What's the matter Rose, one trick wonder? Ha!"

Rose scowls at him and begins to concentrate. Lucian ignites dormant anger from deep inside of Rose. The hurt from never being good enough and pain from the laughter of the students in class, who mocked her, bubbles to the surface. Sadness from never living up to people's expectations and the faces of children laughing start to haunt her. Their voices grow louder and louder.

The light pulses in her hand, growing and charging bigger and bigger. The power increases second after second. Rose's past memories of hazing and being mocked continue to flood her, fueling her with intense energy surging through her body. The energy is then channeled into the magnificent ball of energy building in her hand.

"It's all in how you direct your energy," says Captain David who is watching Rose deal with this emotional ordeal. Tears now run down her face as she continues to release the sorrow of her miserable childhood, and transmit it into her new found skill. Memories of her parents neglect and abuse begin to boil inside her. She remembers how her father turned her back on the family, how her mother turned a blind eye to Rose's needs and desires, and the pain of being alone and having to fend for herself because no one was there for her. No one was there to protect her in her time of infancy. She had no one there to hold her and tell her that it was all going to be alright.

The massive energy ball grows too powerful for Rose to control and it explodes from her hand. The light beam blasts towards the ground and burns a path up to the target. Rose can't handle the amount of force that is being emitted from her hand and she falls backwards. The rampant energy beam wildly shoots past several students then up into the air. Everyone stops what they're doing and stares in shock at the spectacle that has just occurred.

Captain David walks over to Rose and reaches out his hand to help her up, "You will learn to harness that tremendous power, Rose. Let's keep practicing. Everyone back to work!" he yells aloud, he then leans in close to her for some one on one advice, "Okay Rose, let me give you some insight on shooting your photon beam. Us light warriors are powerful energetic beings. We can be overwhelmed by the passion inside of us at times. We must learn to balance and connect with our power. We must not dull the light inside or let it overcome our capacity to manage it.

It was great that you reached into the depths of your soul to gather the inspiration you needed to hone your ability, but too much passion too fast will obviously overwhelm anyone. It has also revealed such incredible potential inside you though. Why don't you try to release the energy sooner?"

Rose sets up again and focuses on the target. She taps into her emotional reserve and lets the photon beam build in her palm. She can feel the strength of the light orb pulse inside her hand. She holds it and senses its energy. The orb has a familiar presence to the light beam that entered into her at the brink of death and entwined with her soul during her transformation.

This light orb calls out for her to be one with it. "Know me, nurture me, and love me. Experience me fully and make me your own, Rose." The light whispers intimately to her soul, "I will protect you and help those you care about. Trust me."

Rose pulls her hand back and thrusts it forward releasing a great energetic blast and nails her target. "Great job Rose," responds David, "Keep it up." She continues to shoot blast after blast at the target. Switching from hand to hand and quickly becoming comfortable with her new talent.

Rose clenches her fist excitedly, "Alright!" she yells, proud of herself for grasping her new capabilities.

Rose and the other warriors continue to practice their barrage of beam blasts for a long while and captain David shouts out a big holler, "Alright, everyone gather round. Great job training, I am happy with everyone's effort. Combat practice is finished for the day." The warriors wipe the sweat from their foreheads, and head back to their rooms to get washed up.

The crowded courtyard that was just filled with action is now desolate, and Captain David says a prayer, "Dear Great Spirit, I ask that you please bless the effort of these young warriors. May you help them know their true strength. Please allow us to be sensitive to your guidance," then David turns and walks to his quarters.

Rose and Larissa are all cleaned up, now relaxing on their beds. Rose sits up with her legs crossed and turns to Larissa, "Tell me what you know about the Dark Forces?"

Larissa climbs over to the edge of her bed to get closer to Rose, "I know of a few different forms. There are the Shadows that roam the land hunting for damaged souls to infect. People who are fearful or hate filled. In a moment of weakness they can latch onto a host and whisper deceiving lies into their head.

Rose recalls her encounter on the Mountain of Strength, "I have come across one before," she replies.

Larissa nods her head and continues, "They can smell distress from miles away. Once they spellbind their prey with manipulations, they tempt their victim to commit acts of darkness: self-hatred, sabotaging of dreams, and destruction of the love inside them. They do all they can to get you to snuff out the light inside of us. If they are successful, then an ugly transformation takes place. They become dark beings hell-bent on spreading chaos."

Struck by the details Rose remembers her battle in the desert, "I encountered a witch before I got here to the Village of Hope. I bet she was one who was completely consumed by the darkness," Rose informs Larissa.

"What powers did she have?" asks Larissa.

"She had these pitch black eyes that would enchant me if I stared into them long enough. She also had control over the Shadows that lurked about. I saw potions and elixirs scattered around her chamber too."

"Wow," replies Larissa.

"Yeah," says Rose, "she turned into a shadow and slipped away at the end of our battle."

Larissa is getting more excited from the shared dark tale and moves even closer to Rose, "On my journey here I came across a swamp in Cassiel. I had to cross over the murky water on a bridge, and when I was about half way over the rickety passage I could hear something splashing. I watched as the head of what looked like a decaying man emerged from the swamp. The darkness had transformed him into some kind of undead mutant.

The monster resembled a human but he had a face like a gargoyle. The skin on his arms was torn off and his muscles were decaying right off the bones! It looked like his body was barely holding together. His limbs where hanging from his frame. You could see the pain and bitterness rotting in his soul through his sunken in eyes. It was like he held a world of death inside his body. He attempted to capture me on the bridge, but I ran as fast as I could. He shot Dark energy beams at me as I took cover in the trees. I just kept running and never looked back."

Rose sits back against her wall, astonished at the tale being told, "It seems like they have similar powers to us, just twisted and demented versions, huh?"

"Yeah, that's what I have heard around here, but no one knows what is to come. Who knows what kind of radical development is going to occur in the near future... any day now," utters Larissa.

The day winds down to an end as the warriors eat dinner together. After dinner, they enjoy their free time. Rose wanders to the outer eastern edge of the Village and spots Kaz sitting in silence. She slowly creeps closer as to not disturb him. He sits in such a deep concentration as if he were on another planet or something, so peaceful. Rose continues to watch quietly for a moment. She then backs away and snaps a stick under her feet, distracting Kaz.

He slowly opens his eyes and remains in his spot of relaxation. He notices Rose tiptoeing away, "Don't worry, I would love some company," says Kaz. He waves his hand inviting her to come and sit with him and witness the beauty of nature. Rose accepts and has a seat next to him.

The wind gently blows and the trees dance softly. The fully blossomed branches shuffle back and forth pushing against one another like a crowded dance floor. The sun shines upon the leaves, and in return they cast shadows upon the grassy field below. Sun-spots glisten as the solar rays evade the leaves and warm the ground. Birds chirp and swoop from branch to branch, while butterflies flutter about. The aged trees drop acorns and prickly pinecones that bring life to the scene.

"Close your eyes and listen," whispers Kaz in a state of bliss.

Buzzing bugs zip around as the wind drawls. The rustling leaves sound like waves in the ocean. Rose becomes drowsy from the heavy peace that is blanketing her and Kaz. Nature's lullaby is swiftly carrying Rose off into a deep slumber. She lays back and enters dreamland.

The sun sets in vibrant purple and orange hues. Smoldering clouds streak the red-hot horizon. The few remaining rays from the sun warn of the coming darkness. At this point it seems inevitable that night shall fall upon the land, and on that note the first star ushers in the nocturnal affairs. The cosmic constellations come out to play.

Taurus charges onto the scene, strutting proudly, and out of nowhere a cluster of stars in the shape of an arrow comes shooting across the expanse, directly at the sensuous bull! Sagittarius aims with envy, for he is the superb beast of this celestial sphere. The racing cosmic ray slips past Taurus, and collides with the scales of Libra. Thrown of balance Libra sends shockwaves through space, rattling resting Virgo. The arrow plummets like a fizzled rocket, nose-diving into the clutches of Cancer, who, is immediately washed away by the waters of Aquarius. Gemini looks on with scorn like a scolding parent. Out of the universal ocean vaults Pisces. The two flailing fish jolt in opposite directions. Leo roars as Aries and

Capricorn butt heads and create a massive
supernova that startles Rose from her sleep.

She awakens to her uncle Layne picking her up off the ground. The moon is shining bright in the clear night sky.

"Hey there sleepyhead, did all the training today tire you out?" asks Layne.

"I guess so. Must have taken a lot more out of me than I realized," answers Rose as Layne places her on the ground. "Where's Kaz?" she asks.

"I woke him up before you and told him to head to his room," replied Layne.

They begin to walk towards the dorms.

"Hey uncle?" asks Rose.

"Yes?"

"Have you seen my mom at all lately?"

"No, I have not. The last time I saw her was back in Conway before I came back to the Village."

"How was she doing?" questions Rose.

"Honestly, she wasn't doing well. I'm sorry."

"What do you mean uncle?"

Layne contemplates if young Rose is ready to hear about the darkness in their family.

"Uncle!" yells Rose, "I can handle it."

Layne chews on his lip for a moment and then drops down to meet Rose at eye level, "Your mother was plagued by darkness the last I saw her. Her mind was haunted by demons night and day. They kept her imprisoned in fear. I tried to talk to her and help her all I could, but some people don't want help, and you cannot help someone who wants to destroy themselves. She felt like she was worthless. The whispers of the Shadows devoured her and she agreed with all their lies," answers Layne and then he continues walking.

"Do you think she's turned into one of the Dark Forces, Uncle?"

"No, I don't. Although the darkness was heavy upon her, she still had a glimmer of hope. She was always proud of the fact that she had given birth to such a beautiful and precious girl. I'm sure she's holding on for you dear. I believe the light inside her, although it may be dim, is still alive."

Rose breaks a smile onto her downcast face, "We'll save her uncle. One day, we'll save my mom," she responds.

Layne and Rose approach her bedroom door. He gives her a big hug and a kiss on the cheek.

"Goodnight Rose."

"Goodnight uncle."

9) Flashing Lights

$\mathcal{R}$ose and Larissa wake up at the sound of the ringing bell tower. The light warriors are up and ready for training this morning. They all rush through the long hallways of the building and down the stairs yelling and screaming as they go. They eat a quick breakfast together and gather in the courtyard. Captain David is also overly energized this morning. He adds to the exciting energy by yelling and wildly waving a giant light sword through the air.

Rose can't believe her eyes! She is amazed at all the surprises each new day is bringing and the new abilities that are being revealed. What a wonderful time of self-discovery.

Captain David approaches the squad and begins the lesson, "I will now demonstrate the power of the light sword." Captain David clenches his fist and quickly expands it. Light blue crystal shards begin to construct in his hand. Large sparks of white light fizzle as the electrified pieces of crystal form a burning sabre.

"This sword here burns extremely hot. It can sear off limbs and decapitate your enemy quite easily. We Light Warriors do not have infinite energy though. Our light energy is depleted as we produce Light materials such as the light beams, swords, and shields. Depending on how much energy you have reserved, you will dish out more or less damage with your light sword. That's why it's important you get your rest Light Warriors, or you better become friends with a healer who can give you a charge when you need one.

The light sword cannot be detached from the body. It is a direct conduit of the power flowing from within you. You can however, deploy and withdraw your weapon at will. Kaz! Why don't you come forward and give us a show?"

"Absolutely, Captain David Sir!" responds Kaz with much enthusiasm.

The childlike man stomps his way to the center courtyard in full tribal style. Raising his arms to the sky, he worships the sun. With outstretched arms he breathes in the energy of the universe. He places his hands together in front of his face like a monk and begins to chant, "White light of Great Spirit be with me now." He thrust his hands down by his waist and produces two radiant light swords. The blue swords sparkle with dazzling white speckles of light throughout them. As Kaz rhythmically waves his arms, the white light sparkles begin to surge out like shooting stars through the night sky. The sparks sizzle and hiss as the swords whirl around. Kaz dances intimately with the swords in his hands, slashing through the air as he swings the dual swords harmoniously. Each movement is a tribute to Great Spirit.

Kaz strikes the two swords together directly before his serious stare. Geysers of flashing lights whiz into the air like fireworks detonating all around him. Rainbows of light flicker and flair as they trail through the air like asteroids falling to the ground. He whips around, spinning and kicking as he sprays halos of crackling little flares with his outstretched swords. Kaz then retracts the two light swords and places his hands down by his side and bows to the squad.

The squad applauds and thanks Kaz.

"Awesome job Kaz, Great Spirit has certainly been honored. Thank you for that," replies Captain David as Kaz heads back into the group. "Okay, now everyone partner up and practice your melee attacks. Let's go!"

Rose and Sydney Blake join together for training. Sydney is a country girl with a goofy way about her, but don't mistake it for weakness or you will deeply regret it.

Rose rehearses creating the energy sword in her hand. She sparks out a light sword and it quickly disappears. She repeats it a few times with the same results.

"Feel it in your whole arm," suggests Sydney. "It is a part of you. Let the energy flow through your body and form the sword, darling. Be one with the sword."

Rose feels the energy in her body. She focuses it into her arm and successfully produces a light sword. She holds the energy in her arm as she feels the sensation of the sword becoming an extended limb. The sword remains; pulsing powerfully. She excitedly waves it through the air.

"Okay! Let's practice," says Rose with a devious little smile.

They begin to lightly spar. Sydney allows Rose to slowly strike back and forth to get a feel for the drift of her blade; the way it slices through the air, and how lightly the sword pivots. Finding the balance of her swing, Rose starts to temper her skills and she and Sydney go slash for slash.

Sydney sensing that Rose is growing more comfortable begins to play around. She takes a few jabs at Rose and teleports behind her. Rose stands in place, trying to sense where she might have gone. Sydney elbows Rose from behind and lightly pushes her.

"You got to be ready for anything in battle," says Sydney. She quickly lunges at Rose and jabs at her again and teleports. Rose spins around and slashes her sword, but Sydney is nowhere in sight.

"Up here Rose," yells Sydney as she rains down a devastating punch, knocking her into the dirt.

Rose punches at the ground a bit upset at her poor reaction speed.

"I'm sorry honey. You got to be able to handle this form of attack," says Sydney while reaching her hand out to help Rose up.

"Don't worry. Let's keep fighting," says Rose while fixing her stance. She won't give up so easily.

Captain David, who has been observing and advising all the warriors while they fight, expresses to Rose she has got to use all of her senses, "Listen closely for any sounds. Try and feel where she is," yells Captain David. "That is the key to defeating the Flashes."

Rose glances over at David for a split second and Sydney takes full advantage. She slices away at Rose who blocks the blows with her sword. Rose and Sydney crash swords together and wrestle to overpower one another. Rose gains the advantage and drives her knee right into Sydney's stomach, knocking her onto all fours. She follows up with another kick, but Sydney teleports. Rose immediately rolls away, trying to put distance between her, and where Sydney may be. She closes her eyes since Sydney is nowhere to be seen. She sets herself in an offensive stance and listens intently.

A moment goes by and Rose hears the slightest blip of turbulence above her as Sydney appears. Rose quickly reacts and raises her sword above her and blocks the attack. Sydney teleports to her right, but Rose is on top of it. She swipes her light sabre and crashes swords with Sydney. She begins to teleport continuously, scattering herself all around Rose, who waits calmly for an opportunity to strike Sydney and end this nonsense.

Rose pays close attention to the pattern of Sydney's teleporting, the sounds and the movements she makes. She closes her eyes and can hear the trail of sound leading to Sydney's next position. She predicts Sydney's next move and throws a fierce punch to her right. Sydney appears and grabs Roses arm, fiercely hip tosses her over her shoulder and slams Rose into the ground. Standing over her, Sydney directs her blade towards Roses neck, indicating the round is over. Sydney retracts her sword and extends her hand, pulls Rose up, and gives her a hug.

"That was quite the challenge. Thank you," says Sydney.

"No problem," she replies, "I almost had you."

They both have a laugh, and head to the sidelines to watch the other warriors finish up their matches.

Rose may have lost the fight today, but she is advancing rather quickly for a rookie. She gave Sydney, a senior student, a good match. Rose possesses a keen intellect, and has great battlefield vision. She quickly perceives patterns, threats, and possible opportunities in battle and will adapt accordingly. This is a great advantage for her and the entire Light Family.

Training comes to an end with Captain David hollering across the courtyard. "Alll-riiight! Great job everyone. That's all for today." The warriors head back to their rooms to get cleaned up, and enjoy some rest.

Rose and Larissa, both having washed up, sit on their beds bored with nothing to do and are seeking some excitement.

"Larissa, if you could do anything today, what would it be?" asks Rose.

"Oh I don't know," replies Larissa, "Probably go exploring."

"Yes, let's do it!" replies Rose.

"You aren't serious, are you?" asks Larissa snickering.

"You bet I am," Rose gets up and runs out the door. Larissa throws her hands up in the air in disbelief and yet can't help following her.

They run to the eastern edge of the Village where a canopy of giant treetops will hide their escape. Rose extends her angelic wings. They unfold with a whipping zap.

"Grab ahold Larissa," says Rose.
Larissa wraps her arms around her torso and they fly up over the giant walls of the Village and out into Kane.

Rose and Larissa glide over hills and zip through valleys. They soar through the air at high speeds. The wind blows through their hair as the girls scream in excitement.

"This is amazing," yells Larissa as she watches the scenery whip by like a passenger in a speeding train. They fly to the northern tip of Kane and rest upon the quiet shore of the vacant beach. Larissa and Rose dig their toes in the warm white sand as they stare out into the ocean.

Along the coast of the beach survives the remains of an abandoned lighthouse. The cracking foundation assuredly holds up the neglected structure. Vines wrap around the base and climb up to the shattered windows of the optic section. The trailing plants restrict the once vibrant lighthouse and leech the life from the ancient structure. The massive bulb of the beacon is still intact, yet lacks a spark to fuel the spotlight. *If not this lighthouse, who will warn the unaware midnight travelers of the treacheries hidden in the dark water,* Rose thinks to herself. *How many have been stranded due to the negligence?* The careless light bearer has surely left his post.

Larissa turns to Rose with a downhearted stare and asks, "Do you ever wish your life was different?"

"How so?" questions Rose.

"Do you ever think about what life would be like if we were just normal girls?"

"Honestly, no I don't," replies Rose. "I understand that my life had to be the way it was for me to be the person I am today. I'm proud to be me." Rose notices the sadness on Larissa's face. She grabs her hands lovingly and extends her heart to her, "What's going on?"

"I guess I'm just homesick is all. I miss my family," responds Larissa, opening up her burdened heart.

"Well that sounds normal to me," says Rose with a smile. "I miss mine as well."

"You have your uncle Layne here," says Larissa.

"I know. I am grateful for that, but I'm concerned about my mother. Darkness has been upon my house since I was young and I hope I can save her in time."

Her response strikes Larissa like a ton of bricks. Here she is sulking over her issues selfishly when there are others much worse off, "Wow, that's right. We're fighting to save everyone's family, aren't we?

"Right, that's why we have to keep pushing forward and can't look back," declares Rose as she jumps up on the sandy shore, exhilarated.

Larissa jumps up and joins her in the excitement.

"You're right! That's what we're doing it for. We're doing it for them," she exclaims.

The two girls get up and run along the sandy shore as they enjoy their time of freedom on the beautiful beach. The whisky waves wash away the smoothed pebbles like the cares of the wayward girls. Larissa has expressed her emotional burdens and Rose has compassionately held her heart through the ordeal. She has gained a new perspective and a much needed boost of encouragement.

"How about we head back to the Village before anyone realizes we're gone?" asks Larissa.

Rose agrees, and the two girls regretfully pull themselves away from the brief escape and fly back to the Village to continue their mission.

The girls return as the nightly activities come to an end. Pencils fall and paintbrushes are laid to rest, as the finishing touches are put on the hexagons and spheres of sacred geometry projects. The warriors of spiritual intellect and power head to their rooms to recharge and prepare for all the beauty that is in store for them tomorrow.

Every day is a gift and an opportunity to better yourself, Larissa thinks while she closes her eyes for the night. Rose wishes her sweet dreams and turns off the lights as they drift into dreamland.

From a single point explodes a spiraling sphere. Expanding in a clockwise motion, the sphere divides into three spirals. The triple spiral spins and releases waves of color as three women emerge. A beautiful young woman grabs a spiral and twirls it like a sacred stick. She wears a floral headdress and prances about like a fairy fascinated with creation.

Grasping the second spiral is a pregnant woman. She selects the spiral and presses it upon her womb. The spiral morphs into a torus. The funnel expels energy downward from her womb, then circulates energy upward above her crown, and pours it back into her womb. The repeating cycle nourishes the seed of life evolving inside the woman.

The third spiral comes to rest in the palm of an old crone. She gazes into the whirling spiral that has transformed into a galaxy. She puts the galaxy to her lips and whispers words of wisdom to all who care to listen.

10) <u>Kinetic Clash</u>

*R*ose awakens to the sound of birds chirping outside as the sun rises. She quietly tip-toes out of the room, so not to wake Larissa, and makes her way to an early breakfast. Rose sits silently in the empty dining hall. A few early birds scamper in and out but do not disturb the peace. Her heart is extra sensitive this morning.

Bowing her head she prays, "Great spirit, I thank you for this day. I ask that you would watch over all of our families here at the Village. Keep them safe and free from the snares of the darkness. Keep the light inside them burning brightly. Please allow us all to train hard, and grow all we can to help rid the world of the Dark Forces. Thank you for allowing me to have come so far. Give me the strength to finish my mission here."

She reminisces about her family and imagines what reuniting with her mother would be like. The joy her mother would feel when she saw her face and the smell of her mother's perfume.

The pesky bell tower rings, disrupting the peace filled morning and the rest of the Village joins Rose for breakfast.

Voices echo as the room awakens and the busy bees populate the dining hall. The hungry warriors fill up on food to fuel today's training session. Day three has come and Rose is more motivated than ever. The passionate fire for saving her family is being fanned as she continues to grow and gain confidence in who she is and what she is capable of.

Her excitement builds as she sees Captain David out in the courtyard preparing for today's lessons. The warriors finish up their breakfast and head out to join Captain David.

"Next, you will receive instruction on the crystal shield. The crystal shield is your main defense against projectiles and melee attack," says Captain David as he stomps before the sleepy warriors who are wiping the slumber from their eyes while they attempt to stand in attention. "The crystal shield can withstand a lot of damage but is not indestructible."

Captain David deploys a crystal shield and throws it up in the air. He then quickly produces a light saber. Captain David jumps into the air and thunders a devastating overhand slash that breaks through the crystal shield, shattering it to pieces. The drowsy warriors are caught off guard by the explosion of shimmering lights and he now has their full attention.

David snickers, proud of himself for the clever alarm clock. "Now, instead of focusing your light energy into a photon beam, direct it into a force field around your arm to wield it as a shield." Captain David peers down the line of warriors, "Larissa, step up!"

Larissa is ready and alert. She dashes to the front of the squad, "Yes Sir, Captain David Sir!" she shouts enthusiastically. She definitely cherishes the opportunity.

"Larissa, as a psychic communicator, the crystal shield is crucial to your survival. While watching over the battlefield and communicating unfolding events to the oracles, you can become vulnerable to attack. Deploying the crystal shield will protect you from any opposing threats. Please demonstrate how to wield the crystal shield for your fellow students."

"Yes Sir!" replies an excited Larissa.

She focuses her energy inside her palm and a small light orb forms. Larissa clenches the light in her fist and cocks her arm tightly as the light spreads around her forearm. Piece by piece a crystal shield constructs from her fist to her elbow. Like frost gathering in the winter, the crystal cubes coagulate into a giant sheet resembling ice. Light shines in shimmering waves through the dark blue crystal shield that extends from her chin to her waist.

Before anyone can comment Captain David swiftly blasts out his light saber and lunges at Larissa. She quickly thrusts her shield upward to deflect the blow. Captain David strikes with another strong slash that is quickly blocked by Larissa. He circles around her slowly. They stare each other down fervently. Larissa's eyes enlarge like a bear backed into a corner. He stalks her like a starving panther closing in on its prey.

Captain David lunges and fires an assault of deadly dagger jabs. Larissa blocks one after the other. The intensity is picking up and Larissa feels genuinely threatened at this moment. Captain David means business.

Larissa kneels down to withstand the barrage beating down on her. She charges a photon orb in her palm, then forcefully stands up, knocks his dagger away with her shield and blasts the powerful light beam. Captain David immediately deploys his crystal shield and deflects the blast of light into the air. He returns with a menacing kick that crashes directly into Larissa's shield and drives her backward.

Larissa skids to a stop, jumps sideways, and launches multiple photon beams before hitting the ground and rolling. The photon beams rocket towards Captain David, who side steps and dodges the beams. He lets out a grin and retracts his saber.

"Very good Larissa," remarks David, "One last challenge."

Captain David drops his hands to his sides and charges two great photon beams. He lets out a gruesome shout as he hurls shot after shot of photon blasts at Larissa. She blocks low, blocks high, and blocks low again. The light beam onslaught continues to rain upon Larissa who is becoming overwhelmed. She has no choice but to withstand the assault.

Captain David's swarm of severe photon spheres persist beating upon the crystal shield. Sparks fly left and right as light fragments ricochet off of the dark blue shield.

Captain David ceases fire and lets out a great big holler, "Now, that's some defensive work. Fantastic job, Larissa! I hope the rest of you were paying attention."

Larissa drops her guard and sighs in relief. "Thank you, Captain David," she replies while walking back to the squad exhausted.

"Excellent technique Larissa, you showed a strong defense and an intelligent offense, perfect strategy for a PsyCom, Great job!"

Captain David takes a minute to gather himself. He wipes the sweat from his brow and grooms his beard before focusing back on the warriors. "Now, depending on your gifts everyone, you will have to develop a unique strategy formulated to your mode of operation. My Flashes, you can set up a shield, block the attacks, and teleport to the opposite side of the enemy and attack. My Kinetics, you can hurl your shield at your target and draw it back to you. There are many different combat maneuvers to discover. Now let's get to work. Partner up everyone."

The squad pairs up and prepares for combat training. "Lucian Luzz, why don't you partner with Rose so the two of you can work out whatever differences you are having, huh?" recommends Captain David.

Lucian turns his smug face towards Rose and smirks, "Humph, whatever."

Rose just shakes her head and prepares for battle.

Some people are blessed with special abilities in life, and others have to earn them with blood, sweat, and tears. Lucian seems like one of those who have had it all come easy. He's ungrateful and arrogant about the gifts he's been given. He's the unruly king type who has not rightfully earned his place on the throne, and now he faces off with Rose who has fought every inch of the way to become who she is.

Lucian and Rose circle around each other, sizing one another up. Rose fairly new to the combat arena deploys her crystal shield right away. *Like a novice*, Lucian thinks, as he uses his Kinetic powers to rip away her shield. It flies through the air and into his hand. "Thanks Rose. I can do just fine on my own. You don't have to help me," boasts big headed Lucian.

Rose grits her teeth and steadies herself. She concentrates deeply, calming down and honing in on every move Lucian makes. Watching him like a hawk. *This guy is not going to play fair*, she thinks. She deploys another crystal shield and produces a light sword in the other hand.

"Okay so you want to play swords, huh?" says Lucian, as he sparks up a light sword himself. Rose angrily dashes across the courtyard sand, jumps into the air, and slashes down on Lucian who blocks the attempt. He counters with a slash towards Rose's waist, but she jumps back and dodges the attack. Lucian follows up with an overhand slash.

He smashes Rose's shield powerfully and knocks her backwards. She dissolves her energy sword and blasts three light beams at Lucian as she falls. The light beams cut through the air like razors toward him. Lucian swipes the first and second beam away, then spins around and deflects the third right back at her. The deflected light beam soars right at Rose, but falls short and explodes at her feet.

"C'mon Rose, give me a challenge. Let's go!" yells Lucian as he taunts her, beckoning her to step up her game.

He shoots two light beams and catches them in the air with his mind. Lucian then raises them up into the sky and sends them thundering down on top of Rose who absorbs the shock with her shield just in time. The powerful blasts shake her up a bit, but she also notices that Lucian had focused his eyes on the beams the whole time he levitated them, a kink in his armor maybe?

"I'd like to see you do that with these," yells Rose, as she blasts two photon beams at Lucian, who catches them in the air. He levitates them towards the sky, preparing to release another devastating thunder attack, but Rose rushes at him with all her might. Lucian sees her out of the corner of his eye and loses focus. The two photon beams shoot off into the sky as Rose strikes at him. He's caught off guard and throws up his shield, blocking her attacks as he backs away in defense. Rose continues to persistently bombard him with mighty slashes.

Lucian ducks left and blocks right. He can't do anything but guard himself against the heavy battering crashing down on him. Rose has the upper hand and wants to take advantage of it. The fierce strikes send sparks shooting from Lucian's crystal shield. Pieces break off and burn into the ground around them. He sweats from the intensity of her offensive assault.

Lucian gathers himself and freezes her arm in place, mid swing, with the power of his mind. He jumps back and levitates into the air. Lucian showers down a cluster of photon beams at Rose from the sky. She immediately deploys dual crystal shields, waits out the hail storm of light beams raining down from inside the protective blockade, and then retracts them.

Rose stares up at Lucian. She peers deep into his eyes and extends her angelic wings. All of the other students stop and watch as her glorious wings unfold and illuminate the battleground.

She takes off into the air and Lucian quickly blasts a couple of photon beams. She dodges one, and another, but the third beam is a direct hit into Rose's chest. She's hammered backwards and lets out a blaring cry of pain as the light beam burns into her skin. The students look on with shock and anticipation. What will happen next?

Rose flails her luminous wings and catches herself in the air. Lucian resumes discharging shot after shot of blazing light beams, trying to keep her at a distance. Although Lucian can levitate in the air he is not too agile. Rose continues to evade the attacks and penetrates Lucian's defenses. She slams into him powerfully and drives a right hook directly into his mouth. Her anger is growing violent due to the sizzling burn on her chest.

She follows up with a furious overhead double hammer punch and Lucian plummets to the ground. He crashes into the dirt below and kicks up mounds of dust. Rose comes soaring through the dust and lands right on top of him, stomping her feet into his gut. Lucian lets out a horrid gasp as she plunges a hard kick right into his ribs. She charges a light beam in her palm and directs it at Lucian's face. He cowers under the pressure, and Captain David yells, "Okay, that's enough!" breaking up the passionate fight.

Bung! Bung! Bung, rings the bell tower announcing to all that time for lunch has come. "Great job everyone. Let's head into the dining hall and refuel," bellows Captain David.

The squad disperses.

Lucian gets up, dusts himself off, and just walks away embarrassed.

Captain David spots Rose still fuming from the heated match, "Hey, why don't you come and walk with me for a minute," he asks her.

She stares David over for a second and is unsure of what he is thinking. He raises up his arm and throws it over her shoulders, taking her under his wing, "You have unbelievable passion and strength. It's quite impressive. I look forward to seeing how you progress through your training. I have not worked with an Angel before, but I am thrilled to assist you in advancing."

"Thank you Captain David," replies Rose, "I intend to give my all Sir."

"Ha! I can see that," he responds, "but don't let your temper get the best of you. Especially, when training against one of our own."

Rose stares up into Captain David's heavily bearded face. Under all that fur he holds a fatherly grin. "I understand Sir. I'm sorry for getting a little carried away."

"Don't be sorry," replies Captain David," I can see that as an Angel you are geared for war. Certain types of light warriors are designed for battle, such as Kinetics and Rangers. They are gifted with precision accuracy and a sharp intellect in action packed situations. I see it powerfully in you, but that entails you work on your discipline too."

Rose shines a proud smile as Captain David acknowledges the warrior inside of her, "I will work on that Sir."

"Be sure that you do. Other types of warriors like Healers, PsyComs, and Sages are more geared towards assisting the Light Army grow and mature. If you were to unleash a passionate outburst on one of them, only Great Spirit knows what might occur."

"I understand," replies Rose. "Thank you for the info." Her mind is intrigued by his words and she continues to grow more curious about the different types of Light Warriors as Captain David shares his wisdom with her.

"Alright soldier, get out of here. Go get some grub," he replies dismissing her.

The hungry heroes run into the dining hall and wait in line to be served. There is chattering of all sorts echoing through the large dimly lit hall. They share rumors of events occurring around

Octairion, and stories of the battles that took place during training. Rose overhears her name a few times but thinks nothing of it.

Little cliques are formed all around the dining tables as the Light Warriors share lunch with their friends.

Rose makes her way through the lunch line. They are serving chicken and vegetables today. She spots Larissa and Kaz sitting with Sydney Blake. Kaz wildly waves his hand signaling for Rose to come have a seat with them. Rose smiles at his enthusiasm and makes her way over to join them.

"Hey Rose," greets Kaz. "How are you settling in around here?"

Rose sits and makes herself comfortable and replies, "Things are going quite well. I'm learning a lot about the gifts I have and how to control them properly."

"Aw that's awesome," responds Kaz, "looks to me like you have a great handle on them already. The way you took out Lucian today, that was something else!" he says with a giant smile on his face, looking to stir up some drama.

Humble Rose nods and thanks him, "What is your story Kaz?" she asks trying to change the subject.

Kaz, surprised about the question and extremely excited the spotlight is now on him, drops his silverware and prepares as if he is about to give an important speech.

"I lived in Hirama, Ahbaram on the northwestern coast of Octairion. I grew up there with my beautiful mother, sister and father. My father was a strong and wonderful man. He loved my mother so much. He treated her like the queen she was. My mother would tell me all about Great Spirit and about his love for me. She was basically the embodiment of his love. She would sing beautiful songs as I lay in bed at night. I will remember them forever." Kaz pauses a moment and puts his head down. The memories of his mother are heavy on his mind.

Rose, realizing that his mother has passed away winces. *Tough topic,* she thinks.

"She got sick and passed away when I was twelve." Kaz pauses again, and an emotional wave comes over him, "I was lost for a while after that. Nothing made sense to me, you know? Everything changed that day. My father and sister took it just as bad as I did. My dad started drinking and lost his job, so my family started living a much different life then; a much poorer life. In those days I had to deal with my own feelings of extreme loss, plus my families. All without my mother there to assist me in it, but that's what transformed me into the Healer I am today."

"I'm sorry for your loss Kaz," responds Rose. She can't imagine how he feels, but she certainly cares for him.

"Thanks, but that is all in the past now. We have the world to worry about. The rumors around here have been picking up."

"You're right, it shouldn't be long now before they attack," says Larissa. All of a sudden the conversation quiets down and a cold reality settles over the group.

"How do you know they're true?" asks Rose concerned.

"PsyComs from the Northern outpost of Cassiel say that they're hearing sounds at night, but no one has seen anything," says Larissa.

The talk of Dark Forces sparks Sydney Blake, "I hear they're like rabid Hyenas. They swarm around their prey and rip it to shreds!"

"I heard their jaws are so strong that they can crack rhino bones!" adds Kaz.

"Sounds like a tough fight," utters Larissa.

"You guys! We shouldn't be talking like this," interrupts Rose. "We were made for this. This is what we have struggled for. The people of the world need us, including our families and our friends. This is what all the hard work on our paths is leading us into. All the pain, all the hurt, we have so much to give back to the world. This is our time. We can destroy these monsters!" she declares with authority.

"Wow Rose, you have quite the fire inside that soul of yours, eh?" remarks Sydney.

"You know it. I'm sorry, but to me, this is such an important fight. I have watched home after home and life after life be destroyed by the Dark Forces. My family is not a family because of the darkness. Some of the most important people in my life have had their lives destroyed by the darkness. So much has been stolen from me, so much time wasted on suffering and all those people out there now are suffering the same, except they are still caught in it. They have not been blessed with the gifts we have and the awareness we possess. They need us to lighten the way for them. They need us to save them from the darkness."

Rose is now standing up and leaning over the table. The rest of the group can see the passion inside of her. Clearly she is prepared for all the change in her life and enjoying who she has become. A once so fragile and gentle soul trampled on by the darkness, has now been transformed into a Light Warrior. Confident and determined, she has been equipped with wisdom, knowledge, spiritual sensitivity, and a heart of gold. Now she has a passion to extinguish the darkness that has plagued this nation. She's really becoming the leader she was destined to be.

11) <u>Spiritual Wisdom</u>

*B*ung! Bung! Bung! There goes the old bell tower ringing in the end of lunch. Commander Layne rises up from his table and addresses the room, "Alright everyone. Let's move into the sanctuary where we will share the wisdom of Great Spirit."

The Light Warriors exit the dining hall and move across the courtyard into the sanctuary. Its tall rooms have such a holy presence. Stone walls stacked two stories high are dimly lit with candles. The hallways have an eerie cavern feel to them. The long dark passages set a tone of sacredness. The warriors walk through in silence. This place is precious to the entire Village.

The students enter into the main chamber and sit along the long wooden pews facing an altar dedicated to Great Spirit. The carved stone alter is filled with half burned white candles dripping with melted wax, and opalite crystals have been placed in the shape of a tetrahedron. Commander Layne stands before the altar with a serious look upon his face. This time is holy to him. His love for Great Spirit is untouchable. Next to him lays an Oracle dressed in white linens. She has been sitting in complete solitude. Set apart for Great Spirit alone. She serves with complete abandonment.

Commander Layne starts the ceremony with a prayer, "Dear Great Spirit, we are yours. Thank you for bringing us into this moment, a moment so critical in time. We thank you that you have chosen us to bring forth your light into the world. Be with us now as we share this time. May you purify our hearts even further, and sanctify our minds. Keep us focused on spreading your love and light to all who need it. May you guard our steps and steady our hands, Great Spirit. Give us the strength to continue upon this path you have chosen us for. Nothing is more important than our mission."

A gust of wind blows through the room and caresses the abundance of wind chimes placed around the sanctuary. A soft jingle of bells fills the air and a peace so heavy falls upon all inside. Great Spirit's loving presence has certainly blessed this holy place. Everyone is so relaxed and now ready to hear from commander Layne.

"This life we have been given is sacred and beautiful. When you are filled with love, life just seems to flow at an amazing and intimate pace. To be at one with the world around you is the ultimate love. To share this love with your fellow man and to admire his skill, to nurture his weakness, and have the same done for you in return is the ultimate blessing. Bearing one another's burdens in love does not mean to handicap your brother when he is fully capable of the task before him. But rather true love will be there for support in any manner that is necessary to help your brother or sister accomplish that task, and grow because of it.

When you are out there on the battlefield, you must be in the moment. Focus intently and listen to your heart. You must be on your toes, if not to keep yourself alive, then to keep the person next to you alive. Your effort in this training camp will carry over into the battlefield. The effort you put into developing your skills is what is going to win this war. To change this world we must first change ourselves, and then assist the person next to us. By making our team here at the Village of Hope number one, we will have a better chance of helping the rest of the Light Army defeat the darkness.

Now I know that there have been rumors going around about the increasing number of Dark Forces and their plans to attack. We believe these are more than just rumors. It's inevitable. Indeed their numbers are growing, but we have no idea of knowing just when they will attack. That is why we must be ready. That is why our training is so important. We have gotten word from outposts further east that large cities have been taken over by the darkness of Drakkar. So for now we wait and continue to prepare for our time to strike. Great Spirit, be with us."

Commander Layne turns to the Oracle, "Blessed Oracle, we consult you. Do you have word from the Great Spirit?"

The oracle stretches her head up in the air as if extending an antenna. She breathes deeply and tunes into the Inner Realm. Her flowing linens wave in the air as she moves around elegantly and methodically, swaying her arms rhythmically as if dancing to the music of creation. She worships Great Spirit with every movement.

She opens her mouth wide and exhales deeply and then speaks in a low soft tone, "Time is certainly crucial. Make the most of your energy use. Feed and water your garden, for a bountiful harvest is in store. Ready your eyes to be widened. Ready your being to be stretched. All of you are going to be exposed to a new world. The spiritual dimension is quickly settling upon your physical realm and life is new every moment. Be aware of the miracles surrounding you every day. Be aware of the miracles that you are. Great Spirit is weaved into every fiber of your being. There is no coincidence in you being here. We need you. The universe needs you.

We stress the importance of your specific roles in this war. Have confidence in yourselves and the power each of your beautiful souls contain. Have full faith that all is working in perfect harmony for the greater good of the universe. Although there are going to be growing pains in this time, when the dust settles and the rubble is sifted, there will be a new dawn Light Warriors. We are dependent upon you. We thank you all for coming so far and we charge you to continue to fulfill your destinies."

The Oracle finishes speaking and falls to the ground in ecstasy. The ambiance in the room is of a quiet empowerment. The Light Warriors look around the room at each other and realize that all of their lives are now united. They are a family. As much as they are uniquely designed individuals, they need each other to accomplish this task. They will need to depend on each other in order to usher in the new era of light on earth.

Commander Layne acknowledges all that the Oracle has spoken, "Thank you, Oracle. As much as we are your leaders Light Warriors, when you leave this training camp and are deployed around Octairion, you will need to depend on your own abilities and intuition. You must absorb all you can in these last days of preparation. Spend time in personal training to customize your strategies. Get to know your skills very well." Commander Layne pauses for a minute and looks over the Army of Light. Their eyes are wide and still attentive. He clasps his hands together and concludes today's message, "Thank you all for sharing in this time with me. Now, how about we take a break and meet in the garden? Corporal Krystah will be holding a spiritual awareness session shortly."

The warriors rise from their seats and begin to exit the sanctuary. As Rose walks up the aisle towards the sanctuary entrance, she is stopped by Sydney Blake.

"It must have been pretty awesome growing up with Commander Layne, huh Rose?" she asks coming up from behind her. Sydney seems like she is being bothered by something deep inside. Rose can see some difficult emotions have been stirred up during the message.

"I was lucky to have him," Rose replies. "He has taught me so much about life."

Sydney bites down on her lip like she wants to speak but can't find the words to do it. She pauses and looks around the empty sanctuary, then back at Rose, "Like what?" she asks.

Rose can read Sydney's eyes even though they hide behind her bangs. She is looking for someone to trust right now, someone to be vulnerable with.

"Well, when I was younger I was taken from my family," responds Rose. "My uncle Layne came to me and told me that this was the beginning of my special journey. He told me I was brave and that I could handle anything that came my way. He really helped me keep my head in the right spot through all the trials I had."

"I wish I had looked at life like that when things started to get out of hand for me," replies Sydney.

"What struggles did you go through?"

"Well." Sydney kicks at the ground, nervous about sharing her wounded side with Rose, "You see, I never knew my real mother and father. I grew up on a farm with my uncle Jack in Edana. Everything was fine when Uncle Jack was sober, but when he would get drunk he'd scream and throw things around the house. He never hit me, but one time he came close to smashing me in the face with a horseshoe he whipped across the yard when he was angry." Sydney starts to tear up but she chokes down her sadness and holds it back.

"I'm sorry Sydney," replies Rose.
Sydney wipes her face and puts up a hardened front like she doesn't care, "Oh its fine, really. I learned to go and hide in the barn and take care of the horses whenever he would drink. They really became my best friends in that time.

Nothing beats the love of an animal, I'm grateful for that. I mean, it could have been a lot worse I suppose."

"That sounds like a difficult life," replies Rose, sympathizing with her. The poor girl is broken and she won't let her guard down.

"It wasn't all bad. I got to spend a lot of time with those horses. There wasn't anyone else around really. You know how much love a horse is capable of giving?"

Rose cracks a smile, happy that Sydney's tone has changed. "No I don't," she answers.

"A whole lot, they're emotional animals. Horses also have detailed memories. They don't forget a thing! They would always get so excited when they would see me coming. They would jump up and run around. I could have ridden those horses forever. But they didn't like my uncle Jack much. I think they could sense what kind of man he was. I can't blame them though. I'm happy to be away from him."

"How did you get to the Village?"

"One day I was out in the stables and Uncle Jack was ranting and raving in the house. He spooked some of the free roaming horses and they went charging. When those horses came running by the stable, they frightened all the other horses that were tied up. The stable was old and rickety, so when the horses tried to run they broke the support beams and the roof came falling down.

I swear I saw it all happening in slow motion. My senses became extremely amplified. I saw so vividly and heard every single sound. As the roof came falling down on top of me, I looked outside and could see myself standing out there looking in. Then next thing you know, I had teleported to that spot where I saw myself and I watched as the stable collapsed. I wasn't sure what had gone on but I knew I'd had enough of that farm. I hopped on Jessie, my favorite horse, and just started riding. I eventually came to a river where I met up with one of the PsyCom girls and she told me about the Village of Hope. We then traveled here together."

"Wow! That is some story. I'm glad you're here with us. We are each other's family now." Rose reaches out her arms and gives Sydney a big hug.

"Thanks for listening to me," replies Sydney.

"Anytime," says Rose as the two girls exit the sanctuary.

Rose and Sydney come to the courtyard where their fellow Light Warriors have gathered. The heat has been turned up around the Village due to all the talk of the Dark Forces. A sense of urgency can be felt. The time of peace seems to be dwindling. It is expected that war will soon break out in Octairion.

Rose looks around the courtyard and the general mood of her fellow Light Warriors seems to be one of confusion. She can't stand the low morale around this place. Her blood boils. She spreads her wings, flies into the air, and perches onto a giant statue in the courtyard.

"Hello everyone, what is going on here? You all look a little down. Is this news of war getting to you all?"

They begin to mutter to each other and someone cries out, "We're just a little shocked is all."

Looking down onto her fellow squad members, the soldiers with whom she will be shoulder to shoulder with in combat, Rose becomes filled with the need to do something about their depressed attitudes. "Well I'm sorry my friends, shocked is not going to save you on the battlefield. Shocked is not going to protect you when the darkness is surrounding us. We must focus and use this time wisely like the Oracle said. We must perfect our abilities and go into this battle with confidence!" she yells into the courtyard.

Slouching turns into attentive listening as some of the warriors begin to perk up a bit.

"We're in this together Light Warriors. We're going to need to encourage each other and push each other to strive to leave here the best we can." The passion inside Rose is unbeatable. Her motivating words and confident determination are certainly a force to reckon with. She dawns a presence of personal assurance that surely draws their attention.

As the soldiers stare up at Rose, they can see this natural leader rising up in front of them. She is definitely someone worthy of following. Her infectious speech and energy spreads around the community and the Village of Hope is slowly being revived.

Lucian Luzz approaches the statue and yells for Rose to come down and speak with him. She glides down and lands in front of Lucian.

"What's up now?" snaps Rose at Lucian whose track record is not getting him any respect.

"Rose, I apologize for the way I have been acting. I can't deny the fact that you are looking to unite us all, and for me to stubbornly impede your vision would do a disservice to the Light Army. I'd like to bury the hatchet."

Lucian reaches out for Rose's hand and she takes it. They shake hands and put the past behind them. Bung! Bung! Bung, rings the bell tower. It is time for Corporal Krystah's spiritual awareness class.

"I'll see you in class," says Lucian and he runs off.

12) <u>An Urgent Tone</u>

Corporal Krystah relaxes in a luscious garden in the far end of the Village as she waits for her students to arrive for class. The landscape is plush with all kinds of topiary hedges. The excited students enter in through a captivating walkway lined with polished stones and puzzling trees carved into spirals. They peer down the many winding paths and marvel over the numerous sculptures. Cascading cubes line the enclosure and mysterious animals are carved into the bushes. A giant seal and her baby lay in a bed of daisies. On the other side, a huge lion stands proud surrounded by an assortment of red and white roses.

    The students make their way to the main court where Corporal Krystah is standing in between two superbly etched statues of howling wolves; ears back and jaws pointed to the sky. The students pile in and fill the benches that complement the enchanting square. Corporal Krystah approaches the students dressed in a purple and black gown with a matching shawl wrapped around her. She stands tall. Her platinum-blonde hair flows down past her pretty face and rests upon her shoulders. Krystah is a wise woman gifted with spiritual wisdom and an intuition second to none. She can read anyone like a book.

Corporal Krystah is a survivor of an internment camp. Years ago there was a war between the desert people of Kane and her people in Houron, Tahein. The desert people wanted to dam up a river that flowed from the Sea of Tearse, located along the southern border of Octairion. They desired to re-route the river and bring new life to the desert, but this river also gave life to Tahein. If they did then Tahein would suffer a drought. No agreements could be negotiated. So the desert people attacked Houron. Unfortunately Krystah was taken captive and separated from her family. She ended up in a prison camp in Kane.

Krystah was only thirteen at the time and was mortified at all she was exposed to at the camp. She was imprisoned in a cell made of rusted bars with a metal slab roof, and stuck out in the open to bear the hot sun.

She witnessed all that went on in the camp: beatings, the defenseless being stoned to death, and innocent people being tortured. The screams still haunt her at night. One face in particular she will never forget. A kind eyed soldier came to the camp and attempted to rescue the slaves and bring them back, but he was caught. They dragged him to a fire pit that lay before their cell, held him down, and seared him with hot irons. They burned his face and body then sent him back to Houron beaten and scarred for life.

She was trapped in the large rusted cage with eleven other people for over a year. In that time she had no choice but to observe everyone around her. She studied the guards and their mannerisms. She tried to gauge their attitudes and predict what they were going to do. She could tell when they were going out to battle because of the tension in their bodies and the nervousness in their hands. She studied everything.

Krystah observed the mental breakdown of someone being tortured for days on end. As bizarre as it may seem, she was fascinated with the human process. The way victims would snap and become frantic. Some couldn't stop screaming and shaking. Other people could take hours of torturous punishment and not say a single word. They would hold their tongues while their finger-nails were ripped out with pliers. Krystah will never forget the way fear and intimidation looked on the faces of her people. It was the main method used in the camp, and it truly made her sick.

Eventually Tahein won the battle and she was set free, but since that time her eyes were opened like never before. She became extremely interested in human behavior and the effect of their circumstances on their psyches and spirits.

"Welcome, my dear beloveds," Krystah greets the students. "I am honored to have you with me today. As you all know, it is essential to utilize this time. Please listen closely my cherished brothers and sisters to the wisdom I share.

When you are out on your own, your mind can be your best friend or your worst enemy. While you are relaxing in your beds or as you are engaging in battle, your conscious thoughts are going to affect your reality. Your perspective on the circumstances and your self-talk during the situations is going to greatly determine the outcome of your condition.

If you are negative, pessimistic, hopeless, or fearful, your energy will be wasted and you will be caught in the snares of the Dark Forces. But I say, remember the love of Great Spirit and the gentle touch of his mighty hand upon our lives and you will overcome. Have full faith that Great Spirit will see you through. Have full confidence that you have been fully prepared for the challenge before you. Granted you are being called. If you are full of pride and stick your nose into business that is not yours, your ego may get the best of you and cause you to fall," says Krystah waving her finger like a stern librarian.

"However, if you surrender to the mystical flow of Great Spirit and allow Him to conduct your lives, I have full faith you will conquer all barriers within yourself that hold you back from fulfilling your destiny. You will be led in the manner necessary to grow and mature into your full potential. The way may not always seem logical, but I assure you the results will speak for themselves if you allow the work to be done."

Corporal Krystah takes a deep breath and exhales as she readies herself to continue imparting spiritual nourishment to the hungry students. They listen intently and watch their beautiful teacher as she paces before them with love in her eyes.

"Know yourselves, be aware of the power you contain," she says pointing to the warriors. "The person who does not need outside approval, the person who does not rely on the good or bad opinions of others obtains one's self. Live Light Warriors and experience all that you are. Come to own your weaknesses and strengths and love them. The person who walks around with a self-possessed spirit is powerful and influential. They handle their lives with such love and care that makes all that they choose to do flourish."

Krystah pauses for a moment after speaking and walks further down the aisle to where the students are seated. She extends her arms with love, "My dearly beloveds, how are we this evening?"

The students crack smiles as the seriousness breaks. A little laughter and positive replies start to echo through the garden.

"Good, I'm glad all is well. Over the last few months I have witnessed many of you develop and grow here in the Village. Oh what a special garden to be planted in! One that is full of such an overflowing abundance of love and wisdom to be shared. I have to say that I am quite impressed with, and honored, to have been a part of your growth. I am certain you all will assist the Light Army in many victories over the darkness. When you are called forth, whenever that day comes, know that you are ready."

Krystah slowly steps back up to the front of the yard and has a seat in a chair carved out of marble stone. A throne fit for a queen indeed. "I would like to talk to you about meditation and how important it is to your lives. In meditation you lose contact with your surroundings, the sights and sounds of the world around you, the busyness of life and the many cares. You find a sacred space within, a place of tranquility and peace. In that space is a quiet and still presence that merely exists.

This sacred space, when known and recognized, is a reference point for you to gauge your current state of wellbeing. Maybe you are overstimulated or greatly depressed. In this sacred space you let go of your control over life and become one with existence. The peace of Great Spirit fills you as you rest in his arms. Through meditation you can bring calmness to yourself and assess where you are out of alignment, then bring yourself back into balance.

During meditation let all the stress and all your worries come and go. Do not try to suppress the feelings, but rather let them come and have their say, then go on their way. When you have dealt with all the spiritual baggage inside, you will return to your sacred space and connect with Great Spirit who will lead you in what to do next. Follow your hearts dear ones."

Krystah gets up from her seat and waves for the students to follow her. She walks serenely and purposely, as if mindful of every step. She guides them toward a giant hedge that is carved into a Phoenix, the legendary bird that rose from the ashes. Pushing aside his tail feathers, she reveals a hidden pathway where a set of stairs leads into a cavern. The students follow as she creeps down a narrow stone staircase.

Corporal Krystah lights five torches along the walls to illuminate the darkened passageway. The walls dampen as the steep descent leads deeper into an open chamber. She drifts her way around the room and ignites three more torches that reveal a room with seven singing bowls, two gongs, and multiple symbols of all types. The sweet fragrance of myrrh incense wafts through the air as they enter.

The crystal bowls lay on a table in the corner of the room. An altar is set up with precious stones, candles, and bells. All the items positioned ceremonially upon it, dedicated to Great Spirit. Etched into the front of the heartwood alter is the same phrase from Master's gravestone, "Be the Light!"

"Please have a seat on the rugs," asks Krystah as she sits in front of the crystal singing bowls and places a thin black linen veil over her head. The ceremonial headdress is decorated with the flower of life geometrical pattern, which is a symbol for the connectedness of all life. Everyone becomes still and silent in the room and Corporal Krystah begins the ceremony.

"This black veil represents the darkness that blinds the world we live in." She reaches for the wooden mallet and holds it in her hand. "These singing bowls produce vibrations when I rub this mallet along the rim of the bowls. The seven different sized bowls create different frequencies. The sound waves from the singing bowls are sensed with more than our ears. You can also feel the sounds with your body. The tones of the singing bowls sync our mind, body, and soul with the perfect state for profound meditation. Please everyone, prepare yourselves to meditate."

Krystah clangs the mallet on the largest singing bowl. The sound reverberates through the room. She then places the wooden mallet on the outside of the crystal singing bowl and rubs it around the rim. The friction sends a beautiful tone resonating through the room. As the note echoes throughout the area, Krystah lifts the veil off of her face, "The ritualistic lifting of the veil represents the light penetrating the darkness and awakening the world." The ceremony has been set and everyone begins to meditate.

A few moments go by and Krystah raises a triangle and clangs it three times, "Let all that is inside you circulate and exit your being. Empty out yourself, make room for Great Spirit to fill you." Krystah strikes the triangle three more times and then returns to meditating.

The group of warriors settle, clearing stagnate energies and pent up negativity. Slowing their brainwaves, they reach a point of deep meditation together and collectively envision the revival of the nation in their minds eye.

The warriors observe five sun bleached monuments that have stood strong for years. The green tinted figures are painted with moss and lay hidden in the depths of a destroyed valley. Men on horses pose triumphantly. They have been enshrined due to their prestige on the battlefield. A faint ghostly figure skulks from the shadows of the petrified foliage and stands before the five horsemen, who are weather worn and corroded from the base up. These heroes of modern warfare were the forerunners of human evolution. They successfully battled the many diverse shades of darkness through time.

The shade studies the statues; the first horseman wears a crown representing his victory over the darkness of the mind. He sits in peace on his mighty steed with his sword in his holster. A quill is now in hand as he writes in a book. Sharing the wisdom of his journey with all who choose to read it.

The second horseman wears a vest decorated with medals for his courage in the face of fear. He is a warrior of true bravery and influence. He raises his Calvary Trooper sword in the air as his horse charges into battle. His eyes peer into the future to a vision of a world free of war.

The third statue is a horseman who rides only in a loin cloth. He's mounted with his arms out to his sides. Completely vulnerable to all attack. His body bears the scars of humanities collective hatred for one another. Thick rounded scar tissue stretches across his back. He is a man who sacrificed himself for the unity of the people and has yet to see his reward.

The fourth horseman races on his sprinting horse with a scroll in his hand. He has word for all of those who will believe. The words of a better way and a brighter day, but yet to this day his message has fallen on deaf ears. The people have failed to heed his words and still live in discord.

The fifth horseman lies upon his horse, completely drained of all energy. He has given his all to humanity. He has paid a ransom of blood so that they may be saved. Will his sacrifice be wasted or will the people see his example of love and change their ways?

The shade, which has had enough of this ancient sight, raises his arms and joins his hands together. In the middle of his palms he charges a dark energy beam. The gloomy purple orb releases bolts of energy that circle around the shade as it expands.

The shade is a soldier for the new darkness that inhabits the earth. He opens fire on the horsemen, launching the massive energy bomb at the statues. The bomb crashes and explodes in the middle of the horsemen, engulfing them in radiation. The energy dissolves the statues, reducing them into a pile of liquefied metal.

The shade then returns into the shadows of the forest and disappears. The puddle of molten metal lies stagnant for a moment on the cold ground of the desolate forest. Just then, a flaming comet plummets from the cosmos and lands in the metallic pool. The comet shatters into a million tiny shards and fuses with the boiling metal.

A trio of angels descends from the heavens and begins to construct a new figure out of the enhanced matter. Laboring with precision and care they give birth to a brand new model.

Meticulously shaping this precious masterpiece, they forge a divine being. From afar the statue resembles a genderless person holding its arms out as if to embrace you with unconditional love. But as you look closer, the body is made up of all of humanity. Person upon person interlocked, woven together to form the massive body of this divine being. They hold onto one another with love, supporting each other fully. Without the strength of *the person next to them this statue would not stand.*

The shade returns from its hidden lair. He notices the new statue that has arose from the rubble of his destruction. In extreme anger, the shade lashes out at the statue. But the divine being is completely unfazed. For as long as the hands of the many are united, nothing can shake this sculpture. Together they are indestructible. The shade continues to attack with no success. Eventually he retreats back into the depths he crawled out of and the statue stands unblemished in extraordinary brilliance.

Just then Corporal Krystah hits a giant gong that sends a reverberating crash through the room, bringing all the warriors back into the present moment and ending the ceremony.

"I hope you all hear the resounding message coming through from Great Spirit. Light Warriors alone you are uniquely designed for your purpose, but only together will you accomplish your mission. You need each other and humanity needs you. A time of quickening is upon us and humanity is advancing at an extreme rate. Unfortunately it is towards both polarities; light and darkness. As we travel down the path of evolution into the realms of superior spirituality we must continue to follow the light! In order to conquer the darkness that is now on earth, we must stand together! Otherwise we will fall.

Darkness such as this has never been experienced on earth. It will take our combined strength to conquer it Light Warriors. We will have to rescue those trapped in darkness and awaken all the remaining humans to gain advantage over the Dark Forces. We must destroy their campaign and take back our nation!"

Krystah smashes the gong once more signaling that class has come to an end. The students exit the cavern and head back into the Village. As they walk slowly through the Village courtyard together, Rose and Larissa converse about the magical ceremony they just experienced.

"That was pretty intense, wasn't it? I have never had such strong visions," says Rose.

"Yeah, being a PsyCom I'm starting to get used to it. The way that I communicate with other psychics is similar," replies Larissa.

"Whoa, that's awesome!"

"I can see both pictures and hear words when I'm receiving a message from another PsyCom."

"That's pretty amazing. Hey, why don't you try and contact someone right now and see what's going on?"

"Okay, I'll try." Larissa sits down on a bench in the courtyard and concentrates. She breathes in deeply, exhales and then freezes.

Rose watches as Larissa shows no signs of inner activity. She just sits there quietly for a few moments completely still. Larissa then becomes more erect as she receives a message. Her back straightens and her eyes begin to move rapidly under her eyelids. Parts of her body begin to twitch lightly and Rose doesn't know if she should leave her alone or try to wake her up out of this state.

A few more moments go by and Larissa snaps out of it. Her eyelids pop open and she turns to Rose.

"Strange noises have been heard again outside of the Cassiel outposts. They are investigating it now."

"So the rumors are true. This all might really start sooner than we believe!" replies Rose.

"You never know. It could have just been some wild animals."

"Regardless, we all have to be prepared," says Rose clenching her fist. "We have to take advantage of the time we have left."

The two girls stare at each other as they take in the grim reality. It is inevitable that one day they will depart from the safety of the Village walls and advance into the unknown.

Night has fallen upon the land and the long day of teaching has come to an end. The warriors eat dinner together and then head off to bed to close out the evening. Rose stares out her window as she lies in bed and reminisces on all she has experienced so far in the Village.

How much longer are we going to be here? she wonders. Her eyelids become heavy while she contemplates. They slowly close and she drifts off to dreamland.

There is a calm that has rolled in on a storm wrecked country. Tornadoes have torn a path of destruction, leaving the cities in ruin. The traumatized people can finally relax for a moment. The storm has been beating on their home for days

*and has subsided for now. The time of panic is over.
Sounds of whipping winds tossing everything in
sight still haunts the victims, who slowly emerge
from their basements, and find what remains of
their lives.*

*A man who was separated from his family
during the storm sheds a tear as he realizes his
home has been demolished, but then he cracks a
giant smile as he turns around and witnesses his
whole family safe and running towards him. The
man embraces his family as he realizes what truly
matters most; their love. No material possession
could ever replace them. Wherever his wife and
kids are is his home.*

Rose continues her training day after day,
sharpening her skills. She is turning into an amazing
warrior. The rumors of Dark Force activity have died
down and the Village experiences a time of
peace. The members of the Village continue to grow
closer as they bond on the training field and in their
free time. Gelling together they unite into a
family. The leaders of the Village can't help but be
proud of the warriors. They have watched them
mature over the last couple of months, and have
grown along with them. Commander Layne has seen
Rose grow up from a child and become an
outstanding person and a valued member of the
Light Family.

13) <u>Challenging News</u>

*O*ne quiet and peaceful day, the Oracle of the Village of Hope receives word from the Oracle of Cassiel.

"We have sent a squad of soldiers on reconnaissance to Drakkar where we have seen the Dark Forces inhabiting the nation. In a town called Allusian, people wander about unaware of the demons that are leeching the life out of them. Dark Shadows are latching onto their backs and sucking them dry of their energy. The darkness has infested the town and is slowly but surely possessing everyone.

The people of Allusian are dead inside. The Shadows feed them lies about their self-worth so that the people parade around trying to look their best. Winning the approval of another would make them feel so good about themselves. Women adorn provocative dresses and men wear flashy clothes that make a statement of luxury that says, 'I am better than the next.' The empty shells attempt to tempt one another so that they can steal the life force of their neighbor. They stare with gaping eyes, trying to absorb all the looks they can, but nothing but the love of the Great Spirit will fill that bottomless pit inside their soul.

Men hunt women looking to seduce innocent victims who are deceived into believing that they deserve to be treated like objects. The media tells them if they are not beautiful and rich, then they are doing it wrong. They are confused and have no idea of what real love is. Women starve themselves trying to fit the image of perfection that the media portrays. All the while their true spiritual beauty is being leeched from them by the Shadows. They twist their minds and blind them from the truth of their divine nature.

'You're not good enough,' 'You're too fat,' and 'You don't deserve that,' are the lies that the Shadows whisper into the ears of their prey. The tortured souls try to escape their suffering with drugs and alcohol. They try to numb their minds and ease the pain for the moment. When in reality they're doing more damage than they know.

They chase after fantasies and false identities that they think will satisfy the craving inside them. All the while they are getting further out of alignment with who they really are. The plastic people mimic who they believe will be accepted and praised. They imitate icons of excess rather than loving and honoring their own inner beauty. They sell their souls to the darkness for the promise of a fake dream and end up robbed of their lives.

Here at Cassiel, we have witnessed a group of savage beasts we have labeled Hunters. Prior to devolving it seems these mobs of humans were full of anger and hate. They committed numerous acts of murder and even cannibalism. Consumed by the darkness inside their souls, they mutated into Hunters. They are monsters thirsty for blood and set on destroying the light, and these demons have been seen stalking just outside our borders. We predict that soon they will be at our front door. So we desperately ask that you would assist us in defense of our outposts in Cassiel and also at the outpost of Tahein. Please act quickly as we foresee an attack approaching in the near future."

The Oracle of the Village cannot believe what she is hearing. "The time has arrived," she yells out in the quiet sanctuary. She blinks her eyes and shakes off the fog from communication and looks to her chamber-maid, "Summon the leaders immediately. We must have an important meeting!"

"Yes Oracle," replies the chamber-maid and she sprints out of the sanctuary in a hurry.

She finds the leaders in the courtyard assisting the warriors. Corporal Krystah is conducting a telepathy class with Psychic Communicators; while Captain David and Commander Layne train the rest of the warriors in hand to hand combat.

The chamber-maid frantically runs up to the elders and interrupts, "Excuse me! Excuse me!" Startling everyone, she now has their attention, "We have just received urgent word from the Oracle of Cassiel. You have been summoned to the sanctuary immediately!"

David, Layne and Krystah look at each other stunned and then rush the sanctuary, leaving the students in anticipation.

Inside they find the oracle sprawled upon a candlelit platform. She lies with white linens draped over her body. Vulnerable and frail, she waits.

Commander Layne approaches.

The Oracle sits up slowly and informs the leaders of the message she has received, "The predicted time has arrived. Action must be taken. Our troops must be deployed to the outposts along the borders of Cassiel and Tahein to defend against the advancing enemy forces."

Captain David yells in excitement as he pumps his fist in the air. He is greatly looking forward to getting his hands dirty on the battlefield.

Krystah and Layne are a little more concerned, but still are ready for action.

"Okay, so we must begin a deployment plan immediately. Divide the troops and arrange a route of travel for every squad," states Krystah.

"I will get on it right away," replies Layne as he runs out of the sanctuary. He dashes out into the courtyard and through a crowd of students.

"What's going on commander?" yells Roger Redcliff.

"Light Warriors, it's time to move out! The Dark Forces are advancing and we have been called for backup. We will devise a plan and inform you when we are done. Prepare to leave in the morning," yells Commander Layne as he continues running to his office.

Rose and all of the other stunned warriors stand in silence for a moment and take in what has just been spoken.

"The Dark Forces are advancing?" says Roger to Abigail Day.

"Back up? Oh my goodness this is really happening," yells Rose as she grabs Larissa in excitement.

"No, no, no, Rose. That can't be right. Can it Kaz? So soon?" asks a shocked Larissa.

All of a sudden Captain David comes screaming out of the sanctuary, shooting light blasts into the sky as he enthusiastically shouts, "Let's take it to them warriors. The moment we have all trained for has finally come. Everyone fall in!"

The warriors hustle into formation before Captain David.

"Day after day we have sweat in this very courtyard. Day after day you have studied the ways of the Spirit in preparation for the moment when you are called upon. Ladies and Gentlemen, it has arrived. Now, I stand here in front of a squad that I know is more than capable of handling this mission. I stand before a group of soldiers who were placed here on earth to fulfill a destiny. A destiny that will reign supreme in the history books, and a path that we must now continue to pave one step at a time. Light Warriors, may we give our all to rid Octairion of the darkness and give rise to the Empire of Light!"

The warriors cheer from the spirit of war that Captain David omits. Rallying behind such a confident leader has a powerful impact on morale.

"Gather your belongings and ready yourselves to travel. We will be repositioning to outposts along the border of Drakkar. Some of you will be relocating to Tahein, while the rest of you will be divided between the northern and southern outposts of Cassiel. Head to your rooms while we draw up plans and we will contact you when we have further instructions." Captain David finishes speaking and then charges off in the direction of Commander Layne's office to assist him in drawing up deployment plans. The warriors proceed to their dorms.

Up in their room, Larissa and Rose converse as they load their bags, "I can't believe it! I can't believe it!" repeats Larissa as the anxiety builds inside her.

"I know! This is it!" says Rose who is becoming more eager as the seconds go by. "We are on the forefront of the battle. The darkness has only been preying on defenseless victims who are vulnerable to their spiritual attacks, but now we will come face to face with them. Real live combat. We will strike them down one by one until we get to the leader of the Dark Forces and liberate the world!" She clenches her fists in anticipation, while Larissa sits on her bed and admires Rose's enthusiasm.

"I sure hope I get to follow you into battle," says Larissa, "you have such a passion."

The darkness that has been upon this world since the fall of man has now fully manifested on the physical plane. Exposed and inhabiting the earth. No longer is the leader of the Dark Forces conducting from the shadows of the spiritual realm. He stands behind his rising army and longs to devour the world in an endless dark. It has taken ages for this era to occur, but the slow evolution of both light and darkness has finally reached the point of eruption.

Whether the darkness used hate, greed, violence, or fear, the light has always attempted to purify and right the wrong the evil has caused. Now humanity faces the harsh reality head on. There is no denying what is happening on earth. There is no denying that the issues must be dealt with now, or else the world will be consumed by evil. To turn a blind eye to the darkness, something that has been done by many for far too long would mean the death of humanity. Those who chose to contribute to the evil have been consumed and are now being used to further the dark agenda. Those who remain in the light are the only hope for the human race.

Commander Layne sits as his cluttered desk examining maps of Octairion. Pouring over the charts he inspects the terrain and makes note of possible dangers. He observes the locations of the outposts and sketches possible routes they will have to travel. Layne is full of emotion as he pieces together the strategy.

"We're really about to engage. The Dark Forces are on the move. How intense!" he says to Captain David who is grasping onto the arms of his chair in anticipation. Dividing the troops up into three squads, Layne plots individual courses for each of the leaders to direct. "Krystah being a native of Tahein will guide her team to the outpost located in western Tahein. You and I will head to the Cassiel outposts. I will take the southern border and you will man the northern."

"Sounds perfect," replies Captain David.

Layne takes a step back and looks upon the map of Octairion, "This is it. The choices are made. Let's inform every one of the plan and we'll head out first thing tomorrow morning."

"Game time is over," says Captain David.

Layne approaches David as the seriousness of their call sets in, "It's been a pleasure preparing the Light Army with you Sir."

Captain David rises from his chair and embraces Layne, "Masters would be proud of you champ," he replies. A giant smile fills Layne's face and the two men exit the office.

The leaders call for a meeting in the dining hall. The troops pile in eagerly awaiting an update. The hall is soundless as Corporal Krystah approaches the podium, "Hello my beloveds. As you know, the Dark Forces are pushing closer to the border of Drakkar and the Oracle of Cassiel has asked for reinforcements to Tahein, as well as Cassiel. We have formed three squads led by Captain David, Commander Layne, and myself. We will post assignments in the courtyard after this meeting and tomorrow morning we will set out."

Uproars of emotional shouts fill the room.

"Listen up!" yells Krystah, "I know these are exciting times but we must stay focused. Let's enjoy this last night of peace together as a Village of Hope family, because once we exit out of those gates tomorrow, boot camp is officially over and conflict

can be waiting around every corner. Head out to the courtyard and grab your assignments. Tonight we will meet back here for the King's Feast."
Immediately the warriors jump up out of their seats before Krystah is done speaking. "Wear your best attire!"

The warriors run out to the courtyard where tables are set up with three stacks of paper labeled group A, B, and C. The packets of papers contain their operation details. Lists with the warrior's names are written out in front of their selected group. Rose's heart is beating out of her chest as she finds her name on stack A: Captain David: Northern Cassiel.

Shocked and confused, she backs away from the table. *Uncle... Why would he? How could he not put me in his squad?* she thinks.

She overhears Larissa shout, "Squad B!"

Kaz yells out, "Squad A!"

The other warriors are hollering about and conversing with their friends, but Rose just stands there in a daze. *Separated from my uncle again?* she thinks to herself. *I have to speak to him right now!* She dashes though the group of people, bumping and pushing the wound-up warriors out of her way as she hurries off to find her uncle Layne.

Entering his office, gripping a hot cup of coffee, Layne hangs his hat and takes a seat. He lights a few candles and settles in his chair. He sips on the coffee as the steam rises in the air. Letting out a groan of concern, he leans back and stares up at the ceiling and reflects on his first battle. In those days no one had developed the powers they have now. Everyone fought with weapons or had hand to hand combat against a human enemy, who held different beliefs as you, or wanted the land you inhabited. A battle of such spiritual dynamic has never occurred. What an experience this will be.

Stomping footsteps can be heard approaching the door. Closer and faster until, CRASH! Rose comes storming into the office.

"Uncle!" she shouts.

Layne spins around surprised, "Where's the fire?" he yells.

"Uncle, we need to talk," says an upset Rose.

"Okay. Sit down," replies Layne.

Rose comes to the side of his desk and slams down powerfully into the chair, "Why are we not adventuring together?"

"I have thought long and hard about this dear. It wasn't an easy decision to make but I feel the best choice was made."

"I don't understand?" she replies with a hint of sadness in her voice.

"The battlefield is an unforgivable place. In times of war I believe it is best to be on your toes. I felt that we would be distractions to each other. I transform when I'm out there. I am no longer uncle Layne. I become a much harsher and more demanding person. War is nothing to take lightly and I feel that my heart needs to harden, and being around my sweet Rose would soften me up."

Rose gazes at her uncle as a glimmer of the reality of war comes into view, "I understand Commander," she replies with tears in her eyes. "I will take your word on it. You have never led me astray."

Layne leans forward and grabs Roses hand. "I love you so much Rose. Thank you for understanding." He speaks with such care. "Captain David is the most experienced officer here. There is no one I would rather have you stationed with other than David. You will gain the most from spending time with him."

Rose gets up and hugs her uncle. Clenching him tight she whispers, "I love you. I will see you at the King's feast tonight," and walks out of his office.

Reflectively walking through the courtyard, Rose observes the Village. So many memories have been made in such a short time. *The Village has given so much to me*, she thinks while realizing that a major change is about to take place. *All the grace that has been poured upon my life is so incredible. What a time of blessing.*

She takes a seat on the lawn and reflects on her childhood, the journey to the Village, and her time spent here. All she has experienced in her young life is about to give birth to the woman she will be forged into from the heat of the battlefield. When faced with difficult challenges, she must take all she has learned and apply it against not only her enemy, but also herself. In moments of pressure will she remain composed? Or crumble under the weight of stress? Is she equipped to handle herself against the little known tactics of the Dark Forces?

Corporal Krystah spots Rose in deep thought. She approaches her sitting before a window, studying her reflection in the pane.

"Hello," says Krystah as she takes a seat next to Rose. The glass portrays a picture of maturity. Rose, youthful and ready to bloom, sits next to Krystah, seasoned and full of wisdom. Both beautiful blondes contemplate the precious sight.

"What's on your heart, dear?" questions Krystah with genuine concern.

Rose looks into her soft blue eyes. They hold such a grand compassion. "You told us that when we are called, to know we are ready, right?" asks Rose.

Krystah places her hand on her shoulder and looks intimately into Rose's eyes. "My dear, with all my heart and soul, I tell you that you are ready. I have witnessed your amazing abilities and leadership skills first hand, but besides that Rose, Great Spirit is moving. I can feel it. We are not proceeding before our time dear. Rather we are being presented with our purpose."

Krystah puts her hands together and positions them on the center of Rose's forehead. The area associated with her third eye and communication with Great Spirit.

"Do not resist the flow Rose. Embrace it!" She raises her hands into the sky, spreading them wide apart as if to open up her being to the energy of the universe. "We must allow Great Spirit to conduct this masterpiece. We must be the instruments of his hands." She then lowers her hands to the middle of her chest, representing the heart chakra. "Following the messages he sends to our hearts and the promptings he nudges us to act upon. Trust he will lead us in conquering the darkness and setting humanity free.

When your back is against the wall, there can be no doubt. When fear is pressing upon you like a boulder laid upon your chest, suffocating you, causing you to question if Great Spirit really exists, know that he does and he has your best interest in mind my child. Great Spirit will lead you in becoming a fully realized soul who knows her full potential as a divine being.

You are a queen Rose. Ever since your first conscious decision to deny the lies of the darkness you have been on a path of freedom from the oppression of the world. Freedom from the crippling enslavement forcing the blind, confused, and deceived souls of our race to break their back for luxury that distracts them from the beauty of which they really are; divine."

Krystah stands to her feet. The passion growing inside has her geared up for battle. Motivated by her anger for the darkness and the way it has caused our people to suffer for far too long. She looks into the windowpane. She leans in and stares deep into the reflection of her eyes. She sees the same eyes that have been looking back at her all her life. "Can we kill these monsters and not lose the light inside our souls?" asks Krystah.

Rose stands up next to Krystah and mimics her actions. "We must rescue the humans who have not been lost. Those who have not traveled too far down the path of darkness and still have a spark of hope in their souls. That is all we need to focus on, Corporal."

Krystah turns to Rose and looks down into her face, "Death has an effect on you that you cannot control. You reach a point where you question how much more you can witness before you are tainted by it." Krystah turns around and begins walking away from Rose, "I will see you at the King's feast," she says and she walks through the courtyard towards her office.

Rose watches Krystah as she walks away. *Tainted by death?* she thinks. *I wonder how much she has seen?* Krystah disappears into her office and Rose turns back to her reflection. *Well, there's only one way to find out if I can take the struggles of battle and that is to face it head on.*

She stares into her determined eyes and clenches her fist as confidence builds. Rose looks up to the sky and remembers the guidance of the Inner Realm. "With Great Spirit I can stand strong in any darkness," she yells out loud. Reassuring herself that with Him she can do all things. She turns from the pane and heads up to her room to get ready for the feast.

14) <u>The King's Feast</u>

Searching her closet for what to wear, Rose
rummages through her wardrobe. "Not the red
dress. No, not the purple one either." She is having a
hard time choosing. She comes across the light blue
dress that she had received as a gift from Larissa a
couple months back. A long dress reaching to the
ground, laced with white around the collar and
waist. Gems are sewn into five circles that wrap
around the skirt of the dress. Elegant blue and white
quartz crystals sparkle in rows about six inches
apart down the outfit. Rose puts on the dress and
twirls about the room, truly feeling like a princess.

     She hears the door creak open and it's
Larissa, "Wow, you look so beautiful. I'm honored
that you would wear the dress I gave you for the
King's Feast tonight," she says as she stands before
Rose in awe. "I'm so excited. Let me get ready too."
Larissa begins to prepare for the dinner as Rose puts

the finishing touches on her make up. "Oh this is going to be so glamorous," says Larissa. "What a wonderful idea for our last night together at the Village."

Rose watches Larissa as she does her make up. She Takes in the angles of her face and observes her mannerisms. After tomorrow, who knows when the two of them will see each other again?

"So you're in squad A, huh?" Larissa says as she pulls her hair back into a ponytail. Rose nods her head and looks away. "I'm in Squad B with your uncle. We will be traveling to the southern outpost of Cassiel where the distress call originated. I have heard that Light Warriors from the Headquarters have already arrived."

"Headquarters?" asks Rose.

"Yeah, the Light Warrior Headquarters in Tahein. Elder Saden head of the Light Army lives there and oversees the training. It's the biggest compound the Light Army has."

"Wow, who did you hear all this from?"

"From a psychic at the headquarters, we contact each other sometimes and share rumors and updates on the darkness."

Bung! Bung! Bung! The bell tower chimes signaling dinner for the last time. Larissa jumps up excitedly. She is beautifully dressed in a stunning white dress with red gem trails shooting down the skirt. She places her hands on Rose's shoulders and whispers, "Let's forget about the war for now, while we still can, and have the feast of our lives!" Then she dashes out of the room and Rose quickly follows behind.

The two girls dressed like royalty run down the corridor. Their jewelry jingling and jangling as they stride. Other students are exiting their rooms and entering the crowded hallway. Everyone is dressed to the nines, wearing their fanciest clothing. They make their way out of the dormitory and gracefully stroll through the courtyard. The men stand around in a circle out front of the dining hall admiring one another's get ups. They complement the ladies as they walk by full of smiles and politely hold the door as the young women enter the celebration.

The smell of pine incense hits Rose's nose the second the door to the beautifully decorated dining hall is opened. Numerous candles are lit and scattered about the enchanting hall. Bouquets of flowers adorn the back walls and are placed as a center-piece on every table. Their lovely dresses flow across the floor as Rose walks side by side with Larissa.

Everyone in the community is well dressed and feeling quite sophisticated tonight. The stylish soldiers make their ways to their seats. They glow with joy as sparks of light fill their eyes. Smiles gleam from ear to ear. A last night of fantasy before a harsh reality comes barging in tomorrow. They delight in conversation and share intimate gazes with those who they have come to love over the last year.

"Hey Kaz, remember that day you slipped and fell at lunch and dropped all your food in front of everyone?" says Larissa as everyone bursts out laughing.

"Very funny, how about that time I smoked you on the training-field?" replies Kaz a bit embarrassed.

"Yeah right, you could never whoop me."

"Hey, what about that time Rose flew into the bushes when she tried to dodge a bunch of light beams from Captain David," says Sydney. The group laughs again. "You were covered in dirt and leaves," she yells holding her belly and pointing at Rose.

"Hey! That's not funny." replies Rose, "What about that time you got yelled at for teleporting into the kitchen and stealing food at night? You're not perfect Sydney."

"I forgot about that," replies Kaz, "Captain David took you in front of the whole army and chastised you. Ha!"

"Whatever," replies Sydney getting a little angry at the comment.

"Don't get upset Sydney," says Larissa, "We all have little mishaps. It's nothing to be ashamed of. One time I lost a match against Roger Redcliff. I miscalculated a shot and nearly took out Corporal Krystah. Roger capitalized with a right hook and nearly knocked me out cold. The important thing is I learned from my mistake and I will be better prepared on the battlefield because of it."

Sydney acknowledges Larissa's humility and holds back the insult she had on the tip of her tongue. "Fair enough," she replies and twists her face at Rose instead.

Captain David approaches the podium and clears his throat, "Welcome to the King's Feast Light Warriors. Tonight we celebrate our last night together here as a family. Tomorrow we dissemble and go upon our respected missions, but we will always be a family. We adventure out to unite with an extended family. You will come to meet brothers and sisters who have been training just as you have and are looking to defend the light, just as you are.

I am honored to have served you here at the Village of Hope along with Commander Layne and Corporal Krystah. The time shared with you soldiers here has been a special one, but tomorrow we move on to the trials of war and we shall serve you in far greater ways on the battlefield. Shoulder to shoulder in the trenches, conquering the darkness and reviving the light one soul at a time!" Captain David slams his fist down as the Warriors rise to their feet in excitement, applauding their inspirational leader. "Together we will keep the light! Together we will keep the light!" yells David.

The whole Village chants in unison "Together we will keep the light!"

"Now, let's feast!" yells Commander Layne.

A whole assortment of wonderful food is laid out on their tables. Delicious roast beef, a giant cooked turkey, and sweet honey ham fills their plates. Followed by steamed broccoli, buttery carrots smothered in brown sugar, and mouthwatering mashed potatoes. The happiness overflows from the faces of these celebrating warriors.

They merrily eat and drink, full of delight, and share stories as they continue reminiscing over the time they shared at the Village together. Afterwards, dancing and singing fills the hall. They laugh and cry as the sun goes down on the Village family for the last time, then Corporal Krystah announces the end of the feast.

"Thank you all for such a special evening. Tomorrow our journey begins. Let's get a good night of rest and we'll assemble in the courtyard first thing in the morning. Goodnight, Light Warriors."

Everyone vacates the dining hall and begins heading towards their rooms. Commander Layne approaches Rose in the courtyard. His eyes fall upon the precious sight of his lovely young niece, all fancied up and full of smiles. "How are you doing?" he asks her.

She spins around in her beautiful dress and curtsies to her uncle, "I'm doing great Sir, and you?"

Layne smiles back and bows to her, "Not too bad," he replies. "Care to take a walk?" he asks as he extends his hand to her. She takes her uncle's hand and they walk off into the night together.

Stepping slowly, Layne holds her close and cherishes this precious moment. He is grateful for the special gift of Rose's presence this evening.

They come to the tall trees along the eastern edge of the Village and Layne releases Rose's hand. "I just wanted to make sure that I took the time to tell you how much I love you." Layne pulls her in for a big hug and kisses her on the head.

"I know how much you love me uncle," says Rose absorbing all his affection. "I love you so much too."

Layne continues to hold her tight; he's taking advantage of the little time they have left. "When you were born I would have never imagined that we would both be here preparing for such an important battle. You were always so fragile and delicate to me."

"Not anymore uncle. I'm a Light Warrior now," responds Rose with zest. Her face shines brightly in the moonlight.

"I know you are," says Layne. "You're going to do amazing things out there." Her uncle is trying to be as encouraging as he can, but Rose can sense a hint of concern in his voice.

"I have trained hard and learned so much here. I am well prepared, and there is no turning back now. Tomorrow we set out to fight for Great Spirit. I know he will bring us back together again. I am certain of that. There is no need to worry."

"That's right," he replies gripping her tighter. "No holding back."

Rose reaches into her dress pocket and fumbles around for a moment, "Hey uncle, do you remember this?" she asks as she pulls out the emerald calcite that he had given her when she was young.

"Oh wow, you bet I do!" replies Layne, surprised to see the crystal. "If you hold onto that, there's nothing that will keep us apart."

Rose takes great comfort in his response and snuggles into her dear uncle. Layne pulls her in for another great big hug, "Let me walk you to your room so you can rest up for the big day," he says and the two of them walk to her bedroom.

Rose lies in her bed. *The next time I open my eyes, we'll be heading out*, she thinks as thousands of thoughts bounce around in her head. *Great*

Spirit, be with us. Rose closes her eyes and journeys into dreamland.

Standing on the rocky ocean shore, the waves crash in; the wind is blowing through her wavy blonde hair. She kneels down and examines the stones at her feet. Picking through them one by one, she tosses aside tiny tonalites and small selenite stones. Digging deeper into the shore, she finds little shell particles and rock shards.

Blues, yellows, and all different shades of orange and red fill every hand full she excavates. At the bottom of the hole she uncovers a mysterious stone in the shape of an eagle. Rose examines the rock in the sunlight and it magically transforms into a real bird and flies away! She holds onto his talons with all her might as the majestic eagle flaps its powerful wings and darts through the sky like a guided missile.

The great bird soars through the heavens, far above the earth, determined to reach his destination. Too high to let go, Rose grasps onto him tightly. The smooth white feathers of the bird wave in the breeze. His eyes peer into the distance as he dashes through patches of hazy clouds. Where is this bird taking her?

Rising closer and closer to the sun, heat can be felt upon her skin. Rose climbs up on top of the giant bird and straddles him. The unruly eagle struggles and roughly tosses about, but she clenches her fists full of feathers and yokes him.

She rides the wild bird until he comes to a rough landing on the top of a mountain. On the towering peak, Rose dismounts the eagle and

168

stands before the enormous creature. He spreads his wings extending them fully into the sky and lets out a loud cry. He then turns back into the piece of stone he had transformed from.

She picks up the stone and notices a carved out piece in one of the nearby pillars. Rose places the eagle into the mold and all of a sudden the sky above her splits open and three Angels appear and land before her. They wear simple white robes and stand together with a heavenly glow. The Angels raise their trumpets to their tender lips and bellow an ominous tune that thunders through the land.

Rose is startled awake from a second trumpet blaring in the courtyard. It seems morning has come and Captain David is outside sounding the wakeup call. She lies there momentarily, gathers herself while taking a deep breath, and then jumps out of bed.

Larissa, who has also jumped up, asks Rose to pray with her before they leave their room for the last time. She agrees and gets down on her knees with Larissa and they begin to pray, "Dear Great Spirit, we thank you for this day. Please be with us as we travel. Thank you for bringing Rose and I together. I ask that we may see each other again in the future. May you guide our footsteps today and get us all to our destinations safely."

They stand to their feet and connect eye to eye. Rose places her hand on Larissa's shoulder, "Be strong and courageous out there," she says.

"I will. You keep that fire inside of you burning bright huh?"

169

"You know I will," replies Rose with a devious grin. She pulls Larissa in for an affectionate embrace. The two young women hold one another for a moment, and then Larissa pulls away. She shifts her demeanor and displays a severe stare, her eyebrows angled down and eyes narrowed, "Let's do this," says Larissa squeezing Rose's hand. Rose reflects her determined glare, and the warriors grab their backpacks and exit the room.

Part Three: Spiritual Warfare

"Even though I walk through the valley of the shadow of death, I will fear no evil for You are with me."
— Psalm 23: 4

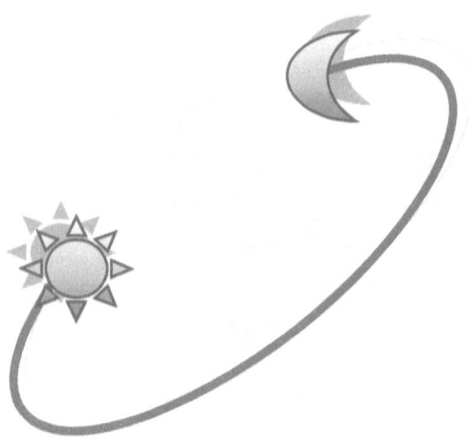

15) <u>First Strike</u>

*O*ut in the courtyard, the sun rises in the early morning sky. The warriors emerge in silence and await their orders.

Captain David taps his foot with an angry scowl. He's all business and eager to deploy. Corporal Krystah and Commander Layne stand behind him in battle mode; hands on their hips and fire in their hearts. David's hand trembles as he overlooks the Army of Light with aggressive eyes. The mood is serious.

"Alright, everyone fall in! Squad A, you're with me. Squad B with Commander Layne, and squad C with Corporal Krystah," orders Captain David.

Dust fills the air as the warriors sprint into formation. Rose gathers into Squad B along with Lucian, Kaz, Sydney, Abigail, Roger and Joey Stalls.

Commander Layne paces in front of the squads, "Once we exit through those gates warriors, I need everyone to be on their toes. It is go time. Now, are we ready Light Warriors?"

"Yes, Commander Layne!" yells the Platoon.

"Let's move out!" roars Captain David as he thrusts his fist in the direction of the entrances.

Marching out through the giant gates of the Village, Layne salutes Rose, she salutes back, and they proceed towards their assigned outposts.

She stares out into the open grassy field under the vast sky and continues to press onward into the unknown. She glances over her shoulder and sees her uncle Layne disappear with his squad behind a group of trees. *I wish I could hold onto him forever*, she thinks, but it is time to face her destiny. *Here we go. No turning back!*

The eight members of the squad travel over hills and trudge through small rivers, everyone remains silent as they trek. Captain David stalks the land as he walks like a mobile mine sweeper trying to pick up any activity. His eyes peer into the trees and scan over hilltops. The rest of the squad follows their leader and does the same.

"Try and tune into the world around you," advises David. "Listen for any sounds or movements that will forewarn you of danger." The squad listens intently but doesn't pick up a sound. They just carry on quietly.

Abigail Day keeps her mind free and clear as they maneuver through the badlands of northern Kane. She needs to make sure she is receptive to any incoming psychic communications. Her brown eyes comb over the landscape. The earth up here is not good for much. The thin branches of dead trees resemble the bare bones of a skeleton. Many decaying trees that have fallen to the dry ground lay in defeat to the harsh conditions.

Roger Redcliff keeps his eyes peeled as they march through the eerie forest. He's ready to fire upon anything that poses a threat, but Lucian Luzz doesn't seem to be as cautious. A murder of crows flees from the trees up above and he nearly jumps out of his skin as the squawking birds scatter.

The group laughs at loopy Lucian, but Captain David is not amused. He looks back and growls at his distracted squad. He rears his teeth and bulges his eyes, then whips back around and stomps forward. He doesn't have to say a thing, everyone got the message; no more joking around.

Kaz and Rose walk side by side down an isle of knotted pines. The dark atmosphere is not helping with her glum attitude. She looks to Kaz who doesn't seem to have a care in the world, "I'm glad my uncle and Larissa are together at least. Two people who I care about and love."

"Hey c'mon Rose, you got me here. That's got to be worth something huh?"

She looks at Kaz and his wild hair. It's pushed back and spikey like a crocodile's tail. His brown eyes are wide and hopeful, a big smile on his chubby face. "Of course," she replies with a hint of sadness and continues to walk through the lane of grim trees.

At the end of the dead forest the Light Warriors reach what looks to be a ghost town.

174

Rundown buildings and neglected shops line the streets. There doesn't seem to be a single soul in this abandoned area. No signs of intrusion or a fight either.

Rose examines the small homes as the squad quietly treks through the main street. *What an eerie silence,* she thinks, *where has everyone gone?*

Captain David spots a large statue of a man sitting on a stack of books, pondering while he reads. The metallic figure rests upon a wide gray-stone base. "Let's take cover behind that statue," orders Captain David.

Their backpacks ruffle and clothes rustle as they hustle forward and hide.

"Abigail, see if you can pick up any incoming communications. Maybe we can figure out if anything is going on nearby," whispers Captain David.

She sits on the ground, surrounded by her alert squad members and opens herself up. The squad peers around the neighborhood with hawk eyes. All is quiet and all is still.

A moment goes by and Abigail comes back, "I got nothing Captain."

David scopes out the town once more. He's suspicious of the desolate town but that is not his mission at the moment. "Let's carry on then," he commands and he marches into the tall grassy fields at the edge of the town.

Passing by stone after stone, tree after tree and plant after plant, the soldiers trudge on. The dullness of the scenery lulls them into a hypnotized stroll. Kaz daydreams as he sleepwalks along the pebbly path. Visions of majestic beings float through his mind. Sydney Blake watches as he blankly stares into the distance. She shakes her head at the spacey cadet.

Roger Redcliff examines a row of pussy willows. He picks off a few of the snowy white buds from the branches and flicks them at a few of his squad members. Joey Stalls, who is already irritable, pushes Roger. In return, Roger shoves him back.

"What's wrong with you man?" replies Roger. "It was just a joke."

Joey Stalls grabs Roger by the collar of his uniform and scoffs at him, "I'm in no mood for a joke!" His face red and blood boiling.

Captain David runs up to the soldiers and stares them down. His presence is threatening and serious, "Do you think this is a game? This is no time for horseplay. The enemy could be awaiting us at-"

BANG! Just then a loud explosion erupts from over the hill. Rose and the rest of the squad fall to the ground and take cover. They pause and listen for a moment.

"Rose! Find a vantage point on top of that hill and see if you can spot the source of the commotion," orders Captain David.

"Yes Sir," she replies and spreads her wings. She launches off the ground and flies towards a large rocky hill facing the direction of the sound. Landing on the cliff, she turns her head to detect any activity. Before she can fix her gaze, there are two dark purple energy beams coming straight at her. She quickly bends backwards and the beams just miss her face. Her eyes open wide from the attack and she spots a valley full of Dark Forces clustered in a burning town.

"We've got company!" she yells as she darts back down to the safety of her squad.

"Okay, everyone arrange battle defenses!" commands David. The soldiers deploy there crystal shields and huddle into a group. "Forward!" he yells.

They march up the hill slowly, ready to engage. Crossing over the crowning of the hill, they spot a crowd of Mavens occupying the outer perimeter of the town. The bulky monsters stand tall with terrifying claws and piercing red eyes. Their terrifying red bodies are plated with thick brown armor-like skin around their triceps and torsos. Frantic people can be seen scurrying through the town streets as well. Shadows are latched onto them, draining their energy as they scream in horror.

The demons open fire on the squad!

"Compound!" yells David as the troops squeeze together tightly and form a wall with their shields. Blast upon blast beats against their barricade. These frenzied demons are thirsty for blood. "Backward!" commands David. The squad then steps back out of sight from the enemy.

"Spread out along the ridge. Joey, set up a distraction. Roger, get in sniper position. The rest of you prepare to fire on my word!"

The crew disperses along the border of the hill and holds. Joey Stalls teleports to the far Eastside and blasts away at the demons, but they block the beams. He teleports to the far west side and continues to fire upon the Mavens, catching them off guard.

Captain David yells for the squad to open fire. They shower the demons with a stream of beam blasts and decapitate the distracted brood. "Take their position!" hollers David and the team sprints down the hill and slides up against the side of a wooden barn. "We've got to take back this town and rescue any remaining people. Let's split into groups of two and spread out along the southern rim of the town and force the enemies north."

Rose and Sydney pair up and head southeast towards a flaming house. They creep along the side slowly. The sounds of screaming and crackling fire mask their footsteps. The girls peer around the corner of the building into the center of the small town. A litter of demons has gathered in the square.

"I think those are the Hunters we heard about," observes Sydney. The collection of Hunters is assembled around a pile of ravaged bodies. Blood drips from their razor toothed jaws. The darkness could not destroy the light inside these brave souls. So instead they tore them limb from limb.

Rose and Sydney, both shocked, try to endure the striking scene. The blood soaked bodies lay on top of one another. The men and women of this innocent little town brutally massacred and desecrated by the evil scum of the Dark Forces. A man still alive in the mound of the dead lets out an agonizing cry, signaling the Hunters to pounce on him and rip him to shreds like ravenous wolves.

Rose flinches and recoils behind the wall. The horrors of war spare no one and waste no time revealing this terrible truth to her. Sydney, who's just as shaken, tries to make sense of the situation, "This is what we're up against. We cannot be intimidated by these demons. We must conquer them!"

Rose snaps back to reality and peers into the violent site, "Okay, let's do this. We'll rush in for a sneak attack, alright?" Sydney nods in agreement and the two girls burst from the side of the house.

Both girls sprint towards the unsuspecting Hunters. Rose jumps, spreads her wings, and quickly propels herself at one of the Hunters. Sydney teleports directly behind another and they both deploy their light swords and simultaneously drive them straight through their victims, slicing them in half. The butchered bodies spurt blood and guts ooze out and fall to the ground. The loud sloshing of body fluids alerts the rest of the Hunters.

Smearing the blood from her eyes, Rose sees a group of Hunters running towards them. With no time to squander, the girls engage. A charging Hunter fires two shots at Rose, who jumps over the beams and plunges her sword into its chest. She then pulls her light sword from the demons cavity, spins around and with a mighty slash, beheads the demon. The head spurts blood as it flies through the air. It plops onto the ground with a soggy thud and rolls to a stop before her feet.

Sydney dodges a severe claw strike and returns with an overhand hack that is blocked by the thick armored skin on the Hunter's forearms. He kicks her in the stomach and shoots several fiery blasts. The beams just miss her face as she rolls away. The irritated demon intensely slashes at her. Gruesomely screaming and charging forward, he forces her up against a wall. His demonic eyes lock on to Sydney and she freezes in fear momentarily.

The monster raises his thick claws to strike, but Sydney snaps out of it and quickly teleports away from the menacing attack!

The beast lets out a thundering cry that draws the remaining multitude of minions to the core of the town. Red Mavens and Hunters come stampeding from the houses, streets, and alleyways and crowd the town center. Sydney and Rose watch as the horde of demons flood the square from all sides and barrel towards them like a tidal wave of death.

"Where is everyone else?" nervously asks Sydney, intimidated by the mass of monsters.

"They must be occupied. We have to do this," says Rose. "Let's show them what we got!"

Launching shot after shot the girls try to fend off the Dark Forces, but there are too many. They obliterate a large portion of demons, but they continue to push closer and closer.

"Keep shooting, don't let up!" yells Rose, starting to feel the pressure.

A vicious Maven jumps high out of the crowd and targets Rose. His eyes widen and his mouth salivates as he closes in on his prey. The demon points his massive claws downward to drive them into Rose, but out of nowhere a super charged sniper beam blast penetrates the demon and blows him apart. Roger is watching over them like a guardian angel!

Multiple photon beams burst from behind the homes. It's the Light Warriors! Seems they were also alerted by the monsters echoing cry. Captain David and Lucian emerge from the right, bombarding demons like a firing squad. Abigail and Joey Stalls appear on a rooftop and release a downpour of fire like napalm upon the mob of malevolence.

Full on war ensues. The Light army pushes back the Dark Forces and frees up Rose and Sydney. Energy beams rocket back and forth through the battlefield like guided bombs. Thuds and crashes boom from the pounding of photon orbs against crystal shields and armored plates. The relentless array of projectiles bombards the evil invasion and enemies fall to the ground. The energy beams tear through the demons like asteroids.

From across the courtyard, Kaz can be seen defending a temple full of survivors and Rose flies over to assist him.

"I'm here to back you up," yells Rose as she swoops down by his side.

"Good, there are about ten distraught people inside. These demons would want nothing more than to strike additional fear into their hearts and transform them into monsters."

"Alright, let's keep these people on our side," yells Rose as she prepares herself to fight off the demons with Kaz.

A group of Red Mavens and Gargoyles charge out from behind the temple and surprise Kaz. But Rose has an eye on them and launches a storm of light beams that strike like lightening. The beams cut through the glaring faces of a pair of Mavens and they fall to the floor. Rose's shots also alert Kaz. He quickly turns to the threatening monsters plowing towards them. He immediately deploys dual light swords and jumps into action. Kaz whips his arm around and slings his saber at two approaching

Gargoyles. He beheads one with a swift spinning slash, and then crouches and cuts another one of the undead monsters legs clear off.

The Gargoyle hits the floor hard and it's oozing skin drips from its back and slops onto the ground. The demon digs its dagger like nails into the ground like a hammer claw and drags its self towards him. Kaz is spooked but he doesn't hesitate. He thrust his sword forcefully and cuts through the face of the Gargoyle, leaving it dead in its place.

Rose sprints to the corner of the temple to see what lies around the bend, and she finds a pack of Gargoyles slithering their way forward. Abigail Day also notices the pack from across the courtyard and hurries to join up with Rose and Kaz on the side of the temple. She sprints over as fast as she can.

"I've heard rumors about those Gargoyles in incoming communications," she yells while trying to catch her breath. "They called them Goyles. The damn things look like they should already be dead, huh?"

Kaz studies the Goyle on the ground. Its grayish purple skin looks like a mask resting on its skull. The decaying body appears to be held together by stringy strands of muscle. They seem so frail.

"They are horrifying, but they also look weak," says Kaz.

"Be careful. They look like their muscles wouldn't work because of the way they just hang off their body, but I'm told they pack an amazing punch!"

Just then the group of the Gargoyles comes around the corner. Kaz and Abigail engage the demons. They slash their light swords from behind the protection of their shields and try to stay away from the monsters powerful arms.

Rose burns a light beam through the chest of one of the Gargoyles and knocks him onto the ground, but her extended arm is caught by the sluggish swing of another. The Goyle latches onto her and presses with extreme force. She tries to pull away but the monster is clamped on tight. She flies up into the air and the demons arm rips from its socket, its hand still squeezing like a pulverizing pincer.

Rose grips the hand and pulls with all her might. She rips free, but the Goyle's nails tear chunks of flesh from her arm. She winces from the pain inflicted by the scratches, then spots Kaz and Abigail struggling down below.

The demons are not dying from the beam blasts that Kaz is firing through their bodies. Chopping their limbs off is only slowing them down.

"You have to destroy their heads to kill these demented creatures," yells Abigail.

Rose dives down and lands on top of the temple. She rains down a shower of light beams that impale the demons through the head and rip into their bodies. The Goyles moan as they fall to pieces on the ground in a sloppy mess.

Kaz slips on the guts and falls backward up against the temple wall. A screaming Goyle lunges at him and pins him down like a vicious tiger. The powerful monster restricts Kaz with one arm. He tries to wrestle free but the monster is too strong. The Goyle raises its oozing hand to strike, and its muscles and skin slide backwards as it cocks its arm. He then forcefully thrusts his nasty claws right for

Kaz's face, but Kaz moves at the last second and the long claws smash the wall and slowly break into it. The nails of the Goyle gradually drive deeper into the temple wall like a pressurized piston.

Abigail comes to Kaz's rescue as he squirms against the wall like a fish out of water. She severs the head right off of the Goyle's body. Blood sprays out all over the temple wall and drenches Kaz as well. Then the demon slowly collapses to the ground.

"Sorry Kaz," replies Abigail to the grotesque sight. Kaz whips his hands down to the side and the demons blood splatters about. "No problem," he replies. "I'm alive."

Rose drops down from the temple roof and joins Kaz and Abigail in a pile of dead demons. "Those things are nasty, huh?"

"You're telling me," replies Kaz sarcastically.

With the numbers of the Dark Forces dwindling the Light Army pushes in for the victory. Lucian produces dual light swords and dashes through a crowd of demented demons. With his extended swords blazing he brutally lacerates legs, arms, and heads. The severed appendages drop to the ground with a gruesome splatter as the dead fall around him.

Captain David ferociously mows down a mass of monsters in the town square. He riddles the demons with sizzling holes. Horrific streams of blood pour into the streets as the carnage wanes. Meanwhile, Roger Redcliff picks off a few oblivious demons on the outskirts of the town. He blasts powerful headshots as he remains hidden on the rooftops.

The claws of the murderous creatures clash against the overpowering light swords drawn by Kaz and Rose. They give their all to defeat the remaining Goyles that are attempting to invade the temple.

Abigail Day runs to back up Joey, who has descended from a two story house with his sword and shield drawn. She trades slashes with the far-reaching claws of a ferocious Maven. They battle back and forth intensely until Abigail is overcome. The crazed Maven knocks her back with a vicious blow and slices her across the waist! Blood gushes from her belly as she falls to her knees and tries to hold in her splattering guts!

Joey screams and runs to her rescue, but is hit hard from behind with a dark energy beam, and tumbles to the ground. The sadistic Maven stands before Abigail, seething like a hunting lion. He places his knife like claw on Abigail's shoulder and slowly drags it across her neck, slicing through her tender skin, and she flops to the ground.

Just a second too late, Captain David drives his sword through the back of the demon, ripping the sword upward through his chest. Tossing the demon to the side, David crouches down and inspects Abigail's wounded body. "Abigail! Abigail!" he yells, but her vacant eyes roll back in her head as she goes limp in his arms. His first casualty dies right in front of him.

Silence falls as the battle concludes. Looking around the town square, Rose surveys the nightmarish scene. Decapitated corpses populate the area. Rubble and ash decorate the once peaceful town. She sees Captain David pick up Abigail's lifeless body and walk through the sea of corpses towards the temple. She is stricken with emotion as it dawns on her that Abigail has died. Rose does not know how to react. Seized by the event, she drops to her knees. Kaz and Sydney run to her side.

"Are you hurt Rose?" asks Sydney.

"I'm- I'm fine," she replies as she attempts to gather herself. "Just a little overwhelmed."

"Yeah, that was some introduction, pretty intense. Everyone seems a little stunned and trying hard to hold it together," observes Kaz.

Lucian from across the courtyard yells, "Is everyone okay over there?" His voice echoes through the square.

"We're okay over here," replies Sydney as her and Kaz lift Rose to her feet.

Joey is still on the ground, suffering from burns along his back. He rolls over to alert the team and melted flesh drips from his body as he yells in pain, "I need some help over here!"

Kaz runs over and kneels down beside him. Examining Joey he notices the giant portion of liquefied skin bubbling on his back.

"Okay Joey, hold still," says Kaz. He floats his hands over the searing burn and uses his shamanic healing powers to restore Joeys wound. Green orbs radiate from his palms as he hovers over the blistering injury and slowly rebuilds the skin. Bit by bit the wound is rehabilitated and Kaz helps Joey up off the ground.

"Good as new," says Joey as he stretches side to side. "Thank you, Kaz."

"My honor," says Kaz as he bows to Joey.

The team runs to meet up with Captain David outside the temple. He is still holding Abigail in his arms and peers into the aftermath of the battle. Darkened clouds have rolled in and rain lightly drizzles as the warriors converse about what has just occurred.

"She was murdered by a one of those damn Mavens. We couldn't get to her in time," says Joey as he puts his head down in regret.

"You tried," replies Sydney.

"Yeah, but it wasn't good enough," utters Joey.

"Enough!" says David. He walks away and gently places Abigail inside the temple hallway then returns outside to address the stunned group.

He removes his hat and wipes the dirt and blood from his brow, sighs, and looks over the warriors one by one with an emotionless face. "This is what to expect," he says, "at any moment, anywhere." He takes a second and gathers himself, "You all did an outstanding job, Light Warriors. I can't express that enough. We stand victorious. Unfortunately we lost Abigail, leaving us without a psychic communicator to contact the other squads or the Cassiel outpost to see what their status is."

"Do you think the Dark Forces have attacked Cassiel?" yells Lucian.

"There's no telling, but we must not worry. We must be aware. Let's head inside. Kaz and Rose, check on the survivors. Sydney, come with me and we will find a place for Abigail. Lucian, Joey, and Roger, stay here and keep watch." David speaks with a sense of urgency. The battle was won, but the war has just begun.

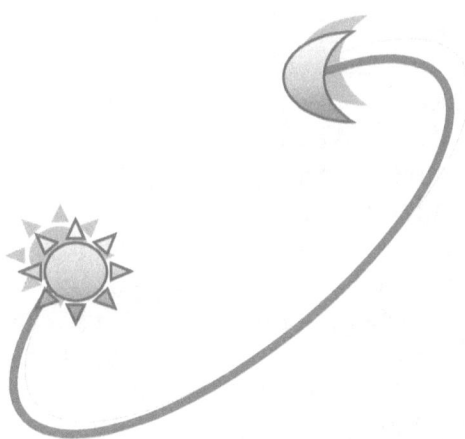

16) <u>Inevitable Trauma</u>

𝒯hey enter in the badly charred doorway. The
glorious temple halls are covered with golden
hieroglyphs. Images of the heavens fill one side
while demons and torture fill the other. Books are
thrown off the shelves and lay all over the floor.
Smashed sculptures and vases are scattered about in
this ransacked shrine.

    David hovers over Abigail. He leans in close
and softly shuts the lids of her empty eyes. He lifts
her up from the ground. Her body droops in his
arms. Blood drips from her severed torso as he
carries her through the stone temple, searching for a
place to lay her to rest.

    Kaz and Rose run off to tend to the survivors.
They come to a group of people huddled in a corner
of the priest's chambers. The frightened people
cower in fear at the sight of the Light Warriors.

Their clothes are torn and blood soaked, and some of the survivors have been severely wounded.

"Don't be afraid. We are here to help you," says Kaz, but the survivors are caught in the grip of fear and do not understand.

Rose kneels down before a mother and her child, "Don't worry, we have defeated all of the demons here. No one is going to hurt you now." She reaches out her hand to comfort the woman, but she screams and slashes her sharp fingernails at Rose, yelling for her to get away from them.

"They're all in shock. Step back Rose, I will use my powers to heal them from their trauma," says Kaz. He rubs his hands together before him, breathes deeply, and opens his hands wide in front of the group of trembling victims. He begins to chant in tones as his palms glow green. His voice echoes through the chambers and the vibration coming from him penetrates the haze of fear that is clutching them.

Shadows start to cry out upon the survivors. Their mouths open wide as they scream from the sound waves blasting out of Kaz. They have possessed the group and were devouring the light inside, slowly transforming them into monsters like them. Eventually they would have turned into dark beings, but the light omitting from Kaz is repulsing the Shadows and exercising the demons.

The screaming Shadows leap from their hosts, and slither away in different directions. The survivors begin to regain consciousness. The people are no longer paralyzed by fear, but traces of darkness are still heavy upon them. Kaz places his hand on the heart of an elderly lady. "Feel the light," he says as he sends waves of energy through her body. The light energy travels into her being and transmutes the darkness. She allows the light to revive her soul and she begins to weep.

Rose embraces the sobbing woman while Kaz continues to free the remaining survivors from the wickedness attacking their souls. "You're going to be fine now," says Rose as she caresses the woman's head.

"Thank you so much. Thank you," says the woman. "It was terrible. I felt consumed in darkness, completely hopeless and lost. Demons where taunting me from everywhere, and threatening to steal my soul!"

"It's over now, we're here to help," says Rose as she starts to cry herself.

David comes to the temple sanctuary. A pale light shines through a mosaic window onto a sacred bench. He places Abigail on the dais and Sydney brings him some linen she had found on a nearby table. "Please help me wrap her in these fabrics," asks David. He begins to lay the cloth over her face. "Great Spirit, we know she is with you now," prays David while Sydney wraps her legs. She watches David as he shows no emotion on the outside, but deep inside he is greatly saddened by the loss.

He continues down to her torso where the fatal wound was delivered. The cloths become saturated by blood as he wraps her in the fabric, "Your will be done, Great Spirit," continues David. They drape a beautiful blue tapestry over her body, decorated with suns, stars, and moons. Now, Abigail must be shown her respect. "Please gather the others," David asks Sydney. She nods and runs off.

Joey, Lucian, and Roger are out front discussing the demeanor of the enemy. "Did you see how determined they were to destroy us?" says Lucian.

"They didn't think or have a bit of fear. They just acted," replies Joey. "Not a single second of hesitation."

"They were just stuck in attack mode," says Roger.

"Hey!" yells Sydney, running up and startling the boys. Joey and Lucian both almost have a heart-attack.

"Whoa, C'mon Sydney, What's going on?" asks Roger.

"Captain David wants us to gather in the sanctuary to say goodbye to Abigail. I'll gather the others. You three head in."

"Alright," sadly answers Joey as he and Lucian walk to the sanctuary. Roger stands and looks out towards the hills, scoping out any possible threats, but he sees nothing and turns and enters the temple.

Sydney hustles into the priest's chambers where Kaz and Rose are comforting the survivors, soothing them from the damage caused by the darkness, calming and loving them.

"Excuse me," says Sydney, "Captain David wants us to gather in the sanctuary to lay Abigail to rest."

"Of course," says Kaz then he lovingly turns to the people, "We will be right back, rest easy," and the group dashes out.

Sydney returns to the sanctuary with the rest of the squad. Captain David asks everyone to hold hands as they pay respects to their fallen sister. Rose watches as Abigail lies wrapped upon the dais. *Poor girl*, she thinks to herself. She looks around at her brothers and sisters. She relishes in their presences: Sydney's fair complexion, Kaz's comforting existence, Joey's tall scrawny frame, Roger's sparkling green eyes and even Lucian's smug demeanor. *Who could be next?* she thinks. They share the moment of silence, and Rose sneaks away from the group.

Overwhelmed she looks for a quiet spot to process all that has unfolded so quickly. She wanders through the temple and enters into a hall lined with six jeweled knights. Crouching onto the floor, she hides in between two of the giant statues.

She attempts to bring herself to a calm meditative state like she has been taught. Her mind is racing a million thoughts per minute. The split second decisions of the battle have taxed her psyche. Haunting demons press upon her conscious. The giant fangs of the Hunters and the dragging claws of Mavens scrape along her mind. Rose tries to shake it off. Breathing deeply, she regains some control as her thoughts drift to her uncle Layne and his squad. *I wonder if he came across any danger,* she thinks. *What if he's hurt or... or like Abigail?*

Rose girds herself once more and concentrates on bringing her mind back into balance. *Let all this negativity go. This was all necessary somehow. Sadly this is the way the encounter had to unfold.* In order for Rose to continue to advance she must allow herself to get used to the stimulation of battle and not be overcome with this surge of emotion, although this certainly was an extreme beginning.

Captain David and the other members of the squad are now gathered around the survivors and asking questions about the catastrophe that occurred in town today. A disheveled old man who's extremely shaken speaks.

"Everything was normal in Tarbeck. The town folks were going about their business when screaming could be heard ringing through the square. I looked up to the hills and I could see the demons descending like an avalanche onto our helpless town. First a pitch-black wave of Shadows swarmed in and began torturing people. You could see another crowd of demons perched atop the hills watching as the Shadows tormented the town. When the time was right the clawed beasts ran downhill and started destroying everything in sight."

Lucian continues listening to the man while Kaz is tending to the wounds of other survivors. Captain David has heard all he has needed to and is growing a little impatient. He knows the Dark Forces are not slowing down and neither should they.

Back in the hall amongst the statues, Rose has brought herself to a relaxed state. The thoughts float from her mind as her conscious becomes quiet.

Chink, Chink, Chink! The sound of clanging metal can be heard approaching. Rose opens her eyes and hovering above her is a phantom knight!

"Hello there Rose, I am Magnus." The phantom spirit floats down in front of her and sits on his knees. "I must thank you."

She stares at the phantom. His platinum armor glows in the light. His face, a metal mask with golden eyes and a golden smile, just floats above his shoulders. His armor is intricately detailed with action filled pictures from ancient battlefields.

"For what?" she replies with a downcast expression.

"For destroying the darkness that plotted to conquer our town, that's what."

"Yeah, we won, but at what cost?" says Rose angrily, a bit discouraged.

The knight falls backward onto the ground and splits to pieces. The sections of his armor scatter across the floor. They clang and bang as they tumble. Seconds later in a puff of smoke he reappears before her completely reconstructed!

"Rose!" Magnus yells as he floats off into the distance. His hands and legs sway oddly through the air.

She gets up from her nook and walks into the center of the statues. Magnus sits upon a figure of an armored man. The adventurer poses triumphantly with his hands upon his large sword as it stabs into the ground.

"This is the sacrifice that has to be made in order to bring freedom to Octairion. The fatalities of war are never sweet, but it is the world you have been called to. In order to taste heaven here on earth you must continue to free humanity from the clutches of darkness."

Rose walks down the aisle of statues to a throne. The tall chair is encrusted with shimmering diamonds and decorated with golden emblems. Could this possibly be the throne of the high priest? She traces the smooth throne with her fingers and looks up at Magnus.

"I understand it's difficult to accept the brutality of what I just witnessed."

"Indeed, but my dear you have been bred for such a task."

"And Abigail, what about her?" cries Rose, now yelling up at Magnus.

"Who knows what is for good or bad? Her time had come. That is something that is between her and Great Spirit. We don't know why that particular moment was chosen. But pay attention to the lessons that are to be learned about her death. Therein lays the value."

Magnus suddenly disappears in a puff of smoke yet again. This time the clouds stay lingering in the air. Rose jerks her head back and forth searching for him, "Are you there?" she cries aloud. Through the fog of smoke a shadowy figure can be seen approaching. Her eyes widen as the tall figure skulks closer.

"Rose, is that you?" asks the shadowy character. Joey Stalls emerges from the smoke. "What are you doing, burning incense in here?"

Rose just smiles and laughs. "C'mon. Captain David is ready to move out," says Joey as he waves for her to follow him and runs out.

Rose looks around the throne room one last time and whispers, "Thanks for the advice Magnus" and exits.

Joey and Rose meet up with the rest of the squad outside. Captain David is standing before the group looking impatient, and eager to move out.

"Light Warriors, we need to be on high alert. The Dark Forces could be anywhere. Joey and Sydney, teleport up to those hills and scope out the area," he commands.

They flash to the bordering hills, investigate the surrounding area, and report back.

"Nothing Sir, just empty planes, it should be safe to move out," reports Joey.

"All clear on my end also," reports Sydney.

"Ok, we're going to carry on with our mission and head to the Cassiel outpost. Let's move out squad!" orders Captain David thrusting his arm towards the sky.

They climb the southern hill of Tarbeck and set out once more to their destination. Now having experienced battle, the team's sensitivity is heightened. They tread lightly and listen closely. Their eyes search intently like a starving tiger hunting its prey.

Passing over rocky dirt paths, they spot tracks from the enemy heading towards the devastated town.

"Spooky, huh?" whispers Joey. "This is where they set up and prepared for the assault." The squad examines the footprints as they continue to march along their path. Terrifying four clawed feet about a foot long that give them all goose bumps!

"They came from the south," observes Joey as the imprints trail away from their route.

"How long do you think they waited?" asks Kaz.

"Who's to know," replies Lucian. "They don't seem to think much. They kind of just thrive on a savage instinct."

"They only had one thing on their minds: to kill anyone who did not submit to the darkness," says Joey.

"They have no conscience, no morals, and they won't stop until they get what they're after. So we need to keep moving warriors," says Captain David as he turns and continues trekking to Cassiel.

Hours of wading through swamps, maneuvering through small patches of forest, and hiking many desolate miles of empty terrain go by. The soldiers prowl the land, edging closer and closer to the Cassiel outpost. Specks of sand, clumps of dirt, and bunches of boring bushes is all that surrounds them. Tottering through trees and over giant roots, the team stays together and persists on the sensory dulling journey.

The warriors come to a large crevice in a mountain side. "Let's make camp inside here," suggests Captain David. "The sun is setting and darkness will fall upon the land soon and I don't want to be caught out in the open unprepared." He swings off the straps to his large backpack and drops it onto the ground, "We are not far from Cassiel. At first daylight we will proceed."

The warriors gather into the fracture and nestle along the sides. Captain David attends first watch and faces the entrance, while the squad attempts to relax.

Night consumes the camp. Nothing can be seen inside or outside of the tight crevice. The cozy camp brings comfort to the warriors. With a moment of peace, they share stories. Captain David overhears from outside as he keeps watch.

"Tell us your story Joey," says Sydney Blake.

"Well, I used to always feel like the world was out to get me. I never trusted a soul. My parents used to abuse me and leave me home alone all day. I was the real tall and skinny kid that everyone picked on in school too. So that didn't help. Needless to say, I didn't get along well with others. I never felt comfortable in my own skin, ya know?"

"Yeah," replies the squad in unison.

"One day I decided to start fighting back. The kids in school were giving me crap and I stood up for myself and whacked the guy in the nose. Everything was different from that point on. I gained some confidence and started believing in myself. I never let anyone treat me that way again. Unfortunately it kind of hardened my heart too, but in this world you have to."

"How did you figure out you could teleport?" asks Rose.

"One day I was walking home and my heart told me to just keep going. Don't enter the house, just keep walking. So I did. I came to this group of people that we're working on the side of a farm. Part of a barn had collapsed and they were rebuilding. I was crossing the construction site when a giant bull smashed through the barricades. As he stampeded, a bunch of wires snapped from the pulleys the men had set up and they whipped me up against the wall. I could barely function because I was hit so hard.

Next thing you know, a wooden beam was coming right at me. Just as it was about to take me out, everything got extremely slow. The world around me almost stopped. I felt this wave of power come over me and I could see myself standing off in the distance. Then all of a sudden, I was standing in that exact spot, watching the beam plow through the wall that I was just up against. Trust me, I was freaked out."

"Wow, that's intense," replies Kaz.

Sydney Blake jumps up with excitement, "My situation was similar."

"Whoa," reply the campers as the excitement is growing.

"How did you get called to the Village Joey?" asks Lucian.

"I said I was freaked out by what just occurred, right? Well I eventually ran into Abigail Day as I kept wandering around," Joey puts his head down and looks away a bit sad. "She told me that this Oracle told her that she wanted us to travel to the Village of Hope together. As if I wasn't spooked enough already, I had Abby claiming she was a psychic and telling me to come with her. If I hadn't just teleported to save my life, I probably would have never believed her."

"How about you, Lucian, What's your story?" asks Joey.

Lucian sits up and adjusts himself while he nervously twists a flower in his hand, "I grew up in Chesterville, Holyoke. My father owned a successful clothing company. Basically I was spoiled rotten. I got everything I ever desired and if I didn't, let's just say there was hell to pay. When I got to school I became a terror. Bullying kids and causing lots of emotional damage. Some were beaten by the darkness, and some like myself, were used by it."

"Well? Tell us how you escaped the darkness, Lucian?" asks Sydney.

Lucian sighs. He's not too proud of what he's about to share. "There was this kid, Adam Snow." *A name he will never forget.* "He was fat and shy, an easy target," says Lucian as he raises his arms in disgust. "One day after school I cornered him and forced him up to the roof. I made him walk along the edge of the building while I taunted him. He did it or else I was going to give him a beating. He ended up slipping and falling off the school. I ran to the side and watched as he fell. My heart sank into my chest. I felt a strange sensation come over me as I saw Adam falling head first towards the ground.

I was overcome with an extreme urge to want to rescue him. The pressure surged inside of my body. I felt as if I had an extended limb, like I could grab him and pull him back up. Sure enough, I caught him in midair and levitated him to safety. I was never the same after that day."

"That's something else!" responds Kaz.

"Hey Rose, how were you called to the Village?" asks Lucian, trying to shift the attention.

"Isis, Spirit of the Waters, appeared to me and told me to travel there," answers Rose.

"What?" questions the group. Captain David intrigued by her answer nudges back into the crevice.

"You saw a spirit?" asks Lucian.

"I've seen a few of them."

"When, who?" asks Kaz.

"Isis, Ahzhaire, and Magnus are their names. They have appeared to me and guided me throughout my journey. I just saw Magnus at the small town we left. None of you have seen anything like that?" replies Rose.

"No," replies Captain David. "That's something even I haven't heard of."

Rose glances at her stunned squad, "I recall angel's coming to my rescue when I was young also," she says.

The squad looks around puzzled.

"I've felt the guiding of spirits, but I have never seen them with my eyes," says David. "Looks like you have some special abilities few may know about Rose."

"Huh. Yeah, I guess so," she replies.

The squad continues to bond a little while longer. Lucian lets out a yawn, followed by Sydney. The yawn spreads around the camp and eyelids grow heavy as the warriors doze off into dreamland.

Rose races out of the crevice and soars into the night. Flying high and free, she fearlessly raises above the planes of Cassiel. Hidden in the night sky, she stealthily travels to the land of Drakkar. Smoke fills the heavens, rising from the ground.

Mysterious mounds are caught on fire and dispersed about the land. Rose, shocked and curious, flies down to see what is aflame in the burning piles.

As she inches closer she can hear screaming. Cries of thousands of screeching voices can be heard in the distance. The scent of burning flesh hits Rose like a ton of bricks. She stops in her tracks as she realizes what is going on. Oh no, she thinks as she darts towards the bodies and tries to rescue anyone she can.

Her eyes fall upon a sight of monstrosity; dismembered bodies are stacked in piles. Decapitated heads cry out amongst millions of mutilated limbs. "Save us! You have to!" cries a disfigured face on the pile, but there is nothing she can do. The damage has been done.

Panicking, Rose cannot accept the fact that she cannot save these people. She digs through the mound of appendages. Tossing aside bloody hands and legs, she burrows into the tower of body parts, but a complete person cannot be found.

As she continues to remove the pieces from the base of the pile, the mound of body parts starts to sway. Unaware, she continues to frantically fling the severed limbs. The mutilated faces continue to scream in agony, "We're suffering, please save us. We have no one. It's up to you!"

From outside of the manmade pile she hears the crashing of blood soaked flesh slopping onto the ground. Turning around to exit, she runs, but she is too slow. The tower of death topples onto Rose and traps her amidst the corpses.

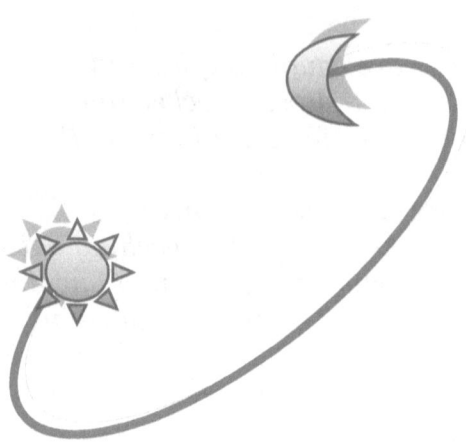

17) <u>A Dark Occurrence</u>

*R*eleasing a blood-curdling scream, Rose awakens the camp in fright. Everyone jumps up and looks to her in suspense.

"What's the matter?" asks Kaz.

"It was only a nightmare," she answers while sweating profusely.

With a sigh of relief, everyone relaxes.

"I'd prefer our annoying bell tower over that wakeup call any day," says Lucian as he gets out of bed and heads outside to get some fresh air.

The crisp morning air fills his lungs. He glances around the forest. All is calm and all is well. The rest of the squad arises and joins him outside. Yawning and stretching, they wipe the stagnant slumber from their eyes and awaken their bodies for another day of adventure.

Captain David hops up and is ready to get a move on. "Okay squad, we can make it to Cassiel by noontime if we hustle onward," he yells and the squad gears up and they continue on their way.

A group of sneaky Shadows watches the Light Warriors from afar. Hidden amongst the shade of the trees, no one spots the spying Shadows. Lurking in the distance, they plot. "Should we attack or go tell the others?" mutters one of the pitch black shades.

The stealthy Shadows watch the unsuspecting squad as they move out of sight, "Let's go inform Kirtaunta," replies the other.

Slithering away, the Shadows comb the land at a ferocious pace. They head into the edge of Drakkar, towards the heavily guarded city of Bronwyn. Dark clouds surround the pinnacle of the sky-scraping fortress located in the core. The Dark Forces infest the land. They dwell like maggots on a decaying carcass. Trains of human slaves are forced into prison camps set up all over Bronwyn and pushed along by Grangers; giant hard-bodied demons that patrol the city.

The burly Grangers stand about two stories high and their muscular arms stretch down to their feet. The furless ape-like demons have a horrid temper and pack a devastating punch.

The Shadows plague all of the slaves that are being forced into the prisons. They inflict tortuous visions and feed off the fear of the haunted humans. All of the monsters in the Dark Forces thrive off of tormenting the poor souls in this hellish stronghold.

Kirtaunta sits alone in his chamber, watching over Bronwyn. His wicked black eyes peer out into the city as a villainous smile dawns his snout. This sadistic monster loves to hear the screams of agony rise to his chamber as he sits in his black and blood red throne; embedded with zircon crystals and metallic silver devil heads. He sees his kingdom growing before his eyes and is pleased. Kirtaunta is the ruler of the Dark Forces here on the physical plane and the most impure evil fills this devilish Minotaur.

Kirtaunta Himilad was the unmerciful leader of a band of terrorists before he mutated into a sadistic half man, half bull. Known for his unrelenting hate for humanity, he led a mob of terrorists in a bullet filled killing spree through a populated city one quiet evening. He and his group of murderers gunned down a multitude of innocent people who were merely going about their daily lives. Slaughtering the inhabitants of the city, Kirtaunta and his gang locked down the area. Dark energy surged inside of him from the Inner Realm, transforming Kirtaunta into the psychotic beast he is now and establishing Bronwyn as the center of dark power. Since that day, Kirtaunta has commanded the Dark Forces in spreading through Octairion.

The doors burst open and the Shadows enter into Kirtaunta's chamber

"Master, Master!" they squeal as they slither before his feet.

"Yes minions?" he replies with a deep bellow.

"We have spotted a group of Light Warriors near the border of Kane and Cassiel. We believe they are the ones responsible for the great losses at Tarbeck."

"Well then, unfortunately we are going to have to send them an upsetting message, aren't we? Gather up an army and go see what they're so interested in." Kirtaunta stomps his heavy black hooves down onto the ground before him. His fleecy reddish brown legs shudder as they hold up his chiseled mortal upper body. A surge of energy blasts down the massive tower and into the city alerting the evil population.

He then approaches an enormous window looking out of his throne room and shouts into Bronwyn, "Dark Forces, the Light Warriors are assembling. They want to put an end to our reign of darkness, but I tell you they will be overcome by our power. None shall stand before us. The light will be extinguished once and for all. Dark Forces, prepare for war!" Kirtaunta's voice echoes from the tower and the demons wail in agreement as they run through the streets in a wild frenzy.

Back in Cassiel, the squad has reached the northern outpost. Surprisingly it stands in one piece. Captain David bangs his fist against the large steel doors of the settlement.

"What is your business?" asks a voice from inside.

"We are the Light Warriors from the Village of Hope," answers David. The sliding of wooden planks and the cranking of leavers can be heard as the door is unlocked.

"Come in quickly," replies a reddish blonde haired man waving frantically for the squad to enter. He slams the heavy metal doors behind them and barricades the entrance once again.

"Hello, my name is Gai Toa'ni," says the concerned young man.

Captain David introduces himself and the squad.

Gai, a bit frazzled, can hardly speak, "There are only a few of us here. The southern Cassiel and Tahein outposts have just come under heavy attack. The rest of our troops have gone to assist them. We knew you were coming so we waited for you here."

Taken aback by the news they just heard the squad freezes. Rose can't help but to think about her uncle Layne.

"Do you have any more information? Do you know if the other Village of Hope squads made it to the outposts?" asks Rose.

"We have no further information. The last communication we received was a distress call from the southern outpost informing us that they have just come under heavy attack. Our troops were sent out about two hours ago and since then we have had no word."

Captain David thinks critically as he inspects the outpost. Large walls forming a sphere surround them. Three small buildings sit from 12:00 to 3:00. The rest of the outpost is dirt arena used for combat training. Basically it's a giant dustbowl.

"Who is stationed here with you?" asks David.

"Including myself, we have three here. They are in the barracks right now. Follow me."

Rushing into the barracks, the squad interrupts a meditating pair of warriors. A slim man with wild hair leads the session. He peers over at the intruding squad, "Hello, I am Malcore. Welcome to Cassiel."

A charming young woman jumps up and curtsies, "I am Shawnti, pleasure to meet you." Shawnti walks over to Rose and stands before her. She stares into Rose's eyes as if peering into her soul."My! You have had quite the difficult road, haven't you?" she asks.

Rose smiles and looks around the room nervously, "I'm sure we all have," she replies

"Indeed, we all have," says Shawnti, "but yours has been darker than most."

Rose intrigued and a bit charmed by Shawnti replies, "why do you say that?"

"I can feel you. I just know."

Rose stares at this mysterious girl for a moment. Her short black hair caresses the line of her jaw. Her beautiful brown eyes almost seem familiar, but she can't put a finger on it.

"What has your path been like?" asks Rose.

"Death," replies Shawnti. "Throughout my life, death has followed me. Those I've cherished most in life have been taken from me and some I could care less about also. Nonetheless, I've experienced a lot of loss." Shawnti becomes sensitive in front of the Family of Light. "It can make you want to harden your heart. Close it up and not let anyone else in," she says as she glances at the new guests.

A tear falls from her face. Rose reaches for her and pulls her in for a hug. Weeping in Rose's arms, Shawnti feels a powerful connection with Rose, a mysterious soul sister relationship.

"Only the strong will let themselves be this open and vulnerable," says Rose.

"Only in the presence of true love, like that in your heart Rose, can the walls be torn down. You have been through true darkness, so you understand what others are dealing with. You have survived the pit of despair, never giving in to the lure of the darkness," says Shawnti.

Gai approaches the girls with great care and joins them in a circle, "Only when you have experienced deep darkness will you truly appreciate the light," he says. "When one has been baptized in suffering and emptied oneself of the ego, a powerful spiritual attitude emerges. You know yourself and the voice that guided you through the night well. Certain aspects of life are no longer important. A part of you dies and life gives birth to the true self inside."

The group holds hands. Malcore and the rest of the squad join. The Light Family shares the sacred space as a spiritual union takes place.

"The sacred truth inside me recognizes and honors the sacred truth inside of you," says Malcore with a great smile on his face.

Rose feels total acceptance from the group. Something she has not felt in a long time. It's as if they have all known each other in a past life. The soul family enjoys the intimate presence of one another. A sense of home fills their hearts.

Shawnti squeezes tightly onto Rose's hand, "I'm glad you finally made it."

"Thank you, we got held up in Tarbeck. The Dark Forces were attacking the town and tormenting its people. We had to help," says Rose.

"Unfortunately we lost one of our own there – beloved Abigail," says Joey.

"I am so sorry to hear that," says Malcore. "Our whole team is out fighting right now. Who knows what is occurring there."

The reunion is broken up by some noise that can be heard outside the barracks. Captain David runs outside and is stopped in his tracks by the sight of a giant Granger. The massive demons head can be seen above the twenty-foot wall. His hands grip the wall and he tries to pull himself up. The Granger peeks his head over, opens his salivating mouth, and lets out a forceful shout. Captain David unloads multiple energy blasts at the Grangers hands and face, knocking him down.

"Ambush!" he yells, signaling the rest of the troops to rush out of the barracks and join David in the combat arena. A flock of winged demons sails through the sky above the outpost. Their black tattered wings carry their scrawny little bodies, while their sharp pointed beaks and talons are reasons to be cautious.

"Those are the Akumies. They are the messengers of darkness. They are sent straight from Kirtaunta, Ruler of Darkness," says Shawnti.

"Which means they came here for a specific reason," responds Gai.

"What would that be?" asks Sydney.

"They may be seeking revenge for Tarbeck, or they're looking for someone in particular," answers Gai.

"Whatever their reason for visiting may be, it's time to defend the outpost. Light Warriors, attack!" yells Captain David.

The terrifying grunts of Grangers can be heard from behind the wall. At the same time Hunters are being catapulted into the arena. Taunting and screaming, the ferocious Akumies and Hunters attack. Dive bombing with their pointed beaks, the Akumies descend from the sky while the Hunters charge.

"Divide!" yells Captain David. "Half attack the Hunters. Half oppose the aerial assault."

David, Kaz, Lucian, Joey and Sydney dash into combat with the Hunters. Rose, Roger, Shawnti, Gai, and Malcore stand back and blast light beams into the sky.

The Akumies strike with lightning speed, evading the rising beam blasts. An agitated Akumi stabs at Sydney who teleports out of the danger zone just in the nick of time. Lucian and Kaz, back to back, fend off the ravenous Hunters. Kaz wielding dual swords slices through Hunter after Hunter with overhand chops. Lucian blocks a vicious claw strike, and Kaz spins around him and rips through the legs of the menacing demon like a chainsaw through a tree! Lucian delivers a death blow to the chopped down Hunter, and then smashes his shield into the multiple approaching demons! Kaz follows up with a double blade slash right through the torsos of the multitude! The monsters cry loudly as they bleed out on the ground, dying slowly.

Joey and Sydney shift around the arena like amazing flashes of light, impaling Hunters as they teleport. Captain David drives his sword through the demons as he wails about the outpost, grunting as he goes, but the numbers keep growing. Captain David, Joey, and Sydney move in closer to Kaz and

Lucian, forming one unit and fighting together. David and Joey join shields, push the advancing Hunters back, and then strike together, shredding the demons to pieces. Meanwhile Grangers continue to hurl more Hunters into the arena from outside the outpost walls.

Roger scores a direct hit to the center of an Akumi, scorching a light orb into his chest and knocking him from the sky. The Akumi plummets to the ground and splatters into a puddle of blood and guts. Four more remain.

Rose spreads her hidden bioluminescent wings, surprising her new teammates.

"You're an Angel?" says Shawnti.

"Yes," replies Rose. "I'm going to engage the Akumies. Try and shoot them down while I distract them."

She leaps into the air and charges straight for the Akumies. She forcefully drives her shoulder into one, catching him off guard and pushing him back. Rose launches light beams at another and manages to clip his wing. From this height, she can see the unbelievably large army of darkness that stands outside the outpost. They're beginning to climb on top of one another and are getting closer to the edge of the outpost walls.

The Akumies chase Rose like ravenous ravens. She flies back and forth, eluding their talons along with many dark energy beams flying into the sky from the droves of land roving Dark Forces.

She flies lower towards the outpost and draws them down towards her squad. Rose lands awkwardly on the ground and skids into one of the open barracks. The awaiting Light Warriors discharge numerous beam blasts obliterating two of the Akumies and damaging another.

Fluttering out of control, the wounded Akumi erratically bounces around the arena. Landing on its feet, the Akumi spots Lucian, unguarded and preoccupied. The beast lunges at his leg and severs it off at the thigh. Lucian screams at the top of his lungs as he falls to the floor! Plasma pours from Lucian's mutilated stub and trickles through the battleground. Now the Hunters can smell blood, causing them to hone in on Lucian like a pack of cutthroat hyenas looking for an easy meal.

Malcore sees Lucian in the reflection of a bloodthirsty demons eye. He looks behind him and sees Lucian crawling backward trying to avoid being dinner for the murderous brood. Malcore uses his power of levitation to pull Lucian into a corner, trailing blood streaks along the way. But the Hunters don't let up! They hurdle over one another to get closer to him. Gnashing their teeth and clawing each other, they ignore the other warriors and ravenously pursue Lucian!

Captain David, Joey, and Roger run to defend Lucian as he screams in pain while gripping his severed thigh. They form a barrier around him and fire upon the approaching demons, but the overwhelming numbers still continue to grow as more and more Hunters are catapulted into the outpost by the massive Grangers.

Loud crashing can be heard from the aggressive Grangers attempting to demolish the cracking stone walls with giant overhand blows. Rose, Shawnti, and the rest of the squad unite to help defend Lucian against the unrelenting forces pressing in. The cornered warriors blast hundreds of beams into the sea of Hunters who flood the arena, but the beasts persist.

Crumbling can be heard overhead as debris falls onto Lucian. He looks up and to his dismay, witnesses a wave of Hunters pouring into the outpost. Climbing on top of one another, they have finally scaled the wall. In an instant he is smothered by vicious Hunters; enveloped in Dark Forces.

Joey and Sydney teleport out onto the edges of the outpost wall and start to shoot downward into the battlefield. Joey mows down a few but is clobbered by a devastating punch from a colossal Granger. He is knocked unconscious and lands amongst a pack of Hunters. They pounce on him and mince poor Joey to pieces!

Sydney, who just witnessed the critical blow, teleports close to where Joey was hit and her ill-fated eyes fall upon the gruesome picture. Joey is being picked apart by the gang of vicious demons! The largest beast pulls at Joey's leg and rips it from his pelvis. The cracking of bones and tearing of skin sends chills down Sydney's spine. Smaller Hunters nip at the limb torn from Joey's body and try to steal it away from the large demon, but he won't let it go so easily. He savagely snaps at them, defending his spoils.

Sydney is lost in the nightmarish scene and flinches forcefully at the clusters of beams sailing her way. She runs along the top of the thick outpost wall, ducking and dodging, trying to stay alive. Sydney jumps and rolls to avoid being taken out by the sniping enemies, but slips on a splatter of blood and loses her balance. She falls off the side and

215

quickly catches herself, hanging on by her struggling fingertips.

An Akumi, who had been patiently stalking her, immediately strikes in her moment of weakness. Swooping down from the heavens, he fastens on to her backside and drills his beak repeatedly into her spine! Sydney teleports into the nearby mountains, but the damage has been dealt. She coughs up blood as she lay dying alone, watching her squad be annihilated by the darkness.

Kaz and Captain David hack away at the predators feeding on Lucian, but the battlefield is far too crowded and David is struck down; sliced through the lower back and quickly losing blood! He fights for his life from the ground. Blocking their attacks with his shield, he counters with deadly strikes and lops off their legs. The Hunters topple onto the ground and begin to chaotically crawl about.

Kaz, who is consumed in concern as he watches his Captain floundering on the ground, is caught by a sneak attack from the groveling demons. The monsters stab their sharp claws into Kaz's legs and pull him to the ground. They bite and rip the muscles from his bones with their powerful jaws! Kaz screams in anguish as he is being eaten alive. David tries to jump up and save Kaz, but he is paralyzed and can't move his legs. His spine has been severed!

Grangers plow through the western portion of the outpost walls. Stone blocks scatter and ricochet as they crash through the outpost's defenses and bulldoze inside. The ill-tempered Grangers begin to destroy everything in their path.

Swinging their massive arms, they pummel herds of Hunters as they rampage towards Roger and Gai.

Roger, who is involved in combat, is snatched from behind. The crazed Granger lifts him high and smashes him into the ground over and over. He rams Roger's skull into a pile of rubble, snapping his neck. He picks him up once more. This time driving his legs into the ground and shattering his femurs! Then the Granger pitches him across the outpost and blood spills from Roger's body as he flies through the air and splatters against a wall. The blood-soaked beast roars and beats his chest like an insane gorilla celebrating his kill.

Gai charges up a pile of dead bodies. Drenched in blood and screaming, he leaps through the air. He deploys dual light swords and plunges them into the face of the homicidal Granger, who's still beating his chest. The burning hot swords rip through the demons skull and blast out the back of its head. Gai hangs onto the swords and his bodyweight pulls the blades down the brawny build of the Granger, ripping the monster into fragments as he falls to the ground.

"This is insanity," yells Gai standing in a pile of Granger guts.

"We have to keep fighting!" yells Rose as she deals a death blow to a stumbling Hunter. Blood squirts from the monster and splashes into her mouth. The plasma coats Rose's tongue. The taste of iron at the back of her throat has her gagging.

"We're not going to last much longer if we don't start racking up the kills. We're dropping like flies!" yells Malcore a bit worried as he surveys the tidal wave of Dark Forces still flooding the arena.

Just then, a wall of looming Grangers presses in on David. He's bleeding profusely up against a wall and the fact that he is helpless to assist his struggling squad is killing him all the same. The remaining few warriors quickly merge on their wounded Captain and form a wall of defense.

The large Grangers don't hesitate for a moment at the threat of four puny humans opposing them. The three Grangers separate and the outside two lunge forward at the group of warriors. The warriors scatter out of the way of the Grangers giant mitts attempting to scoop them up.

Malcore double rolls and finds himself behind a recoiling Granger. He produces a light sword and wields it above his head like a stealthy ninja. He steps softly and quickly like a samurai, awaiting any kind of backfire. He silently steps up close behind the oblivious monster and unloads a sneak attack.

Malcore frantically slashes at the tree trunk like leg of the demon, leaving deep lacerations with every hack. The snarling Granger attempts to reach back and swipe away the aggravating attacker, but Malcore swiftly evades the giant haymakers. He sidesteps in between the muscle bound monster's legs and continues to chop away.

Rose, Shawnti, and Gai scramble around David, trying to keep the Grangers distracted as they jump and dodge the demons flurry of attacks. Meanwhile, Hunters have noticed all the commotion and start to surround the squad as well.

Rose attacks the group of Hunters in a horror-fueled fury as she witnesses the bodies and fragments of her squad strewn all about the outpost.

She spots clusters of demons feasting upon the remains of the fallen. There is no saving them now, she just tucks away the pain temporarily and continues to kill anything in sight.

Finally, Malcore cuts through the muscle and bone of the Grangers leg. Snapping and cracking bones pop as the Granger loses his footing and tumbles to the ground, kicking up a giant cloud of dust. The wide and absurdly heavy body of the demon flattens several Hunters that were lost in pursuit. Gai capitalizes on the opportunity and sprints over to the grounded Granger. He drives his sword into its skull and instantly executes the intruder.

Shawnti, who was hovering around Captain David, is snatched up by a Granger. He lifts her up to his big ugly face and opens wide his salivating jaws. Shawnti can smell the stench of decaying flesh on the breath of the disgusting monster. She pries away at his fists and burns light beams into his hands, but the demon proceeds to move her towards his mouth.

Malcore and Gai rush to rescue the damsel in distress. Right before Shawnti is shoved into the Grangers mouth, the giant fist of the demon is frozen stiff. Malcore has focused all of the strength of his mind on halting the feed.

Gai produces dual swords, jumps high, and plunges a sword into the waist of the massive demon. He then pulls himself up, stabs into the Grangers chest with his other sword and continues to climb up his body as the powerful demon is restricted by Malcore's mind control.

Gai makes his way down the bulky bicep of the Granger and hacks away at the monster's wrist. A pack of Hunters is beginning to crowd around Malcore. He can't keep this up too much longer. Rose has her hands full with multiple enemies and Captain David is doing what he can from the battlefield ground.

In just a few slashes, Gai has penetrated the thick skin of the Granger. The weight of Shawnti in his giant hand helps Gai rip through faster. He slashes through the wrist bones and the clenching fist rips away and plummets to the ground with Shawnti still in his grasp! Malcore breaks his concentration and runs over to assist her. Gai runs back up the arm of the flailing Granger and launches a devastating beam blast into its eyes that burns into its head and boils his brain! The monster falls backward to the ground and rumbles the earth as he crashes down.

Malcore has released Shawnti, and they've come back to support Captain David.

"You guys got to get out of here," yells Captain David. It's beginning to feel a little hopeless on the battlefield. "C'mon, I'm a goner anyhow. I've been almost cut clear in half. I'm barely hanging on. Leave me and go help Rose."

Shawnti looks over at Rose, painted red from a shower of blood that is pouring from the countless Hunters she is relentlessly slashing apart. Then Shawnti looks back down at David, "Are you sure?" she asks.

"I'll only weigh you down, get out of here!"

Malcore, Shawnti and Gai leave Captain David's side and go to back up Rose.

Another enraged Granger approaches Captain David who has given his all on the battlefield today. The knuckle walking Granger stands over him and consumes David in a massive shadow. He stares up at the behemoth and taunts him, "Show me what you've got you big bastard!"

The Granger grunts and snarls loudly before he proceeds to raise his enormous leg and stomp repeatedly. The demon continuously lifts and heavily stomps. The ground quakes as David is pulverized into the dirt.

Rose is lost for a moment as she feels the quaking of the ground and turns to witnesses her Captains demise right before her eyes. She stands in shock as the group comes to back her up.

The warriors struggle to survive; the infestation of darkness has choked the life out of them.

"We have to get out of here!" yells Shawnti.

"I agree, lets retreat," replies Rose. She doesn't want to admit it, but they can't win against this powerful army.

Rose grabs Shawnti and spreads her luminous wings. Flying over Malcore and Gai she yells for them to retreat. Malcore attempts to grab Gai but he refuses.

"Hold onto me and we'll levitate out of here," insists Malcore.

"Wait one last thing. Make sure you all get to a safe distance." Gai stares seriously at Malcore. "Come get me when I'm done," he finishes.

"Okay," says Malcore. Looking at Gai, he nods – understanding what he must do.

Rose, Shawnti and Malcore fly to a cliff in the distance and watch as Gai is encircled in demons.

Inside the outpost, Gai looks around at the massacre that just has ensued. The once boring dust bowl has become a morbid blood bath. Bodies of his fallen comrades are strewn about. Corpse upon corpse of the Dark Forces lay amassed.

Gai, full of righteous anger, focuses every last volt of energy he has left and spins like a super human-powered turbine. He generates more and more power as he spirals with great speed. The clouds darken and howling winds gust as he begins to glow. Stunning rays of light shine from his being like an exploding star.

His voice thunders through the outpost and Gai releases a blistering wave of radiation that evaporates everything in a hundred yard radius. The explosion sends a shockwave through the land, kicking up dirt and rocks into the air. The group of Light Warriors observes in wonder as they watch the globe of devastation obliterate the majority of their enemies!

When the dust settles, Gai can be seen collapsed inside a gigantic crater, depleted of all energy. The prevailing Dark Forces drop into the crater and frantically charge towards Gai. They will not quit until every Light Warrior is dead. Rose darts down from the cliff and scoops Gai's exhausted body up out of danger. Malcore grabs ahold of Shawnti and the group flies away from the blast zone. They are no match for the enduring Dark Forces, so they retreat north.

18) <u>A Haunting Suspicion</u>

*B*eaten and bruised, the worn out warriors land before an abandoned castle along the shore of Drakkar. A large stone dwelling that hasn't been touched in years. The surrounding shrubbery, wildly overgrown, reaches to the second story windows, which are lined with rusted bars.

"This will do," yells Malcore. "Let's head inside and recuperate."

They enter in through a crumbled wall in the back of the castle. The ruthless weather of the coast has not been kind to the fortress. The ancient wooden floors creak as the warriors make their way through a soiled kitchen. Dirt and leaves have blown in from the opening and cover the room. Pots and pans rest on the stove and the dinner table has fallen to pieces in the corner.

Shawnti coughs as she clears the cobwebs in the doorway leading to the family room. Rose carries Gai to a sofa and places him down to rest. Finally able to relax for a minute, she plops onto a rug in front of a fireplace and passes out. Shawnti keeps guard as Rose and Gai rest, and Malcore investigates the castle.

Shawnti sits in a chair by an open window and watches Rose as she sleeps. *This poor girl has just lost her entire squad,* she thinks. Knowing loss well, she can relate to Rose's pain.

Malcore silently creeps back into the room, "The stairs leading up are demolished. I levitated up to check it out, but it's just a bunch of useless junk. So I guess this is where we stay for now." He sits down next to Shawnti and joins her in keeping watch. "I don't even have words to describe what just occurred," he says.

"So don't try to," replies Shawnti rather sassily.

Malcore takes a hard look at Shawnti. She's just studying Rose with her hand rested on her chin in deep thought. Her blank stare says it all; she is completely enthralled with this girl.

"What is your fascination with her?" asks Malcore.

They watch as Rose nuzzles into her crossed arms on the floor.

"There's something special about this girl," she says.

"Why do you say that?" asks Malcore.

"My heart is telling me so. I know our meeting is far more meaningful than coincidentally being stationed together. I feel more aware around her, more sensitive, like we were destined to share this mission."

"I saw the way you opened up to her,"
"From the first moment I saw her, I knew."

Rose, tossing and turning for a few moments, finally awakes. Blinking the sleep from her eyes, she releases a feline-like stretch. Still half asleep, she smiles at the pair and scoots over to the blackened fireplace. She just sits there quietly and stares into space. Looking over at Malcore and Shawnti once more, inhales deeply, and then exhales. Everyone remains silent for a few moments.

"Have you heard of the alchemy process?" Rose asks, still staring into the distance. Malcore and Shawnti nod yes. Rose turns to them with an inquisitive gaze like she's trying to make sense of all that has occurred. "In the beginning phase of our lives, it's like we're shaped or molded by the world around us. We're helpless to the impact of the hand of fate, right?"

"Yeah, when we're just children," replies Malcore.

"Then I matured to a point where I realized something was definitely wrong. I became aware of all the impurities inside of me. Kind of like the raw material in the first stage of alchemy. Then I was forced to deal with the muck inside: the fear, guilt, shame, all the ugliness that was contained inside this immature vessel. The heat from my trials in life exposed all of these hated impurities."

Malcore and Shawnti nod their heads and just continue to listen.

"Society's view on my situation was like a giant magnifying glass pointing out what was wrong with me – my disorders. Labeling it how they saw it.

I was so hard on myself for not being perfect. Becoming aware of the darkness inside of me was similar to the blackening stage of the process, where the raw material turns into a black liquid. It consumed me in depression for a while, but my desire to grow and heal was more powerful. I've been following my heart in the continuation of the process ever since and going with the flow of the universe. I never would have imagined that what we just witnessed would be necessary to somehow prune us of unneeded qualities, but I feel strangely unattached to it all at the moment, like somehow I can accept it all. I don't even want to question why it had to happen."

Rose finishes speaking and then stares blankly at the wall. Her bottom lip quivers lightly.

Shawnti's heart breaks as she watches this devastated girl fight to keep it together. She can see that Rose is suffering some trauma from the stress of the horrific battle experience. Shawnti walks over and sits with Rose against the fireplace, and places her arm around her. Rubbing Rose's back, Shawnti attempts to comfort her.

The loving embrace of Shawnti provides a nurturing shelter for Rose to breakdown inside of. Tears build in her eyes and stream down her face as Rose cries hysterically. Shawnti wraps both arms around her and holds her tight. Emotions storm inside Rose. They well up and pour out, wave after wave of heartache. An unbearable sadness rips through her. She tries to speak but can barely whimper.

"I... can't... I," cries rose, sobbing into Shawnti's chest.

Malcore's heart wrenches as he sits and witnesses Rose express the great sorrow. Gai, still passed out, sleeps through the ordeal.

Having experienced similar distress before, Shawnti doesn't waste her time telling Rose it's going to be okay. She knows that Rose is going to have to process all of the disturbing encounter before she can move past them. Telling her otherwise would only prolong the state. She just holds Rose and hopes that the love inside of her will be enough to get her through.

Malcore can feel the weight of the stress pressing upon him as well. He gets up and goes outside to get some air. He comes to the backyard of the castle and paces along a speckled cobblestone walk way.

The tension of the situation is dense, he thinks. *We all definitely need to rest and settle down, but this war is not over. Gai is worn out, Rose is managing the best she can right now, and Shawnti is preoccupied with her. What can I do?* Malcore kneels down and prays, "Great spirit, help us. We need you."

Inside, Rose and Shawnti quietly hold each other on the ground. Shawnti combs her fingers through Rose's hair, who has calmed down but is still emotionally drained.

Suddenly, an object falls in the room above them and rolls across the upstairs floor. They both look up to the ceiling.

"Malcore?" yells Shawnti startled by the sound.

No one answers.

A dragging noise can be heard scraping along the floor like the nails of a struggling victim.

"The stairs are destroyed, I don't know who could be up there," says Shawnti as the castle begins to rumble. Crumbling pebbles fall and dust is kicked up all over the gloomy room.

Malcore comes running in.

"Are you okay?" he yells as the castle abruptly stops quaking and everything goes silent again.

"We heard something upstairs," replies Shawnti.

"Come with me and we'll go check it out," says Malcore holding his hand out to Shawnti. "Wait here Rose, we'll be right back."

They rush out of the room and enter the hallway where the demolished stairs used to lead to the second floor. Shawnti listens closely but the noises have seemed to stop. "Grab a hold of me and we'll fly up," suggest Malcore.

"Okay, but we must be prepared for anything."

"I know," he replies nodding his head confidently.

She wraps her arms around Malcore and they zip up to the second story room. Clouds of dust are kicked up as they land. The old wooden floors cry out announcing the presence of investigators.

"Looks like no one has been up here in years," says Shawnti as she wipes her finger across an antique glass table, smearing the thick coating of dirt.

Malcore looks around the room but nothing seems out of place. It's just a bunch of old trunks and furniture.

Downstairs, Rose watches over Gai, who remains passed out on the couch. Out of the corner of her eye she spots someone standing in the far side of the room, facing a portrait of a rising moon. She is a pale, thin woman. A tattered gown is wrapped around her frail figure. The woman turns around slowly revealing the sunken in face of a tormented soul. Her eyes hold the sadness of a thousand years. Limping toward Rose, she drags her decaying legs as she inches closer.

Rose jumps up off the ground and faces the spirit woman.

"Do not be afraid Rose," says the tortured soul. The woman continues to step closer to Rose and slowly lifts her frail hand. "Come with me," utters the woman. She places her hand on Rose's shoulder and they both disappear.

Shawnti and Malcore return from upstairs. "We didn't find anything," yells Malcore as the two of them realize that Rose is nowhere to be seen. They search around the room but find nothing. "Wait here with Gai, I'll look around," yells Malcore and he dashes out of the room.

Rose appears in the center of a large cathedral. Painted glass windows fill the room. There are portraits that line the walls. Some depict the beauty of the universe: stars shooting through galaxies, a creek flowing from a mountain, fire blasting from volcanoes, and one of a new born child.

The child lies in the hands of an angel, sleeping peacefully with a smile of content on its face. The baby is surrounded by everlasting love and care; protected and provided for. The floor of the room consists of white and tan tiles forming a swirl that curls throughout it. Rose looks up, and to her amazement, is a pearl encrusted dome. Along the circular balcony sits the seven archangels. Dressed in elegant armor, they rest with their wings folded and weapons holstered. The circle of archangels observes Rose with emotionless faces - they silently stare.

Rose hears footsteps approaching and quickly looks down. The once tormented old woman has become a vibrant lady full of life and beauty. She wears a wavy white gown and a golden crown that comes to a point in the front.

"Welcome Rose," she says with a giant glowing smile. "I am Eva, Queen of the Inner Realm, and this is the Council of Angels. We have brought you here because we are astounded with your will to survive. You have adapted and rose to all that has been asked of you. When taken to the depths of your soul, you would not be defeated. From a child, until now, you have been dealt a heavy portion. Abused and neglected as a baby, outcast as a child, and tortured by the death and destruction of darkness. But somehow, your spirit remains unbroken. We praise you!" The Archangels raise their weapons and cheer for Rose.

"We have kept a close watch on you my dear. You did an exceptional job on your journey to the Village of Hope, your tests and trials through the mountains and desert, surviving being tortured in Kaylark's dungeon, and now you have witnessed the brutality of war, death, and loss. So much for a young person to handle, but you have found the way. Coping with an emotional burden that could cripple, you have endured."

The Angels stand and cheer once more.

"Follow me Rose" asks Eva.

"Wait," she responds.

Pausing, Eva glances over her shoulder, "Yes Rose?"

"I'm tired of just blindly accepting all of this. I'm tired of feeling powerless in this whole thing. It's my life that is at risk here. I am the one who has to deal with the trauma from this screwed up path you're congratulating me for surviving."

"The whole universe is at stake Rose, if the darkness should overtake the light, humanity will be lost," responds Eva without the slightest bit of sympathy.

"Well maybe humanity should be lost. I have received so much hate from the people of the world. There are so many blind fools out there giving into the darkness. Just let them become slaves and rot. I'm losing friends because of them!"

"I understand you are perturbed Rose, you have been through a lot."

"Don't try to change my mind!" yells Rose.

Eva turns to Rose with a stern look, "All will be lost if you do not keep fighting. You have come all this way. It would not be wise to turn back now."

"My heart is telling me otherwise, I'm tired of being a tool for Great Spirit."

"We are all instruments of Great Spirit. There is the way of grace, which is to follow the lead of Great Spirit. Then there is force, which is to oppose him. To oppose Great Spirit would erase all the hard work you have put into your evolution. Not to mention, you would become tainted by darkness. Is that what you want?"

Rose stays quiet.

"That choice is for you to make, but your destiny, and the destiny of the universe depends on your choice," says Eva as she turns around and walks away. "Follow me," she asks again.

Rose does not refuse this time, but follows Eva into a small side room. She leads her to a pool of water contained in a stone sphere. A golden edge of crystals adorns the peculiar pool. Eva stands over the pool and moves her hand across the water, causing little waves to ripple throughout.

"I have brought you here to show you the state of Octairion." The ripples become still and a picture can be seen in the water. "This is the Southern outpost of Cassiel," says Eva. The pool shows a pile of rubble and death. Rose's heart sinks to her stomach.

"My uncle Layne!" she yells. "Where is he?"

Eva moves her hand across the pool once again and a dungeon appears. Layne is bound in dark energy restraints and is thrashing back and forth.

"He is a prisoner of the Dark Forces inside of Bronwyn; the main city of Drakkar. Kirtaunta, leader of the darkness is holding him. It seems he knows of you Rose," says Eva.

"Me?" replies Rose, surprised.

"Yes, his minions have reported back to him about an Angel who has been wreaking havoc on his army and he has taken quite an interest in you."

Rose stares deeper into the pool.

"He has taken your uncle amongst other Light Warriors in hopes of drawing you to himself," says Eva.

Rose stands back and questions her, "What does he want with me?"

"We don't know for certain Rose, but you are far more special than you know. There are not many who could withstand the trials you have, nor possess the abilities you do."

Rose is not fond of the fact that she must continue on the path of war. She feels forced, but her uncle has to be rescued. He would do the same for her at the drop of a hat.

"So where do we go from here?" she asks.

"Tahein, Corporal Krystah is at the Light Warriors Headquarters with a large army. Her outpost came under heavy attack and she was forced to retreat."

Again, a burden has been placed upon her shoulders, but Rose will also be united with an army to help her rescue Commander Layne. The dangers of war are the least of her worries at this moment. Rose will do whatever it takes to find and rescue her uncle.

Newly motivated and passion filled, she's ready to get back to her squad awaiting her in the castle, "Alright, I accept. But know this, if it weren't for my uncle being taken captive, we might be having a different conversation."

"Oh young Rose, don't let your anger get the best of you."

"It won't, and neither will you," replies Rose. "I'm doing this for myself."

She turns her back to Eva. In turn, Eva has had enough as well. She places her hand on Rose's shoulder and sends her back to the physical world.

19) <u>Heavenly Headquarters</u>

*S*he appears back in the castle's family room. Gai is no longer on the couch, and Shawnti and Malcore are gone too. She can hear faint voices in the distance. She follows the voices until she finds the trio resting on a porch made of branches. The gnarly sticks are woven together and crafted into twisted railings. Hanging vines and knotted wood decorate the obscure creation.

"You're back," notices Gai.

"You too," says Rose with a laugh.

"What happened? We have been looking all over for you," questions Shawnti with heartfelt concern and a look of relief on her face.

Rose comes out onto the porch and takes a seat in a chair made out of a tree stump. "I was taken to the Inner Realm."

"The Inner Realm?" questions Malcore with a confused look on his face.

"Yes," responds Rose. "I can see the spirits of the Inner Realm, and I was taken by one. She informed me that the southern outpost of Cassiel was destroyed and that my uncle Layne and other Light Warriors were taken Captive by the Dark Forces."

Okay, so now what Rose?" says Malcore jumping to his feet.

"There is a large army waiting for us at the Tahein outpost. We are to travel there and lay siege to Bronwyn, where Kirtaunta, Ruler of the Dark Forces, has the Light Warriors captive."

"Sounds like a trap," responds Gai, a bit thrown off by the ordeal.

"Maybe so, I was told that Kirtaunta has an interest in me, and he has my uncle, so I have to go regardless. I will face what awaits me there."

"Okay, let's get to Tahein then. We can strategize with the troops there," suggests Shawnti. The group agrees. Rose grabs Shawnti and extends her wings, Malcore embraces Gai, and they soar off to Tahein.

Flying through Cassiel, they witness the destruction left behind from the Dark Forces: towns in rubble, smoldering villages, and body upon body strewn about. Flying over the southern outpost they observe the outcome of the battle, a warranted distress call.

Slain members of both sides are spread throughout the area. They shout to alert any survivors as they scan the site, but only the crackling of fires can be heard.

"Let's investigate," suggests Rose.

"I think we should just let the dead lie," replies Shawnti.

"I think we should check it out," retorts Malcore.

"Let's head down," decides Gai.

The group soars down into the ruins of the outpost. Rose scans the area and the results are catastrophic. The outer walls have been demolished, and sticking out of the rubble are arms and legs suited in blue and white. Crushed Light Warriors! Where the barracks once stood now lays piles of charred building materials. The crew runs over and examines the wreckage.

"If anyone is under there, they're gone. The smoke would have choked them out by now," says Shawnti as she kicks a heap of charcoaled wood. Rose just stares at the ascending smoke cloud in disbelief.

"I never would have thought that this was going to be the outcome. We left the Village so full of promise. We had no idea what we were in for..."

Gai and Malcore walk further into the outpost. Stepping over the only two dead demons they spot in the whole place, they come to a horrid sight of brutality. The shredded remains of the Light Army!

The demons left the scraps of what little they did not eat. Limbs, random bones with fang indents, and piles of intestines are spread about the surface of a massive pool of blood.

Gai looks to Malcore, feeling sick to his stomach. "I don't think they need to see this," he says.

Malcore looks over at Rose and Shawnti still kicking around the burned pieces of wood, "No, they don't."

The two of them walk back over to the scavenging girls, "You guys find anything?" asks Malcore.

"No, nothing here yet," replies Shawnti as she jumps off a pile of wood. "How about you guys?

Malcore nervously fumbles out, "No, nothing where we searched either. We should get back on course. We don't want to waste too much time."

Shawnti can hear nervousness in Malcore's voice. She gives him a questionable stare and he looks away. She knows something is up, but she leaves it alone. She trusts Malcore's judgment.

"Okay, let's head out," she replies.

"Hold on one second," yells Rose as she uncovers someone in the debris. The face has been damaged beyond recognition, but she notices familiar looking black curly hair. Her stomach drops inside of her, *Could it be Larissa?* she thinks. There is no way for her to know for sure. Rose gets caught in a moment of distress and Shawnti runs to her side.

"Do you think you know her?"

"I don't think so," replies Rose staring at the severely burned body. She turns to Shawnti and shakes the shock off. "Let's get out of here."

"Let's do it," replies Shawnti, and the group sets off into the sky once again.

As they soar over the plush valleys of Tahein, Rose gets lost in a day-dream. She pictures Captain David's smile and the time he jumped up on the dining hall tables during a morning spiritual devotion. He would get so passionate. Then she pictures Kaz. She can't believe he is gone. Any time she needed a shoulder to lean on he was there. What a beautiful heart.

Gai, who is wrapped around Rose's waist, studies her as she processes her deep emotions. Her flowing blonde hair blows in the wind as her crystal blue eyes peer into the distance. He's amazed by her majestic light wings. They move elegantly like a swan as she glides above the clouds. *It looks like blue lightening is rolling through her ghost-like wings,* he thinks as they flutter at high speed.

"Hey Rose, this is quite the remarkable ride," Gai says to Rose, trying to lift her mood.

She looks down at him and notices the love in his blue eyes, so warm and inviting. Life flows freely through them. She stares into the light inside; gentle, caring, and pure, evidence that he had spent time with Great Spirit, so genuine and sincere. Rose gives him an appreciative smile in return and keeps on soaring.

The crew passes over a beautiful creek flowing through a patch of dense forest. "Hey, why don't we head down and recharge for a minute? I'm starting to feel a little low on energy," says Gai.

"Sure, sounds like a good idea," replies Rose. She signals Malcore and they soar down.

The Light Warriors land on the shore of a rocky creek. Gai jumps from stone to stone like a scurrying cat as he makes his way to the water on the rock filled beach. Rose and Shawnti sit on a fallen tree that has landed along the bed of rocks, while Malcore picks up a big sword like stick. He runs over to the nearest tree like a ninja in the night, and strikes the tree repeatedly with perfect samurai form. A look of fierce determination fixed in his eyes.

Malcore was made for battle. He has the spirit of a tiger raging inside of him. Every step he takes is so full of energy. His eyes opened wide to the miracle of every moment. He lets every second pass by with gratitude as he spars with the trees of the beautiful forest. His thick brown hair flows like a raccoon tail as he strikes.

Gai has made his way to the steady flowing stream of life giving liquid. He kneels down and scoops handfuls of water to his mouth, quenching his thirst. He then sits down on a large flat stone and meditates.

"I can't believe how devastating the ambush was," says Rose relaxing up against the fallen tree as she peers into the stream. Shawnti stands beside her tossing pebbles around.

"It looked as if they never stood a chance."

"How are you so comfortable with death?" asks Rose with love, wanting to know more about her friend.

Shawnti can feel the love and joins Rose against the log. She picks up a fallen leaf and plays with it in her hand.

"I have had my Papa and my brother both die of disease. As they lay there sick and dying in their beds, I could do nothing but watch as they faded away together. There was no food, no medicine, and no doctors to make them better. We were poor and lived out in the country side of Edana. My mother and I would scavenge all we could, but we had no one."

Shawnti locks eyes with Rose and allows her into her heart. Intense emotions can be felt by both girls.

"My mother and I could not transport two large men as much as we wanted to. All we could do was pray. Day and night, but they never got well. My father spoke about death as if it was ok. Nothing to be afraid of, 'just the passing from one life to the next,' he would say as he lay dying. Papa tried to share all the wisdom with us that he could before he went." Shawnti looks out into the stream at Gai. She watches him sit so peaceful and serene. "First my Papa went, and then my brother shortly after."

"I'm so sorry Shawnti," replies Rose, who is open to dealing with any sadness that might start to pour out of Shawnti, but her face is weighed down by a cold stare.

"I dealt with all of the difficult emotions then. I didn't hold them in. The loss, grief, regret, and even anger towards them for leaving me were all expressed and then let go. It was a dark time of my life, but I made it through and I guess that is why I am comfortable with death."

Rose is ready to care for Shawnti, but she can see that she doesn't need it. Her soul has become forever changed by her struggle.

"You're lucky to still have your uncle. Even if he is captured, he is still alive and we have a chance to save him."

"We will save him," replies Rose.

Shawnti, a little low on faith, reveals a little half smile. "Let's get going then."

Arriving at the Tahein headquarters, they spot a vast fortress built into the mountain side. The giant stone wall slithers around the city inside like a constricting snake. Towers have been erected along the protective barrier, constructed at supreme vantage points. Stationed Rangers occupy the large turrets that fly the flag of the Light Warriors Army; a blue and white star tetrahedron on a gray backdrop. The city inside looks quadruple the size of the Village of Hope, maybe even quintuple.

Thousands of deceased Dark Forces line the perimeter outside the massive walls. They don't spot any Light Warriors amongst the dead.

"Looks like they were prepared for an invasion," says Rose as they approach the front gates.

A path has been made through the wall of lifeless bodies that crowds the entrance. A small hidden door opens up on the monumental iron gates as the warriors approach the entryway.

"Oh yes, more survivors," belts out an oddly shaped man with a long beard. He jumps up and down in excitement and the four sapphire gems that are braided into his beard bounce as well. "I am Tolstice, keeper of the watch, pleasure to have you with us."

The group enters in and their eyes fall upon a sight of wonder. Highly skilled Warriors engage in combat with one another in the obstacle filled combat yard. Explosions of light beams are bursting in the air like detonating stars. Collisions of swords and shields spray sparkling crystal shards as the warriors spar. Kinetics hover in the air, dodging beams from attacking Rangers. Flashes engage in sporadically shifting battles as they collide and disperse. Looks like easily three hundred warriors populate the training ground.

Behind the drilling warriors lies an extravagant city, filled with buildings of all sorts. Rows of barracks, lavish dining halls, and salient sanctuaries amongst other unidentified places. Rose spots a building with a hanging wooden sign that reads "library."

A building! Not just a room for a library like at the Village, but a building, she thinks.

The aesthetically pleasing architecture of the city is crafted from what looks like shimmering platinum. The white gold buildings are embedded with numerous assorted blue crystals; azurite, celestite, and kyanite to name a few. Beautiful gardens filled with many different types of blue flowers decorate the walkways; thistles, anemones, and tons of forget-me-nots catch Shawnti's interest.

"Welcome to Light Warrior Headquarters," says Tolstice with a twinkle in his eye, "Come with me, and we'll check in with Elder Saden, head of the Light Army." Tolstice wobbles back and forth as he leads them through the illustrious city, decorated with emblems and statues galore. Monuments dedicated to the brave souls who have kept the light alive throughout history. One statue in particular looks to be shinier than the rest; a large marble sculpture of a sophisticated looking man, middle aged, wearing aristocratic robes.

"Jonathan Saden," reads the display name, must be one of Elder Saden's relatives.

"Forever loyal to a brighter future" reads the quote below. The crew gazes around the wondrous courtyard in awe.

"I've never seen anything like this," says Rose.

"Yeah, I was grateful for the shack we shared at the Village of Faith. Check us out now," blurts Malcore.

Shawnti and Gai shake their heads up and down in agreement with him.

"The Elder's chambers," announces Tolstice, who opens the white diamond studded door for the group, and waits outside.

Commotion comes to a halt, as the round table full of Elders sets their eyes upon Rose and her comrades. Fancy dressed men and women who have never seen the battlefield surround an extravagant round table. They are all adorned with silky robes and glistening jewels while they converse day and night about matters of the universe.

"Hello Rose, please have a seat," asks Elder Saden. Rose takes a seat at the table of Elders. Shawnti, Malcore, and Gai sit on a bench near the back of the room.

"Great Spirit be praised. You made it here safely." Elder Saden wears blue and white robes, and a tall self-important hat. He was born into the line of high status Saden's, so needless to say all the authority he has been given was inherited. This man leads with his ego in the name of Great Spirit, and the rest of the elders follow suit.

"Corporal Krystah speaks highly of you Rose. She says you are a natural born leader. She also tells me you're an Angel," says Elder Saden. Rose stays silent and just nods her head in acknowledgment.

Elder Saden speaks with a slur and his face is blotchy and greasy. He looks like an old scrooge, but besides his appearance, Rose's heart feels as if this man is untrustworthy.

Saden glances around the room at all of the inhabitants.

"We have lost a great amount of troops recently. We were caught off guard by the ambushes that struck the Cassiel and Tahein outposts. We severely underestimated the amount of troops the darkness possessed."

Rose just stares at the man angrily. His fat lips slopping as he speaks. *Severely underestimated is not the word,* she thinks. *More like carelessly!*

"We sent out about two hundred troops from here to assist the outposts, sadly all were lost. Losing communication with the outposts left us unaware of the carnage that was spreading through the land. The darkness hit hard and fast."

Shawnti, Malcore, and Gai listen from the back of the room. They know all too well what he means.

"Now, we understand that Commander Layne and a group of soldiers were taken captive in Bronwyn. We have sent a squad of seven to scope out the land. We can assume the darkness will be waiting for us to rescue the captives so it's best we have an idea of what we are walking into."

"We?" interrupts Rose. "Where were you when my whole squad was murdered, and my uncle captured?"

The table of Elders gasps at Rose's disregard for authority.

"Great Spirit expects obedience young lady," snaps Elder Saden fervently.

"Does he? How do you know I am not listening to him right now? I think *YOU* demand obedience Elder. Why do you think he favors you over me?"

Outraged, Elder Saden yells for Tolstice, who pops his head in through the door.

"Get Corporal Krystah for me please," asks Elder Saden, and then he focuses back on Rose. "Indeed I have not been a part of this war physically, but I am very much a part of it. Every one of us is," he says as he points to the members of his council. "You see, we all play a different role. Your generation, and all beings born today, are far more advanced. You are evolving past where our older bodies are capable. So that is why your path consists of the battlefield dear. You see, we did not choose this for you, Great Spirit did."

Rose is not enjoying the speech from Saden. She can sense the manipulation in his tone and feel the ugliness inside of him.

"After all, look at you, you are an Angel," says Saden.

Just then the handle turns and the door pops open. Corporal Krystah limps her way in with help from Tolstice. A laceration extends from her abdomen to her thigh along the right side of her body - it's been covered in bandages. She is helped into her chair, and groans as she settles. Krystah struggles to release a smile for Rose, she is happy to see her. Rose smiles back and begins to speak.

"I am sorry Corporal Krystah. It is hard for me to accept the fact that fighting this war is my destiny. The violent battles, friends falling on all sides, and having to fight for a cause that I did not choose has taken its toll."

Corporal Krystah leans forward and winces in pain, "I regrettably know exactly what you speak of Rose. I spoke to you of the un-welcomed changes that come along with war and death. Your response to me was that we must fight for those who have not been consumed by the darkness, but I think now you have a better idea of what I meant, don't you?"

Having seen the hellish reality of war Rose responds, "I do."

"This war is going to continue with, or without you Rose. Please do not think that this is all meaningless. I stand here wounded for this cause, but I know that imminent death waits if I choose to cringe in the sight of this harsh certainty." As Krystah leans in closer to her, the light from the candles on the table flicker on her face. "We have survived a demoralizing beginning to this war, beloved. Who knows what is for good or for bad? We must keep our eyes upon the vision of light and pray that we can accomplish our purpose before the monstrosities of war harden our hearts. We have come too far to turn back now."

Corporal Krystah's words strike a chord with Rose and she sits for a moment and lets them simmer. She looks to her friends, and then over to the Elders as she contemplates all she has been told.

"I understand the weight of my choice," she responds. She looks Elder Saden in the eyes, "And I mustn't compare my life to another's."

Saden raises his chin high and smiles back at Rose with forgiveness.

"I have seen your potential and believe you will thrive as a leader here," says Corporal Krystah.

Elder Saden chimes in as well, "We also see your potential Rose, and your obvious passion for what you believe in. We nominate you to be a leader in the Army of Light, granted you accept."

Rose doesn't even have to think about the responsibility that has just been presented. She welcomes the task of being a leader and looks forward to the challenge, "I accept. Let's prepare," she responds.

Elder Saden rises with enthusiasm, excited about her acceptance, "We await the return of the squad of seven and the news they bring. We shall give word for all leaders to prepare their squads. Rose, you and your friends are assigned to Barracks J where your new squad awaits."

20) <u>Blinding Light</u>

*R*ose, Shawnti, Malcore, and Gai leave the office and head out into the headquarters. Walking through the military style town, they come across a refreshments tent, grab some food, and sit down to eat. A band of Light Warriors populates the tables around them - enjoying a hot meal.

"That was quite the spectacle Rose," says Gai.

"I'm sorry, but everything just built up inside of me. I felt powerless, like I didn't have a choice in the matter."

"Believe me, we understand," says Shawnti talking about her and the guys. "When we were training at the Village of Faith in Ahbaram, we had the strictest leaders you could find."

"Yeah we did," replies Malcore. "They taught us a lot though. I give them that."

"We had table scraps compared to what this place has," says Gai.

"Not to mention the chapel/library/dining hall we all shared, and how about the ruff nights bunking together with all the other men in one small room. These guys here at the Light Headquarters have it pretty good."

Rose recalls her time at the Village and how special it was for her. Although it was not as luxurious as this place, it abounded with love. From the sound of Shawnti and the others, it sounds like things could have been much worse for her.

As Rose overhears Gai speak about their teachers at the Village of Faith and how they crammed Great Spirit down their throats, her mind drifts back to when her uncle first told her about Him. Great Spirit was not something that she had discovered on her own.

"Ever since I can remember," says Rose interrupting Gai, "I have been told what to do and how to live. It's like life has just been happening to me, as if I am just a victim to Great Spirit. We're told it's for a purpose," Rose raises her finger to the sky, "*He*, has a plan. Part of me thinks it is true, but another part of me believes that there is far more to it. Like it's far more personal than anyone of these people can know. They all want to tell us how our relationship to Great Spirit needs to be, and what he wants for us, but my heart has been telling me different."

Gai stops eating and places his fork and knife down, "I agree Rose. Human nature is far more complex than most of us give it credit. We want to label things good or evil, but sometimes we're just confused. We live the way we were raised to be, and do what comes naturally to us. Others want to live for the light, but have dark roots buried under their cloaks."

"Exactly!" yells Rose. "Some of these light beings make me feel as if they are just trying to control me. Like their intentions are rooted in darkness. As much as they shimmer and shine like a lustrous piece of holy gold, they are rotten inside."

Malcore looks around the table. It seems a light bulb has lit up in his head. "Do you think that the darkness has infiltrated the Light Warrior ranks?"

"My heart tells me there is something amiss, I can't tell you why, but I just know," says Rose.

"The original distress call from the southern Cassiel outpost, none of us were there, right?" asks Shawnti.

"No," replies the group in unison.

"All the survivors were taken captive," says Malcore.

"Then how did they know?" replies Rose.

Gai is beginning to get a little shook up.

"Okay, before we get too deep into this, its only speculation," he says trying to calm down the witch-hunt.

"Yes, you're right. I do think we should pay extra close attention to our intuitions. Let's not try to figure this out with our minds, but let's feel our way through this with our hearts," says Shawnti.

The tension is rising.

"I need to take a minute and clear my head," says Rose as she gets up from the table and walks away from the group.

Breathing deeply as she strolls through the Headquarters. She comes to a waterfall pouring from the top of the mountain into a canyon. Sitting at the edge of the canyon, she relaxes herself. Taking in the beautiful landscape, peace falls over her.

"Great Spirit, I pray to you for clarity. You have been with me my whole life, guiding me, supporting me, and protecting me. Please help me to discern the truth inside of those claiming to be your people. Help me to not misjudge my instincts. If there is darkness masquerading as the light, may you reveal it to us? Speak to our hearts Great Spirit. I want to do your will. Not the agenda of the darkened. Help me not to doubt myself, or misstep. Lead me in your way." Rose finishes her prayer, gets up, and stares into the sky. "Uncle Layne. I am coming for you." She releases her worries and heads to Barracks J.

Entering into the barracks, her eyes fall upon her squad sitting in the common room. Young men and women just like her, all with their own unique stories, personalities, and abilities. She hesitates for a moment as she thinks of how many will be lost. Shaking her head, she refocuses. *No, that is not the way to approach this. I must have no fear. As a leader I need to guard my mind more aggressively from dark thoughts. I must keep my wits. They depend on it*, she thinks to herself.

The members of the squad rise from their mats and stand in respect of their new leader. Shawnti, Malcore, and Gai are already amongst the troops.

"Hello everyone, I have been elected your new squad leader by the Elders. Would you all please join me?" Rose takes a seat on the ground. The squad joins her in a circle. They sit staring at one another.

"This is our unit. Let us quiet ourselves and blend our souls in silence." The warriors relax in a moment of solitude. "Let's share a little bit about ourselves. My name is Rose. I am from Conway originally, but was raised in Holyoke. I was trained at the Village of Hope. Commander Layne, my uncle, is being held captive in Bronwyn and there is nothing I desire more than to rescue him."

She glances to her left; a dark haired boy with blue eyes sits. He looks confident and sophisticated.

"Hello, my name is Noah. I came from the coast of Kane. I am one of the Flashes. I have been training here for one year now and look forward to serving you on the battlefield Rose."

"Thank you," she replies. "So you have not seen battle yet?"

"No," he replies.

"Have any of you?" asks Rose as she looks around the group. No one in the squad raises their hands. Rose sits amongst a squad of soldiers who have not been exposed to carnage outside of these walls.

"Well, um, hello. My name is Zia. I'm sure you saw all of the Dark Forces piled outside of the headquarters," says the long-haired girl. She is tall and strong looking. "Our rangers and best marksmen took them all out. Most of us watched from the ground as they manned the walls and annihilated the enemy."

"Thank you Zia," says Rose. She looks to a boy in the back of the room. "You in the shadows come closer please and share."

The boy creeps from the dimly lit corner, his face scarred from his mouth up to his forehead.

"My name is Shane. I came here from Cassiel." He looks away uncomfortably and he steps back into the dark corner.

"Are you ashamed of who you are, Shane?" asks Rose.

"Not really. It's just hard to have your past written upon your face. Others can try and hide their wounds, but mine is the first thing you see. You know, it's kind of ironic, I am a Healer. I can help countless others, but I'll never be able to take this scar away," replies Shane pointing to his face. He drops his shoulders and slumps to the side.

Rose cannot relate or comfort the boy. Not knowing what he has been through, she leaves him be. "Thank you Shane," she says and he makes his way back to the corner. A vibrant young man jumps up next.

"Hi! I am Ethan. I am also from Holyoke, Rose." The blonde haired boy has a smile the size of the moon upon his face.

"Awesome," she replies, "where about Ethan?"

"I am from Westerville, Holyoke, and you?"

"I lived in Easterlin," replies Rose.

"So we were on different ends. I lived with my family in the poor town. My past is not as dark as most peoples I think. We went long periods of time without food, and we didn't have proper clothing. Sickness and disease ran rampant through our town, but we all loved each other dearly. Our community was always by each other's side doing what we could for one another. So we suffered the pain of poverty, but love was abundant.

Then one day I was out in the barn and I could hear my father screaming wildly. He was working on the stone wall and a giant boulder slipped out of place and fell on top of him. I ran out and tried lifting the giant rock off my father, but there was nothing I could do. The tension built inside me. All the crazy emotions I was feeling enraged me! I felt my whole body surging with power. I was staring at that rock crushing my dad's arm, and next thing you know I felt like I could lift it with my mind. Sure enough, I did. I focused real hard and picked it up off him and placed it on the ground next to him. Thank Great Spirit he was okay. Two cracked bones was all.

I didn't really know what happened, neither did my father, but since then I would hide out in the barn and practice lifting stuff all the time. One day, Mira comes along and tells me that there is an Oracle looking for me and she wants me to come with her. It was my invitation to come and be trained at the Tahein Light Warriors Headquarters. I knew I had to say goodbye to my family and go. My heart told me so. So I traveled up over the Mountain of Strength with Mira, and we made our way here."

"Wow! Thank you for sharing your story Ethan," replies Rose.

A beautiful young girl raises her hand and frantically shakes it.

"Hello, I am Mira from Ethan's story!" she says and waves hello to Rose in a comical manner.

"Nice to meet you, Mira, why don't you tell us about yourself," asks Rose.

"Okay so, let's see, I am one of the PsyComs. You already know that. I really find it to be quite an exciting gift. The fun that can be had is endless you know?"

Rose just stares and wonders about this girl, about her squad. How naïve are they really? How well have they been trained, and how well will they adapt?

A muscular dark haired boy stands up with a serious look on his face. He paces around the room a bit authoritarian like.

"I am Jacob, nice to meet you Rose. I have not seen war yet, but, I don't underestimate it either. Not only is it my life in my hands when I'm out there, but the universe is also at stake. I hope we can all help you rescue Commander Layne and bring home the victory for the Light Warriors."

"Jacob, tell me about the training here at the Headquarters?" asks Rose.

"We were trained in combat by Corporal Aidon. Unfortunately he was lost at the southern Cassiel outpost."

The squad J members are hit hard by the comment. A lot of them still mourn the loss of their Corporal.

"The Elders of the HQ shared wisdom with all of us daily. We would also break off into our special abilities classes. Captain Leal trained Kinetics and Flashes, while Commander Reece trained the PsyComs. Captain Leal is the head trainer of our army, and Commander Reece is second in charge. Rose, I assure you that we are trained well, although we do not have firsthand battlefield experience, we have trained hard. I believe I speak for the squad when I say we are well prepared for war."

The squad stands up together and cheers, "Light Power! Light Power! Light Power!" They raise their fists into the air and the camaraderie encourages Rose.

"Very well, I am excited to meet all of you and see your enthusiasm. Shawnti, Malcore, Gai and I have seen the battlefield and I would just like to say that it is nothing to be taken lightly. The enemy is ravenous but can be defeated. We have to be smart and work together out there. I will give my all to you on the battlefield, and I ask that you do the same for the person next to you. United we will conquer the darkness and free this world!"

Rose spreads her wings exposing her angelic nature. Blue light fills the barracks, shining from the energy in her bioluminescent wings.

"We will march on Drakkar and repay the darkness for all that it has taken from the world!" The squad looks to their leader in awe and with pride. Rose's aggressive spirit can be felt and is fusing with the enthusiasm of her squad.

Later on that evening Rose and her new squad are enjoying the beauty of the Headquarters. Noah and Mira have offered to give their new squad leader a tour around the city. They walk down the cobblestone pathways that line the common areas of the charming community.

Traveling through the "high traffic" section, as Noah called it; Rose observes a street of buildings.

Mira, who is super excited to be Rose's tour guide jumps out ahead of the group and jumps into action. "Okay Rose, over here we have our big beautiful library. Not one of my favorite places, but if there's anything that you have an interest in learning about, it's in one of the books there," says Mira pointing to the large building. Four Columns stand strong at the top of the staircase leading to the entrance of the stone building. Rose takes notice of all the different types of crystals that are implanted into the structure of the library.

"Next we have the medical facilities. If you aren't feeling well or if you are having some kind of issue, we have Healers and Sages inside that would be glad to assist you in any manner they can." Mira waves her hand towards the building like a game show host revealing a fancy new gift. The young girl has a knack for entertainment. "After that is the meditation rooms, inside you will find a quiet place to enjoy some peace. The rooms are filled with altars dedicated to Great Spirit. They are stocked with all kinds of ceremonial tools and trinkets like candles, crystals, and incense. Lots of stuff like that. Oh, and singing bowls too! Those are my favorite!"

Rose looks around the community and notices that more and more crystals have been embedded into the infrastructure. Amber calcites are in the streetlights, green amazonite and fluorite crystals are inside the flower pots and scattered in the gardens. All kinds of quarts, amethyst, and opalite crystals have been thrown in the center fountain. In the middle of the large fountain stands a bronze woman pouring water into a circular stone pool embedded with gems of all kinds. She dawns a wreath of flowers around her head, and spills the water from a jade encrusted bowl clenched in her hands.

"What is with all the crystals inside of everything?" asks Rose. Noah steps in and answers the question.

"Every crystal holds its own special essence. So when you add crystals to something or carry them on you, they add their essence to your overall vibration."

Rose remembers the stone that her uncle Layne had given her. She reaches into her pocket and there still remains the smooth emerald calcite. She pulls it out and Mira and Noah take notice.

"Oh that's beautiful Rose. Where did you get that one?" asks Mira.

"From my uncle, he told me that as long as I hold onto it nothing will ever keep us apart."

"Exactly!" yells an excited Noah. "That is the energy that your uncle charged into the crystal."

"Charged into the crystal?" asks Rose.

"Yeah, if you hold it tight in your hands and focus your love and energy into the crystal, it will absorb the vibrations and become a part of the crystals energy. Then wherever that crystal goes, it will carry the special essence that has been absorbed and affect the world around you."

Mira who is not enjoying sitting in the background clears her throat and begins a history lesson.

"During the construction of the Light Headquarters, they held a mass charging ceremony in which everyone around at the time came and prayed over a ton of different stones and crystals. They spent time with all of the crystals and made sure that a special bond was created before they were imbedded into the different parts of the city. Protection was prayed into the gems that were placed into the crystals of the walls. Wisdom and growth were harnessed into the sanctuary crystals, and health and wellness have been prayed into the crystals that lay in the fountains.

On their own every crystal already has its own essence and qualities they represent, but when you charge them or pray over them it becomes much more sacred. You are united with the energy of the crystal," responds Noah. He reaches into his pocket and pulls out a red jasper stone.

"This is what I carry," he says brandishing the solid red stone with black streaks through it, "It is said to protect you from the evil of the darkness. But to me it represents the passion I will need to fight on the battlefield."

"Wow, that is awesome. Thank you for informing me on the power of the crystals," responds Rose as she clenches tightly onto the small calcite in her hand. *Nothing will keep us apart uncle. I will rescue you,* she thinks and then puts it back in her pocket.

"Hey! Why don't we go meet up with the rest of the squad," suggests Mira who notices Rose's disheartened expression.

"Good idea. Let's go," replies Rose and the group heads back to their barracks.

21) <u>Cavern Crawl</u>

*R*ose, Mira, and Noah enter into the barracks and an uproar of conversation is filling the common room. A debate is occurring as Shawnti and Ethan trade opinions in a rather loud yelling match.

"I'm not going to feel bad about what I have been blessed with!" yells Ethan.

"That's not what I am saying," replies Shawnti. "Look, what it seems like to me is that you all lived a pampered life with the luxury provided for you here in the Headquarters. What we have experienced," Shawnti points to Gai and Malcore, "was much harsher conditions at the Village of Faith in Ahbaram."

"So what are you trying to say that because you have had less, that you are better than us?" shouts out an angered Zia. She sits hunched over

261

with her hands on her knees, looking quite aggressive.

"Not exactly, but when you have gone without, you know how much less you really need to survive. It awakens something in you that can't be understood if you don't go through it, and a lot of stuff in life becomes meaningless."

Shawnti looks to Gai and Malcore, but they didn't start this squabble and they are not getting into it.

Rose has entered in and sat amongst the squad.

"Rose, what do you say?" asks Ethan.

"We each have our own individual path to walk. As much as I would want to think that suffering more than some high and mighty aristocrat makes me more important to Great Spirit, I'm not," replies Rose.

Shawnti is becoming emotional over the argument. She stands to her feet and addresses the squad, "All I'm trying to say is I'm concerned with the attitude that you guys have towards the Dark Forces. You have a fantastical view of what the reality of the battlefield is. This is not a fairytale!"

"Look Shawnti, I don't think you have any idea who we all are and what we have been through," replies Shane. "You can judge us from our appearances or what you say you feel from us, but in my book actions speak louder than words. If you think you're so much tougher than us, then why don't you challenge Zia to a Cavern Crawl?"

The squad's faces fill with excitement and they begin to rumble about and yell, "Cavern Crawl, Cavern Crawl!"

"Yeah, what do you say Shawnti, are you up for it?" asks Zia who is not backing away from the offer.

Shawnti shakes her head angrily, *why did I have to open my big mouth?* she thinks.

Gai nudges her from the side, "C'mon Shawnti, show them how tough you are," he says holding back his laughter. She scowls at Gai and curses him with her threatening stare.

"I don't even know what a Cavern Crawl is,"

"Only one way to find out rookie," says Ethan with a sarcastic tone. "Got to travel the path, what do you say?"

Shawnti has just been fed a heaping portion of karma and now she has to put up or shut up.

"Oh alright, I'm in. Let's go."

"Yes!" yells Zia who is pumped to put this girl to shame. She slams her fists together and the squad exits the barracks.

They make their way to the base of the huge mountain located in the backend of the Light Headquarters. A large cave opening has been dug out on the east and another on the west.

"The Cavern Crawl," announces Ethan standing before the squad. "For those of you who don't know," the group of Headquarter originals laugh, "this mountain is where all the crystals used in the construction of the HQ were excavated. Inside the big tunnel there are inclines, declines, straight shots and curvy canals. The rules of the challenge are simple: one person at the east entrance, another at the west. When I say go, you enter in and maneuver the intersecting course. First one to reach the opposite exit wins. That is... if you can make it out in one piece!"

"Easy enough to understand, Shawnti?" asks Zia as she steps up to Ethan.

"Yup, I get the gist," replies Shawnti.

"Good. Shawnti since you are our guest here at the HQ, and we are generous and moral people, we would like to offer you the choice of east or west."

"What's the difference?" she asks.

"No difference in particular, both of you will have to make your way through all of the same obstacles in the end."

"Okay, I'll take the east."

"Alright, Zia you got the west. Ladies, why don't we head over to the entrances and prepare to settle this."

The squad applauds as Shawnti and Zia hustle over to the cavern openings.

Alright, I got myself into this. I'll do my best, thinks Shawnti as she reaches the dirt path leading into the cave.

"Oh and ladies, the use of special abilities is prohibited inside the tunnel, and when you cross paths, contact is allowed. Best of luck to you both, LETS GET READY!" yells Ethan.

Zia stares into the dark tunnel and drags her feet through the dirt like a bull getting ready to charge. Shawnti stretches her legs a little bit and then squats down and prepares to sprint.

"Alright ladies, here is the countdown!" yells Ethan with his hand in the air holding up 3 fingers, "3, 2, 1, GO!"

The excited girls blast off into the tunnels. Shawnti stomps her way into the giant wide open cavern and sprints through an entryway towards a narrowing shaft. The walls continue to close in as she becomes more and more cramped. Her head almost scrapes on the ceiling of the tunnel now and she has to drop down onto her knees and crawl in the dirt. Tiny shards of red crystals can be seen sparkling in the dirt as the light from the entrance is being cut off.

Shimmying through the tight passage on her belly, she eventually comes to a pitch black room. Shawnti becomes a bit claustrophobic and slightly freaks out as she attempts to examine the rocky cavern. *Keep it together. Stay focused. Nothing will ever break you again,* she says to herself trying to keep her cool.

Walking slowly in the dark she uses her hands to feel her way through. There is an eerie silence and damp moisture filling the air as she rounds a corner and spots a light coming from the whole in the ceiling. She nervously staggers closer and spots a giant pile of boulders that she has to climb in order to make it to the light filled passage.

With no time to waste, she immediately jumps up onto the boulders. Using both arms she pulls herself higher and uses her legs to support the lifting. She begins to sweat a little bit. The rigorous climbing is warming her up and her adrenalin is pumping as she hurdles the stones. Slipping rocks fall from under her as she scales the rock bridge and makes her way into the lighted entryway.

She peers down into the dug-out tunnel and sees that it is lit up by a string of dim lights. She can also hear the faint echoes of footsteps from someone running her way. *Got to get moving, can't keep wasting time. I can't let this novice beat me.*

Shawnti runs down the slick slope that is slippery from limestone residue that has mixed with the precipitation. She falls to the ground and slides her way into a room full of giant stalagmites, stalactites, flows stones, and columns. Shawnti also notices Zia entering in on the opposite end.

"You're never going to beat me if this is as far as you've gotten Shawnti. Looks like you don't know how to navigate the darkness as well as you think do you?" yells Zia as she barrels towards Shawnti. Her burly frame sways side to side like an enraged elephant as she strides through the maze of stalagmites.

Shawnti pays her no mind and continues to sprint through the cavern. The floor is really wet from small streams of water that are leaking off of the stalactites. Shawnti splashes through them as she runs with her eyes locked onto the exit, but Zia has another plan in mind. Right as she crosses paths with Shawnti, Zia shoulder slams her and knocks her onto the ground. Shawnti smashes face first into a puddle and is drenched in water. Zia crouches down and grabs Shawnti by the collar of her Light Warriors uniform.

"I've had girls like you thinking that they were better than me my whole life! I thought I escaped all of that when I ran away from home and came here," screams Zia. Her chubby cheeks are beat red and tears are welling up in her angry eyes.

Shawnti is now realizing that her ignorant comments hit a lot harder than she noticed. "I'm sorry, that was not my intention. I was just trying to give you guys some advice but I see now that I went about it all wrong."

"You're damn right you did. You have no idea what any of us here have encountered. You have this damn holier than thou attitude because you think you have witnessed true darkness. Try living my life Shawnti. Try walking in these shoes!" yells Zia as she starts to cry. Shawnti picks herself up off the ground and witnesses the hurt and pain that is pouring from this girl.

"Honestly, I apologize from the bottom of my heart. It really was a stupid comment and I don't want to be that way." Shawnti places her hand on Zia's shoulder and attempts to care for her. Zia wipes the tears from her eyes and turns to Shawnti.

"I know you don't want to be that way, and I'm glad that you see now what your rude comments caused. Even if we are rookies Shawnti, why would you want to fill our minds with doubt?"

Shawnti gasps at the illuminating question.

"I didn't realize that is what I was doing. You're right." Shawnti drops her head in shame. *How foolish of me,* she thinks.

Zia grabs Shawnti's chin and pulls it up towards her face. "I forgive you, but I'm still going to smoke you in this Cavern Crawl!" she yells as she pushes Shawnti and runs towards the slippery slope leading out.

Shawnti filled with disgust for her high-minded attitude just turns and walks her way towards the western exit.

She slowly trots down the smooth stone tunnels and thinks about her life and the way she has conducted herself.

I think I have been bitter for all these years. I feel like I have been dealt such a heavy hand and I hold myself above others because of it. That's so wrong of me. She shakes her head, *foolish pride.*

Shawnti comes to a fork in the path, she listens quietly to the left side and she can hear droplets of liquid plopping onto the ground. Then she moves her ear to the right and can hear the cheering of the Light Warriors, *"Zia! Zia! Zia!"*

Shawnti eventually makes her way out of the western opening of the cavern. Zia stands confidently amongst their proud squad.

"C'mon Shawnti, don't look so down!" yells Ethan.

"Yeah it was only your first attempt. Don't be so glum," yells Mira

Shawnti drags herself up to the squad. It seems her crawl through the cavern really humbled her.

"I'm sorry you guys. I shouldn't have acted that way towards you. I don't know who I thought I was."

Ethan looks over the squad with a sympathetic face. He connects eyes with Shane who agrees. "We forgive you Shawnti, and believe me we know that you were just trying to help," says Ethan, "Now come over here and give us a hug. You're still one of us you know."

A smile cracks on the gloomy face of Shawnti and she joins the squad in a giant group hug. The warm embrace of Squad J calms her down.

"Okay Squad, why don't we run through some drills since we're out here," suggests Rose.

"Yes ma'am," replies the squad in unison.

"Pair up!" yells Rose and the squad breaks up.

Inside the Elders chamber, Tolstice mans the doorway as the Squad of Seven stands before the board of Elders. The Seven wear customized white suits that are layered with blue studded armor around their collars and torsos. The mysterious men are covered in dirt like they have been sleeping in a bush all week.

Elder Saden rises, "What news do you have for us?" he asks.

An older man with a weathered face steps forward. "Elder, we traveled the path between the two mountains that leads to Drakkar. We did not see any enemies along the way. It took us about one day to reach the mountains and another day to reach the fortified city of Bronwyn. From the top of a hill about a mile away, we watched the city for hours. Stationed outside the city walls are countless hordes of demons waiting on guard. Inside there seemed to be tremendous amounts of activity. They live like animals Sir. Like crazed beasts locked inside a cage, waiting to get out and kill. There are many prisoner camps inside Bronwyn. We witnessed a returning horde with captured humans transport them inside. The humans were beaten half to death and possessed by Shadows.

In the center of the town stands a giant dark tower, possibly made from obsidian. I have never seen anything so black. From time to time we would

269

hear Kirtaunta roar from his throne. Dark energy would flow down the tower and into the city, inciting a frenzy amongst the inhabitants. Screams of the humans would send dark energy into the tower fueling whatever is going on inside, we assume.

We did not witness anyone leave Sir. It seems the Dark Forces are holding tight. They are certainly waiting for us to come and rescue Commander Layne."

Elder Saden acknowledges the men, but he doesn't seem too concerned. "Good work, good work. Thank you gentlemen," he replies. He waves his hand to the door. "Leave us to discuss our plan of action. Go spread the news around the Headquarters, tell everyone we will move out in the morning." Elder Saden dismisses the squad of seven and they exit out of the chambers.

The Elders converse in the candle lit room, shadows dance upon the walls as the flames rise in their eyes.

"He's discovered more than I expected," says Elder Saden.

"Enough to keep the Light Warriors hopeful," says an eerie voice hidden in the dimness. A woman dressed in dark robes reveals herself. She slightly lifts off her hood, revealing her beautiful lips and sensuous jawline. She waits a moment for the door to be locked by Tolstice, and then she removes her hood completely. It is Eva, Queen of the Inner Realm! She has somehow infiltrated the Light Warrior Headquarters and seems to be conspiring with the Elders. She peers into the face of Elder Saden with her sparkling blue eyes. "Make sure they head out in the morning Elder. King Theron is growing impatient."

"King Theron! No I wouldn't want to upset the King. I swear everything will be in place. Rose has arrived and we will make sure she is sent into the trap. They will be deployed in the morning most definitely," replies Elder Saden.

"Good, I will go tell Kirtaunta that everything is set. He will send the Dark Forces to await the Light Warriors between the two mountains and put an end to this battle. Make sure they travel that way Elder. And make sure Rose is with them." Eva leans into Elder Saden and kisses him on the cheek. He shudders, entranced by her alluring presence.

"Yes Eva," he utters as she slowly paces into the dark corner and disappears.

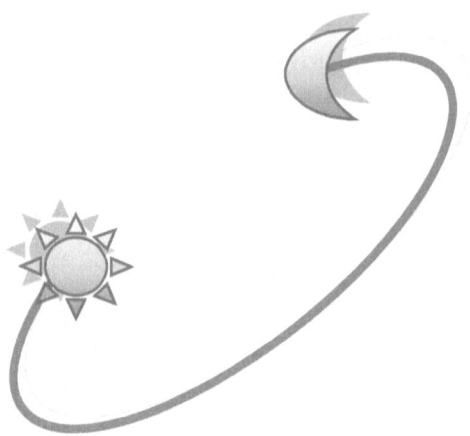

22) <u>Devious Disorder</u>

$\mathcal{N}$ight has fallen in the headquarters and the squad has settled into bed. Yelling can be heard from outside the barracks. The Squad of seven is running through the city awakening the sleeping warriors.

"The land has been scouted. Warriors! We move out in the morning," they shout as they storm past Barracks J.

Rose jumps up out of bed and runs outside. The Squad of seven has gathered in the courtyard on top of a large wooden platform. A crowd of concerned Light Warriors have gathered around them.

"Listen up! We have come from the city of Bronwyn, the stronghold of darkness. A clear path has been mapped out and we deploy in the morning," yells the leader of the Seven.

"So soon," yells a voice in the crowd.

"Yes, Elder Saden commands it. Your leaders will be briefed and then we will head out."

"What did you see?" yells another.

"Clear paths into the city. They are sitting ducks inside. We will catch them with their eyes closed. We will defeat them and take Drakkar, conquering the darkness once and for all!" yells out the man with confidence.

The crowd of Light Warriors seems to be divided by the urgent news. Some cheer at the announcement and head back to their tents, while others look around confused over the unexpected message. Rose heads to Corporal Krystah's tent and finds her standing out front.

"Corporal Krystah, it seems we are leaving for Drakkar first thing in the morning."

"Yes beloved, the Light Army will march on Drakkar. We will have the upper hand and stomp the Dark Forces into the ground, defeating Kirtaunta and freeing Octairion from the oppression of darkness."

"Can we be certain they are not expecting us to attack? They are holding Commander Layne. They know we will want to rescue him."

"Certainly they do. I believe that is why Elder Saden is having us move so quickly, to catch them off guard. I don't think they would expect us so soon. Especially after the multiple defeats we have suffered as of recent. Little do they know our massive army will be knocking on their door in no time." Corporal Krystah looks over Rose with her pale blue eyes, "Are you ready Rose?"

"I am ready for anything Corporal," she responds.

"Good. Then go get some rest and I will see you in the morning. Goodnight Rose."

"Goodnight."

Rose heads back to her barracks. Shawnti is lying up in her bed. Rose comes over and lies down next to her and they share their thoughts.

"Are they saying tomorrow is the day we head out?" asks Shawnti.

"Yes it is. Although I feel that something is amiss," says Rose.

"Why?"

"I just feel like it is happening so quickly."

"Well then it is best we be on our toes tomorrow. Elder Saden has made the call, which means that ready or not, good feeling or bad, we head out in the morning. In the end it doesn't matter what we feel about the situation does it? When we are out there tomorrow you must lead your squad in a manner you see fit. That is where your authority lays."

"You're right. Let's get some rest. Goodnight," says Rose.

"Goodnight," whispers Shawnti and she falls back to sleep.

Arriving in Bronwyn, Eva has teleported her way into Kirtaunta's lair, but she has taken a new form from the vibrant Spirit Queen Rose had witnessed. She is now dressed in black tattered rags and dawns the face of a hideous old witch.

"Kirtaunta!" she cries as she approaches the giant Minotaur staring out the landscape window.

He holds a large black scythe in his hand as he gazes into his kingdom.

"Ah, Akua, you bring good news I presume?"

"Absolutely, I would like to inform you that Elder Saden plans to deploy his troops first thing in the morning. They will travel the way of the two mountains. I think it would be wise for you to oppose their advances. Ambush them at the mountains and make them suffer!"

"Thank you for this information," says Kirtaunta with a low drawling grunt. He stomps his way over towards Akua. His massive hooves clack on the ground as he stamps.

"This is good news," he replies as he looms over the small witch. "How can you be so sure?"

Eva, or Akua, does not flinch at all. She stares right into the fiendish eyes of the inquiring Minotaur, "I have my ways. Do you doubt me Kirtaunta?"

Kirtaunta doesn't doubt her, but something inside tells him she's not sharing everything she knows.

"I will carry out the ambush and complete my mission Akua," he responds.

"Very well," she replies with a proud look of satisfaction.

Kirtaunta turns from Akua. "KAYLARK!" he roars through his chamber. His bellowing cry resounds through the fortress and Kaylark comes slithering in to his chambers.

"Yes Master," replies the evil Queen of Kabal Desert.

"You shall lead the Dark Forces in an ambush where the two mountains meet and destroy the

Light Army. Crash down upon them like a black cloud and choke the life out of them!" He clenches his fist tightly as his anger builds.

"Yes Master Kirtaunta. It would be my pleasure."

Kirtaunta turns to Kaylark. "Make sure you bring the Angel back alive," he says in a threatening manner.

"Yes master," replies Kaylark and she leaves his presence.

Kirtaunta slams his scythe into the ground and a shockwave of energy spirals down the tower and spreads through the city, drawing the attention of the dark inhabitants. The monsters stop what they're doing and glower up at Kirtaunta standing in his window. They await his every desire.

"Minions, we march tonight!" His cry echoes through the land. Frenzied demons begin to wail about, jumping around the city as they howl and scream. Grangers pound their chests like drums amplifying the intensity. Mavens slide their claws together releasing a cynical song of slicing like butchers sharpening their blades!

All the while Akua watches Kirtaunta with a plotting look of deceit on her face.

Back in Tahein, morning has come. The trumpeter steps out of his tent. Dust kicks up from under his boots and mixes with the mist of the early morning air. Elder Saden meets him in the courtyard.

"Sound the horn. Let's get this show on the road," he says. *More like send these cows to slaughter,* he thinks as he releases a chuckle.

Pressing his lips to his horn the trumpeter plays a tune, awakening all of the warriors.

The cold mountain wind blows through the headquarters as the troops arise from their beds. Rose steps out onto the yard, her armor strapped on tight, set for battle.

She lines up with her squad.

"Let's take it to them. Once we head outside of this city, expect anything. The enemy could be around any corner, awaiting us just over any hill. Be on high alert," she commands. The natural born leader takes her position and falls into the battalion.

Commander Leal stands before the army. His armor shines in the sun. His slicked mustache and five o'clock shadow suit him perfectly on this dark morning. "Light Warriors, today is the day we have prepared for. We leave the protection of these giant walls and march upon Drakkar. The enemy is located in the town of Bronwyn. They have multiple captives held prisoner there and a giant army guarding them. But they are no match for us Light Warriors. We will storm the city walls and take the town!" yells Commander Leal.

The eager rookie soldiers cry aloud and bang their light swords ferociously against their crystal shields. Those who know what they're going up against stand a bit more quietly, as the images of the beastly Dark Forces flash into their heads.

From the side, Elder Saden can be seen motioning for them to get going.

"Yes, yes. Get a move on now. We don't have all the time in the world," he says rapidly waving his arms back and forth. His fat belly bouncing as he jumps.

The giant gates of the headquarters screech as they are slowly pulled open. "Forward!" yells Commander Leal and the footsteps of the marching battalion begin to thunder throughout the city. Multiple squads, side by side, set out with the common goal of destroying the darkness.

Rose cannot believe the size of the Army of Light. Warriors as far as the eye can see. They pass under the solid stone overpass above the entrance, many for the first time. There are rotting mounds of Dark Forces decaying on both sides as they exit. Piles of the dead welcome majority of these Warriors to their first day of battle.

"The fate of Kirtaunta is the same as those who have fallen beside you!" yells Commander Leal. The Light Warriors cheer in agreement, raising their swords to the sky.

"Halt minions!" yells Kaylark, leading the Dark Forces into position where the two mountains meet. Her thin straw-like hair waves in the wind as her black robe beats in the breeze. A vision of mayhem fills her dark mesmeric eyes and a bewitching simper of ruin upon her senescent face.

The vast Dark Army of demons spread across the land like a smothering blanket of darkness. Murderous Mavens flail their claws in preparation to skewer the Light Warriors. Hordes of Hunters rally in packs scattered throughout the area. They spring and charge about stirring up excitement. Gigantic Grangers stomp their way through the terrain, and a gang of slow treading Goyles skulk up the rear.

With the hatred of the light fueling their desire for blood, the Dark Forces come to a stop in their destination.

"We will await the Light Warriors here," yells Kaylark from the top of the mountain.

Thousands of years ago a river had carved a division in between the giant mountain, splitting it into two separate mountains. *The perfect place for an ambush,* thinks Kaylark.

Mavens and Hunters migrate to the entrance of the path and hide along the ridge. They gnash their teeth and scratch at the ground to ease their ravenous desire for death. Grangers and Goyles hide near the exit of the division, waiting to devour them in a monstrous onslaught of power. The Dark Forces plan to trap the Light Warriors inside this crucible of death, surround them on all sides, and snuff out the Light Army forever!

23) <u>Chaotic Conditions</u>

$\mathcal{T}$he feet of the stomping warriors resemble the sound of a thousand brave horses galloping through Tahein. The rocks quake and lakes ripple as the tremendous Army of Light travels the land.

Determined, the warriors march. Their eyes scan their surroundings as they press forward like hungry lions seeking prey.

Rose observes the focused warriors dispositions. *No signs of fear or hesitation*, she thinks. *Are they really this confident, or have they no idea of the murderous beasts that await them?*

Nevertheless, the soldiers continue to cover the land like a wave of elephants driving their way to their destination. The Light Army trudges on until the two mountains are in sight.

"We march forward, through the opening between the mountains," yells Commander Leal.

Immediately Rose receives an intuitive blast to her heart. Something is wrong. *This does not feel like a good idea*, she thinks, as a surge of adrenaline fills her body. Rose breaks rank and runs up to Commander Leal.

"Sir, I don't feel like we should march through that route before we investigate it," says Rose.

"Girl, it's already been investigated. Get back in line with your squad. We're marching through and we don't have any time to waste."

"Sir, but my heart-"

"I don't care what your heart is telling you!" Commander Leal yells into Roses face. His eyes are pitch black and filled with tormented spirits. The demonized eyes remind Rose of someone she has seen before.

Kaylark, she thinks as she recalls the evil witch from her past.

"Get back in line!" he yells again, but Rose knows something is definitely going on. She spreads her luminous wings and flies into the air. The warriors stop in their tracks and watch in amazement as an Angel soars from their ranks. Malcore flies after her; he's not letting her go at it alone. She speeds towards the mountains to inspect the area for the safety of the army and Malcore follows close behind. As she gets high enough to see over the ridge of the mountain, she spots a woman. Her long black hair and dark robes still blowing in the wind.

Their eyes connect.

"Kaylark!" says Rose, shocked but not surprised.

Kaylark knows exactly who it is flying her way and foiling her plan.

"Attack!" she cries with a blood curdling scream as the Dark Forces expose themselves and charge towards the Light Warriors. Rose turns from the advancing hordes of demons and bolts back to the front lines of the Light Army.

"She's a traitor! A traitor!" yells Commander Leal pointing towards the incoming Angel. "She just alerted the darkness."

Rose swoops down and dropkicks Commander Leal to the ground.

"Light Warriors, I am no traitor. Your commander has been hypnotized by the evil witch who stands atop that mountain. We were being led into another ambush!" she yells to the army. Over her shoulder an immense army of demons can be seen charging down the mountain like an avalanche.

Commander Leal hisses at Rose from the ground, his pitch black eyes bulge from his head, and his skin turns pale as swollen blue veins become visible. He charges a beam of dark energy in his hand revealing to all, that he is definitely possessed. Commander Leal blasts the energy orb at Rose. She dodges it, produces a light sword, and beheads him on the spot. The army watches as his body falls to the ground before them.

"Light Warriors, the enemy approaches. The only thing that matters now is destroying the demons that descend that mountain. This is what we are here for. This is our destiny, ATTACK!"

The Light Warriors follow Rose's lead and engage the enemy. Dashing Rangers run to occupy the fortifying rocks to the east and west and begin to unleash light beam blasts. Kinetics press to the front lines of the battalion and mentally catch the beam blasts coming from the stampeding enemies, repelling them back into the charging monsters. Waves upon waves of demons fall to the ground as the beams rip through their legs and torsos. Grangers hurl gigantic boulders from atop the mountain that come crashing down like meteorites into the crowd of Light Warriors. Distracted units are crushed instantly.

Rose meets up with Shawnti and the rest of her squad. "If we work together we stand a better chance," she advices. "We must watch each other's backs when close combat ensues. Do you all understand?"

"Yes," the squad replies.

Rose peers into the battlefield. Psychotic Mavens drag their claws along the dirt, kicking up dust clouds as they sprint closer to the battalion. Jaw snapping Hunters rush right alongside them. The lurking Goyles slowly creep from behind. Massive Grangers are scattered about, drudging through waves of demons as the Dark Forces advance from both mountains and pour out from the channel in between.

"Alright, let's go. Charge!" commands Rose thrusting her sword towards the advancing enemies.

The stampeding armies collide like wild bulls, smashing and crashing into each other as they attack. Sizzling of swords against claws and clanging from shields and armor boom through the battlefield. Rose and her squad form a circle. They orbit around one another, slicing and blasting beams, destroying all dark beings that penetrate the perimeter.

Noah and Ethan stand back to back, sidestepping and slashing at advancing Hunters. Ethan trips over the leg of novice Noah who is bewildered like a deer in headlights and fumbling about. Malcore picks Ethan up off the ground as a clawed foot comes slamming down where his head just was.

Malcore deploys his sword and trades attacks with the challenging Maven while innocent Noah continues to watch and shake in his boots.

"Get with it man!" yells Malcore. He has his light sword drawn above his head and is wrestling with the giant claws bearing down on him.

Ethan backs him up and slices through the abdomen of the monster and then turns to the startled young man, "Listen Noah, if you don't snap out of it, you're dead."

Noah crinkles his nose and grunts. "Alright, I can do this!" he yells out. He doesn't really have a choice anymore as a Maven launches at him and tackles Noah to the ground. The trembling boy comes face to face with death as the monster attempts to impale Noah with its sword-like claws. The Maven continuously stabs at the ground like a frantic fisherman trying to spear some dinner.

Noah quickly snaps into survival mode and rolls around on the ground, avoiding the striking claws. He kicks his legs and sweeps the feet of the Maven out from under it and the demon falls to the ground. Noah teleports up, but not out of harm's way, and the rising demon throws himself on Noah. Noah holds back the Maven with one arm and with his free arm he blasts a serious shot that explodes the demons head, covering virgin Noah in his first bloodbath.

Noah pushes the heavy, limp, and headless body of the Maven off of him and tries to breathe.

"That'a boy Noah, let's keep it up!" yells Ethan, and the squad continues to fight on.

Flashes zip throughout the mass of Dark Forces, slashing apart the oblivious enemies as they translocate about the battlefield.

Mavens climb upon each other's shoulders and launch into clusters of unsuspecting Light Warriors. The demons drive their claws into the young men and women, pinning them to the ground and then shredding them to pieces.

Healers rush around to anyone they can possibly help while trying to stay alive themselves. Blood flows from pockets of devastation scattered around the battleground. Screams fill the ears of the inexperienced warriors, and a wave of fear spreads throughout the land that strikes dread into the hearts of the frightened Light Army.

The vicious demons can smell the cowardly scent waft through the air. They shriek aloud and roar in excitement – hungry for more!

Rose can sense the weakening morale spreading through the army. She must oppose the fright before the Dark Forces capitalize. Rose calls to Malcore, "Let's beat back the demons," she yells as she charges light beams in both her hands and spreads her majestic wings. Malcore gets the drift.

"Fly with me," she yells as she jumps up into the air and soars over the army. "Kinetics engage aerial assault!" she screams as she races through the ranks and a flock of Kinetics begin to rise from the battleground and join Rose in the air.

The airborne warriors hover high into the sky and dive bomb into the multitude of enemies like a swarm of attacking bees. Slashing and blasting as they descend, the warriors split the titanic mass of demons in half, right down the middle. Heads roll and limbs fly as Ethan drops from the sky with his light sword extended, mowing down numerous demons, slicing them in pieces as he rips his sword down the aisle.

Malcore produces dual swords and picks up an extreme amount of speed and drills into a pack of Hunters, mincing them like a meat grinder. Blood spurts all around as he spins like a cyclone.

Rose hovers above the Light Warriors in full angelic beauty and shouts, "Light Power!" with her sword raised high. A surge of power flows from her being and penetrates the hearts of the Light Family, raising their spirits and empowering them to battle on. They shout back to their leader, encouraged and exhilarated, and continue to fight.

Kaylark watches the battle from the top of the mountain as the Light Warriors push back the darkness. Enraged she calls in an aerial assault of her own. The Grangers uproot trees and heave them amongst a pack of Light Warriors, chopping them down as the trees steamroll the troops. They continue to pitch the trees like arrows flying through the sky; they slam into the ground demolishing anything in their way. Horrific cries can be heard as soldiers are smashed to bits. Blood spews like a fountain from the dreadful carnage, but the Light

Warriors don't give up. They hack and slash their way through the Dark Forces.

Gai gets knocked to the ground and a Hunter leans over him with his gaping jaw wide open - looking to devour him. Gai crawls backward on his hands, trying to escape. Saliva drips down the jagged teeth of the ravenous Hunter as his eyes lock onto Gai. He wants to wolf him down so bad he can taste him. The Hunter snaps towards him, and Gai just barely gets off a canon blast of light energy and explodes the head of the Hunter. Blood and guts splatter all over the surrounding Warriors to their dismay.

Zia trades slashes with a pack of Red Mavens. She raises her shield in defense and blocks a devastating slash. She then deflects another strike with her sword and pushes back a few of the crazed Mavens, but more press in. The swarm surrounds her and bears down upon Zia. She spots a dead demon on the ground and picks him up by the legs. Zia twirls around the demon, knocking back the suffocating monsters. The colossal claws extend from the dead Maven and carve away portions of the monsters; ripping off faces, decapitating limbs, and slicing demons clear in half as she spins!

On the other end of the battlefield, a giant Granger stands before Jacob and Mira looking for a fight.

"You up for this Mira?" asks Jacob.

"You better believe it," responds Mira as she poises herself for battle.

Jacob runs and jumps off of Mira's shield, launching him into the air like a falcon. He sprays a barrage of beam blasts as he soars towards the brawny beast. The Granger blocks the light orbs with the giant armor plating of his forearms and Jacob follows up with a dropkick. He pushes the sturdy Granger back a step, hardly enough to phase the mammoth monster. The Granger then swings his huge fist, Jacob jumps out of the way, and the Grangers high-powered fist slams right into the ground, causing a tremendous earthquake that smashes apart the earth!

The shockwave throws Jacob and causes Mira to stumble. The beast comes charging for her, but Jacob and Mira recover and slow him down by shooting a flurry of beam blasts. The Granger throws up his arms to block the light beams and continues to press forward through the bombardment.

Mira breaks away and slashes the Granger in the leg, dropping him to his knees. Swinging around to his backside, she follows up with a nasty strike ripping through the Grangers back. The gash causes the Granger to cry aloud and become infuriated. He pummels the ground as he attempts to crush Mira and Jacob like two little bugs, but they are too quick. They dodge his rapid punches and Mira slashes the other leg, grounding the Granger.

Jacob stands over the beast and hacks away at his shoulders, but the Grangers skin is so thick it takes multiple strikes to tear through. The Granger throws a backhand punch and swats the pesky pest away, flinging Jacob into a giant boulder headfirst. Dragging himself with his overgrown arms the monster crawls after Jacob who is dazed after the intense collision.

Mira attempts to deter the Granger, but with a giant roar, he swipes her away too. Ethan and Shane spot the stalking beast closing in on Jacob. They jump on the back of the Granger and slash away at him, but the monster is not slowed down. He raises his fist and Ethan slashes the face of the beast, but nothing is stopping him. He cocks back and unloads a devastating punch that splatters Jacob into the boulder and shatters the rock to pebbles. Horrified, Ethan and Shane continue to attack the Granger until he collapses on the ground and dies.

Sweat drips from Roses face. *What an intense battle*, she thinks as she observes the chaos. The numbers dwindle as each army suffers great losses. The Light Army fights with such passion, attempting to rid the world of the evil darkness. The Dark Forces go berserk as the rampage continues, neither side letting up. They will fight until the end, for this is what they were made for. Destiny unfolds in this ominous war zone.

An agitated Maven slashes at Rose, interrupting her deep thoughts, she blocks the attack with her crystal shield and jabs her sword into the demons gut. He screams in pain as his intestines slop onto the ground. In the distance Rose can see Shawnti engaged in combat with a pack of Hunters. Blood, sweat, and dirt paint the face of this incredible warrior. Hacking away at the demons with the fierceness of a tiger etched into her eyes. Hand over hand she combines shield strikes with sword slashes, knocking the Hunters out cold and delivering them into hell where they belong.

The Light Army fights their way to the base of the mountain. Kaylark has seen enough. Waving her hand over her head, she signals for another aerial strike. A black cloud of Akumies emerge from behind the mountain. The merely one hundred soldiers left of the Light Army cannot compete with the one hundred plus grounded demons and the now emerging multitude of Akumies. Out in the open they don't stand a chance.

Overwhelmed, Rose yells for everyone to, "Move into the channel between the two mountains," hoping the cover will provide an advantage.

The Light Warriors run backward into the passage, blasting light beams as they back pedal. Trying to obstruct the approaching demons and survive as long as they can.

Darkness falls in the waterway as the Akumies fly overhead and blot out the sun. They dive from the sky and rocket through the passage. At extreme speeds, they pick off Light Warriors left and right, impaling them with their piercing beaks. The warriors fight with everything they have left, dodging and attacking, but the darkness is bearing down and overpowering the light.

The Hunters, Red Mavens, and Grangers push in from the entrance and the Akumies attempt to skewer the soldiers from all angles. The intensity builds as Rose watches her comrades being preyed upon like fish in a barrel. Everyone is shooting light orbs as they fight for their lives.

Panicked cries begin to echo off of the mountain walls.

"We don't stand a chance," yells Shane

"If we run, we're goners. If we stay, we're dead too," yells Ethan.

Hope is being strangled from the trapped Light Warriors. Rose becomes extremely frustrated. Anger builds inside of her as she fumes with rage. She trembles with fury as power surges through her body. The vision of her fallen comrades fuels the ferociousness waiting to erupt inside her. She charges powerful light beams in both of her hands. Quaking and gritting her teeth, she seethes with emotion as the beams continue to expand. She faces the over-packed opening of the channel. Monsters topple over one another. They leer and snarl as they target the pinned down warriors. They can smell death and crave it with every bit of their hate filled souls.

Rose raises her hands above her head, and thrusts them forward, detonating an incredible explosion of light. The Dark Forces are disintegrated by the heat of this immense beam. Her teammates fall to the ground and shield themselves from the blinding light expelling from the stunning shower of energy. Rose directs the beam upward and then discharges it into the sky, annihilating majority of the ground troops and a huge portion of Akumies with the devastating attack. She then collapses to the ground, depleted of all energy, hoping she has given her squad a fighting chance.

Kaylark descends from the mountain peak, quite impressed with Rose's display of dexterity. *Maybe that's why Kirtaunta is so interested in this little twit*, she thinks as she lands in front of the remaining group of Light Warriors. "You've all fought well indeed, I applaud the effort," says

Kaylark with an evil grin upon her face. "I ask you all to surrender peacefully and be our welcomed guests in Bronwyn, or die where you stand! The choice is yours."

The Light Warriors prepare themselves to finish out the war. Clenching their fists and cocking back their arms they show no signs of surrender. Noah teleports and attempts to sneak attack Kaylark. She blocks multiple punches and responds by driving her dagger-like fingernails into Noah's neck. The rest of the squad stands frozen as he hangs from her nails like a stuck pig. Choking on his own blood, he gurgles and coughs, attempting to stay alive.

"I will ask once more, surrender or die," says Kaylark as she throws Noah's body to the ground. He crashes down face first like a ragdoll.

Shawnti looks down at Rose collapsed on the ground. She glances at her tired and weary squad and then turns to Kaylark and admits defeat. She falls to her knees and surrenders.

"Wise choice," responds Kaylark.

She shoots dark energy restraints that wrap around the Light Warriors, constricting them from movement and draining all of their power. "Seize them!" she yells. Akumies fly down methodically, snatch them up in their threatening talons, and carry the warriors away.

Kaylark picks up Rose; her body limp in her arms, "I'll make sure you get to Kirtaunta myself," she says with a chilling grin that reveals her sharpened teeth, and then she slithers away into the shadows.

24) <u>Violent History</u>

Slowly awakening, Rose opens her eyes. She can only make out a blurred figure as she regains consciousness. Her weakened eyes begin to focus and she can see a girl on the other side of the dark room. She has jet black hair and sickly pale skin. The girl sits in the corner with her eyes closed, tightly hugging her knees.

Rose stands up and examines the dungeon she has just mysteriously woken up in. She's entrapped in a smothering stone cube with no windows or doors. No way in, and no way out. Mild heat can be felt rising from the rocky ground. Light seems to seep in through the cracks in the walls. Barely enough bleeds in to illuminate the dimly lit dungeon.

Rose calls out to the morbid youth huddled in the corner, "Hey, where are we?" but she does not

293

respond. The ghoulish girl just sits still in complete silence.

Rose decides to relax and listen to her heart. *This place is not normal... What happened to my friends... my uncle?* She sits for a short time and allows all her thoughts to wash away. Opening her eyes, she examines the girl. *Is she alive? I wonder how long she has been in here.* Rose calls out to her again, and once more, she remains mute and motionless.

Rose slowly gets on her feet and explores the stone walls. Dragging her fingertips along the rough and jagged blocks, she searches for any sign of a door or even a crevice to dig at.

Squinting, she peers into the pinhole's that release light into the cell, but the source cannot be seen. Rose turns from the empty walls and again studies the youth. "Enough of this," she says as she tiptoes towards her.

Her heart races as she slowly approaches. Inching closer, she can see scars along the girl's arms and legs; thick, time worn wounds. *Possibly from some accident before she was trapped in here,* she thinks. Nervously, Rose stands over her breathless body. She reaches out and shakes the frail frame of the girl.

"Hello, are you okay?" Her body quickly jerks and uncurls as the girl falls limp to the ground.

Rose jumps back and shrieks. Her blood soaked clothes resemble Rose's and her... her face too. Rose's eyes open wide in surprise. *She looks just like me when I was younger,* she thinks.

"Who are you?" she screams.

The girl begins to gurgle and convulse on the ground. Rose continues to back away as she twitches and rattles, flailing her arms about and spewing a disgusting black sludge from her mouth. Choking and coughing, the girl repeatedly bashes her head against the stone blocks.

"What is wrong with you?!" yells Rose at the extremely disturbing sight.

Instantly, the girl freezes and then snaps open her eyes. She turns her head to Rose with a devilish stare, "What is wrong with me?" she says with a deep, crackling scream. "You are what is wrong. You never cared for me. You let them torture me, taunt and abuse me! You could have stood up for us. But you were too much of a coward, like always!"

The demon child tries to get up. She shifts awkwardly with rigid and aggressive movements, like an evil puppet. "I am the sum of the afflictions, which you have allowed!" she screams as she targets Rose.

Stumbling backwards, Rose crashes up against the stone wall, stunned by the sight of her tormented inner child.

"You couldn't save us, just like you couldn't save your friends. You were too weak!" yells the demon spawn.

Rose's heart breaks inside of her as the ghoul picks at her deepest darkest wounds. Lurching up to Rose, she continues the verbal assault.

"You were always too scared!" she viciously screams in Rose's face. Rose flinches as the intimidating demon tries to break her spirit. "No wonder why everyone hated you!"

Confused, Rose submits to the abuse. Part of her feels guilty and ashamed of her past, but the other half feels that she did all she could. The mocking from the demon girl twists and manipulates her mind.

The ghoul turns her back on Rose and walks away. "But then again, no one really wanted you around in the first place."

"What did you just say?" angrily responds Rose

"I said no one ever wanted you!" she yells as she lunges toward Rose.

Rose throws up her feet and kicks the ghoul away. She springs up and runs at her and launches a powerful kick across her face.

"It was not all my fault!" she yells as blood spurts from the demons mouth. "I didn't know any better!" yells Rose as she forcefully stomps the chest of the ghoul who cries aloud from the attack.

Peering up at Rose from the ground, the ghoul laughs psychotically. "Real tough beating up a child," she yells.

Rose fumes with anger from the insult. She thrusts another kick but the ghoul catches her leg and pulls her to the ground.

She rolls on top of Rose and shrieks excruciatingly loud in her face. Rose attempts to charge a light beam, but only sparks zap out; she has no energy left. The demon girl tries to claw at Rose's eyes, but she blocks the attack with her arms. The ghoul's claws slice into her arms and she rips her nails down to her elbows. Rose cries out from the pain.

"C'mon, you can do better! You're not really that pathetic, are you?" yells the demon as she begins to pummel Rose.

Punch after punch pounds on her face, the ghoul seethes viciously as she attacks her. Rose reaches up and grabs the demons hair and pulls her down into her body. She rifles a heavy right hook and knocks the ghoul off of her, sending her flying up against the wall. Rose leaps up and dashes over to her. Grabbing a fist full of hair, she violently smashes the ghouls face into the wall repeatedly. Tears run down Rose's face as she cave's in her skull and kills the demon.

Rose drops down to her knees and cries hysterically. The poor girl just revisited the horrible pain of her youth, but she has no time to sulk. The dungeon begins to quake. Dust and pebbles fall to the ground as a slate door opens. Rose covers her eyes as a blinding light fills the room. From the doorway emerges a woman dressed in black robes. The heavy door slams shut behind her.

The woman runs over to Rose bloody and beat up in the corner. "Are you okay my Rosy?" says the woman as she falls to Rose's side and tends to her cuts. Rose looks up at the beautiful woman.

"Mother!" she yells. Overwhelmed and shocked, Rose can't believe her eyes.

"Yes, my angel," says Jan. They warmly embrace each other. A moment Rose has waited years for.

A whirlwind of emotions engulfs Rose. Sadness, hate, guilt, and relief come from the terrifying experience she has just survived. Love, safety, and confusion come from the precious reunion of mother and daughter.

"Oh my Rosy, I've missed you so much. Have you missed me?" asks Jan.

"Of course I have. I have thought about you so much!"

"Good, well mommy's here to stay, no one is going to take you from me again."

Rose smiles and enjoys the comfort of her mother's hug. "How did you get here? Where are we?" asks Rose.

"Oh that doesn't matter. The only thing that matters is that we are together Rosy."

That manipulative tone reminds Rose of her mother's dark side and stirs suspicion.

"I was always good to you right honey?" asks Jan.

Rose pauses. *Is my mother delusional, or does she not remember all the neglect and abuse she made me suffer through?* she thinks.

"Right, Rose?" Jan asks again with a subtly aggressive tone.

Again Rose pauses. The poor girl is being torn between easing the tension between her and her mother, and being true to herself. For years Rose catered to her mother, passively accepting her mother's emotional outbursts. It was the only way she knew how to survive. But Rose is not her little girl anymore, and she won't be stepped on.

Astonished by Rose's silence, Jan pushes her away. "I have done so much for you. I had to put my life on hold and raise you. How can you treat me this way?" Jan places the blame on Rose just like she always has. She's too weak to admit the truth to herself.

Rose stands to her feet. She's not going to lay down this time. "You never loved me. You only cared about yourself!" she yells.

"How could you say that? I did everything I could," replies Jan

"You're a liar. You ignored me most of the time and constantly belittled me."

"You were too stupid and lazy!" screams Jan as her face turns red. "You couldn't do anything yourself!"

"I was a child," says Rose, defending herself.

"You were a mistake! I wish you had never been born!"

Jan's cry resounds in the cell.

Rose's heart shatters into a hundred pieces from the harsh comment. Struck by the hurt from the one person who should love her, tears well up, but Rose won't let them fall. She's not worth it.

"Aw, I'm sorry honey. You know how mommy gets sometimes. I didn't mean that. You forgive mommy don't you?" says Jan, her tone growing increasingly manipulative.

Rose just stares into her mother's eyes. The woman who she loved as a child is now completely lost in darkness. Hate fills her, and she *allows* it. All of the evil, death, and despair she has experienced lately has taken its toll. A shard of darkness enters her soul and invigorates the anger within.

"I hate you!" she screams at the top of her lungs.

Jan is outraged by the disrespect. "How dare you talk to me like that? I'm your mother, you respect me."

"You are not my mother," cries Rose. The darkness is taking root inside her aching heart. Rose stands her ground. She moves aggressively towards Jan and yells, "I hope you suffered every day from the pain and regret of your choices. I pray it haunts you forever!"

Jan is overcome with fury. Her eyes turn red and she morphs into a demonic monster. Her face becomes gray and wrinkled, ravaged by years of self-loathing. She lunges at Rose and pins her up against the wall by her neck.

"Who do you think you are?" she screams in a devilish voice, as she strangles Rose. "Listen to me. I know what you are made of. You are my daughter." Jan gazes into Rose's eyes and attempts to demonize her. "Feel the anger and hate pulsing through your body. Don't resist it."

Rose is becoming entranced by the glowing eyes of her mother. Darkness starts to spread through her being. The temptation is too much to deny. The cell of devastation she is trapped in has left Rose susceptible to the lure of evil.

As the dark energy fuses with her body, the demonic power amplifies her strength. She grabs her mother's hand from around her neck, and forces it back, snapping it at the wrist. Jan cries out in agony as her bones crack and she drops to the ground. Seems her plan to control Rose has failed.

Rose slowly pursues her mother as she tries to crawl away like the coward she is.

"No, don't! You're meant to be one of us!" says Jan.

Rose produces a violet energy sword. The blue light energy that once fueled her is mixed with the dark energy that is now pulsating through her and infecting her being. "I will never be like you!" she yells, and drives the sword into her mother's heart. She stares into her mother's face as she passes away and doesn't flinch once at the shocking sight.

Rose finally has a moment to settle. She breathes deep and looks around the murder scene. The dead ghoul and her mother lay slain. She's soaked in blood and intensely stimulated. She attempts to calm herself, but she can feel the dark energy flowing through her being.

How did this all get so crazy? she thinks as she continues to breathe deep, *I did what I had to do...*

Rose can feel the pull of the darkness trying to arouse anger and hate in her soul, but she chooses to relax and cope with the impulses. *I have to regain balance and composure. I won't let this darkness dominate me.*

The haunting whispers of the darkness continue to irritate her mind. They won't let up so easily.

"She was your mother. You caused all of this!" the lingering voices mock her.

Her heartbeat increases and she becomes agitated. The inner battle mentally strains Rose and she drops down to her knees and prays. "Great Spirit, please take this burden from me. Soothe the demons tormenting my mind. Give me the strength to overcome."

Rose gets up from her knees, *Alright. I can't let these negative thoughts fester. I have to get moving.*

She examines the entryway where her mother came in and it is completely solid stone. She will have to break through somehow.

Rose hacks away at the wall with her energy sword, and continuously blasts at the wall with energy beams. Slowly, she chips away at the stones. Chunks break away and more light fills the room. Excited, Rose hastens her pace. Firing beams with both hands, she blasts a hole big enough to crawl through. She squeezes through the small opening and finds herself at the bottom of a massive tower.

25) <u>Final Ascension</u>

*R*ose stares ahead at a narrow winding staircase that leads up into the obsidian tower; it seems to go on forever. With nowhere else to go, Rose scales the immense flight of steps. Round and round she goes, climbing higher and higher, step by step. Driven by the desire to find out where she is, and who awaits her at the top.

      For the first time in a while Rose feels free. She can finally make her own decisions. Liberated from other people's opinions, she knows who she is, what she is capable of, and no one is going to stand in her way.

      She spots a platform up above and pushes herself to go faster. Driving her legs, she races up the steps. *Let's go, you can do this. Move it.* She's found a new confidence in herself and is more motivated than ever. Conquering the demons of her past has allowed her to hurdle the barriers that stood in her way. Feeling her true potential, Rose believes in the woman she is more than ever.

She rounds the staircase and arrives at the platform. Rose spots a doorway that is blocked by a Dark energy force field. She approaches the entrance and checks inside. To her surprise, bound in Dark energy restraints is her uncle Layne and multiple Light Warriors. They hang unconscious, drained of all their energy, confined like captive animals.

She fires a couple of shots at the force field, but the solid wall of energy is impenetrable. She yells to the prisoners, but no one responds. Rose has no choice but to continue up the spiraling stairs. She looks up into the heights of the tower. *Maybe I can find some answers up there,* she thinks as she darts up the steps.

At the top of the staircase, she arrives at a big room with a massive throne in the middle. She circles the giant oval shaped room and comes to the front of the throne.

"I have been awaiting you," says a monstrous Minotaur seated in the chair. His deep, dark voice sends chills down her spine. "I am Kirtaunta, Ruler of the Dark Forces."

The mammoth beast towers over Rose. His tremendous horns stretch a daunting two feet each. Kirtaunta rises from his throne. His gigantic seven-foot frame stands erect. His huge hooves hammer the ground as he makes his way to the enormous opening that overlooks his kingdom.

"Ever since I can remember, the so called light, has been trying to rid the universe of the darkness. But I tell you Rose, you cannot have light without darkness. From the beginning of history, the light has failed to rid the world of darkness. Yet still, they attempt to foil the dark agenda. They don't see that we are one and the same, just different extremes. I tell you, murdering and stealing is just a means of surviving. Anyone is capable if pushed far enough. It's the nature of the beast, really."

Kirtaunta backs away from the window and takes a few steps towards Rose, "Those of the light are always looking to tame the beast inside, while I'm merely looking to set the animal free."

"You're looking to enslave us and make us into hate filled monsters like yourself," replies Rose.

"I am a product of evolution, you see. We are just on opposite ends of the scale. You chose to work through the damage, where as I chose to use it to my advantage."

"You're deranged!"

Kirtaunta laughs and looks over at the enthusiastic girl. "I'm thrilled to finally meet you Rose. I have been told that you have quite the fire inside of you. We could really use an Angel like you on our side. I can see the darkness is already flowing through your veins."

"I will never surrender to the darkness inside of me," she yells, glaring into the vile bullish face of the demon. His pointed ears hang below his piercing horns and sharp teeth show through his angry scowl.

"You say it as if it was such a bad thing, Rose. Do you know what kind of power you would possess? I know you can feel a bit of it enticing you now, exciting the passion within. You would be unstoppable," says Kirtaunta as he slowly paces around her.

"What the darkness has done to our world is nothing I want to be a part of. You have destroyed countless families and ruined our society. You are the reason for all the pain and hurt in the world."

Rose watches Kirtaunta closely as he circles. He rubs his hand along his chin, and opens his hands like he has nothing to hide.

"Am I?" he questions Rose. "I cannot force anyone to do anything. The humans make choices all on their own. They wake up every day and have the power to do right or wrong. It's not my fault that so many of your kind choose to do wrong, Rose. The darkness merely capitalizes on your faults, and then evolution does the rest. The same spirit that flows through you is also in me, but you Light Warriors want to separate yourselves from that truth and label us your enemies."

Rose shakes her head in frustration, "We have different intents. I want unity and love between people."

"Maybe you do dear, but take my word on this, as ruler of the darkness; I know that not all of those in the light care for the world as you do. I tell you Rose, you are caught in a losing battle. You are being misled by the light. No matter how hard humans try they can never annihilate their primal nature, and that will always lead to the infiltration of darkness."

"That's not true. I will weed out the phonies after I'm done here. Now release my friends!" says Rose raising her fists to Kirtaunta angrily. Kirtaunta throws his hands up and shakes them about, not taking Rose's threat seriously.

"Okay, I understand your reasoning, but we have quite the predicament. One, the Light Warriors want to destroy me. Two, they are my hostages. If I let them go, then what leverage will I have?"

"Leverage for what?" asks Rose.

"Well, you can join the Dark Forces and let the darkness that resides inside you magnify your soul, or I can kill the Light Warriors trapped inside my dungeon. You see, the choice is all yours, Rose. Will they live or will they die? It all depends on your decision."

Rose grits her teeth and clenches her fists. She looks like she's getting ready for a fight.

"Are you sure that is what you want to do?" asks Kirtaunta. He powerfully slams his hooves down, shaking the whole tower.

Rose blasts two energy beams at Kirtaunta. Spreading her wings she takes flight. Kirtaunta quickly blocks the energy beams with the thick armor like skin on his forearms. Rose comes darting at him, and he smacks her away like a tiny fly. She soars through the air and slams up against the wall.

"You don't know that you should fear me yet, do you? You are quite confident, I can see that Rose. But I think it would be wise for you to fear me," threatens Kirtaunta. He stands across the room relaxed. He raises his arms to his waist and stands high and mighty, confident in his immense power.

"I have heard all kinds of rumors of the Angel girl who escaped from Kaylark's dungeon and slaughtered multitudes of my minions. But Rose, I'm not impressed. I suggest you submit to the darkness and rule the world with me. I will give you true power and authority. You will lead my armies in taking over the rest of Octairion. How does that sound?"

"I'd rather die!" responds Rose, still slumped against the wall.

"So be it!" says Kirtaunta. His eyes glow an intense red and he lowers his horns. Targeting Rose, he blows smoke from his nostrils and charges. The massive Minotaur fiercely stampedes towards her. Rose attempts to dodge the attack but Kirtaunta is too quick. He side-steps and collides with her, crashing Rose into the wall. He picks Rose up and slams her into the ground, pinning her down.

"We can do this the hard way, or the easy way," says Kirtaunta.

He presses all his weight down on top of Rose in an attempt to dominate her. She cries out in pain from the severe pressure bearing down on her.

"I will never surrender!" yells Rose. She spreads her wings and tries to propel Kirtaunta off of her, but her attempt fails. Kirtaunta's colossal bulk does not budge. Rose tries to flutter about and escape his clutches, but he pins her down with even more force.

"Give it up! You are not strong enough to overpower me Rose. Save your strength and submit!" He places his huge hand upon Rose's head and rams it into the ground, pressing her face into the stones. "I will squash you like a bug!" he screams.

Rose is struggling under the weight of the compression. She cries out in distress and Kirtaunta lets go.

"Now, it doesn't have to be this way. You are fighting a lost cause," says Kirtaunta. He gets up off of Rose and walks back towards his throne. "What do you say?"

Rose knows there is no way she can beat Kirtaunta in combat alone. "Alright, I agree," she answers. Extremely distraught with her head down to the ground, "I'll submit," she utters.

"Wise," says Kirtaunta.

"But I want to see my uncle first," demands Rose.

"Of course you do." He lets out a bellowing roar, "Kaylark!" he yells, summoning her to his chambers.

The evil witch creeps in traveling amongst the shadows. "Yes Master?" she replies.

Kirtaunta places his hand on a group of levers in the corner of the room. "Retrieve Commander Layne," he commands and he releases the levers, disabling the force field.

"Yes Master!" answers Kaylark, and she slithers away to get Commander Layne.

Kirtaunta begins to pace around the room. "You see Rose, you will become more powerful than you could have ever imagined. At my side, we will be truly unstoppable." He extends his hand and points to his throne, "Come have a seat."

Rose gets up and slowly makes her way to his throne. She takes a seat.

"It's got a good feel doesn't it?" asks Kirtaunta.

"Don't think I'm happy about this. I'm only doing what is necessary to save the ones I love," replies Rose.

"Indeed you are. How honorable of you, it truly is a win-win situation. You may see the darkness as a bad thing, but I promise you, when you feel the power pulsing through your being, you will know you made the right choice."

Kaylark returns with commander Layne. He's bound with Dark energy restraints, depleted of all light energy, and badly beaten.

Rose and Commander Layne lock eyes. She jumps up from the throne and runs to her uncle, but Kaylark steps in her way and attempts to block her path.

"Stay back!" yells Kaylark with her arms stretched out.

Kirtaunta interrupts, "Now, now, Kaylark let them share one last moment. After all, Rose is our family now." Kirtaunta kneels down and watches as Rose and Layne hold one another.

"If I don't surrender, he'll kill us all uncle," says Rose with her eye's full of tears.

"Don't worry, there's not a more noble way to go out than a sacrifice to save others. May Great Spirit be proud. I know I am," says Layne. "My sweet Rose, it's amazing to see the woman you have become. You have survived all that this life has thrown at you. Knocking you down over and over again, but still you keep getting up. You surely are an inspiration, and I will never let your memory die. No one can ever put out your light."

With eyes full of tears, the two embrace each other.

"Okay, enough! Come take your place on the throne," commands Kirtaunta.

Rose lets go of her uncle and faces her destiny. She walks to the throne, having done all she could. Her moment of truth has come, for there is no greater love than to lay down your life for another. She will surrender her will to the darkness.

Kaylark approaches Rose seated in the throne. "Gaze deeply into my eyes," she says as the demons in her pupils begin to swirl. The horrifying faces of the trapped souls spin at mesmerizing speed and Rose falls under her control. As Rose stares into her eyes, darkness is being transferred into her soul. It starts to devour her precious heart and taint her.

Rose twitches as the darkness spreads.

"Don't fight it, let it consume you. Think of the power you will possess," says Kirtaunta, proudly watching as Rose is contaminated by the evil flowing into her soul.

Commander Layne is burning on the inside while he watches his dear niece be converted into a monster right in front of his eyes. His blood boils as the very darkness he has fought against his whole life is taking away the most precious gift he has ever been blessed with. He shudders as fierce emotions rage within.

Kirtaunta looks on, his eyes widen as thoughts of power, destruction, and death, ravage his brain. *Oh the mayhem that she will cause. The lights only hope now lost*, he thinks.

Rose is now heavily entranced, she looks like a zombie as she becomes lost in Kaylark's eyes. Dark energy is alive and surging through her system, increasing the power in every cell of her body, and mutating her into an unstoppable demon.

After a few moments she is almost fully demonized, merely a flicker of light remains, and then she will be evil forevermore.

Kirtaunta stands in front of his giant window, "We shall reign until the end of time!" he announces to the city of demons, and then turns back to Rose. "I'm glad you brought your uncle up here, he will be the first death of your massacre!"

Kirtaunta's devastating words crash upon Layne's ears, and he is pushed over the edge. Anger swells inside of him and he pulls at the restraints around his hands with all the power he can muster.

Silently, Akua appears in the room, but no one can see her! She walks over to Layne struggling in his restraints and assists him in breaking free! What is she up to? Is she for the light or for the darkness?

Screaming, Layne pulls apart his restraints with the help of Akua and then she vanishes from the room unseen!

Layne rushes at Kaylark and tackles her onto the ground, breaking up the hypnosis!

"No!" yells Kirtaunta and he strikes Layne with a beam blast that burns into his abdomen. Kirtaunta runs up and smashes Layne with a powerful backhand that knocks him across the room.

Rose arises from the throne, purple flames blaze in her eyes! Immense power erupts from inside her. She picks up Kaylark by her throat and snaps her neck like a twig. She tosses her body through the air and annihilates her with several powerful beam blasts.

Kirtaunta and Rose face one another. Glaring eyes connect from across the chamber. Kirtaunta beats his chest and roars to display his power, but Rose is unfazed. She remains silent in the standoff.

"I tried so hard to be your ally, but now I am going to enjoy murdering you. Prepare to die!" yells Kirtaunta.

Rose smirks. Clenching her fists, she prepares herself for battle.

Kirtaunta charges at Rose with lightning speed, snarling and growling as he picks up even more speed. He lowers his menacing horns and locks onto Rose. She spreads her wings and just barely dashes away from his devastating attack and flies to the opposite side of the room.

Kirtaunta skids to a halt.

"Is that all you got?" taunts Rose.

He slams his fist into the ground with rage, and charges again. Galloping ferociously he targets Rose once more. He leaps into the air and nosedives straight towards her, but he misses. Rose rolls out of the way and Kirtaunta crashes right into the tower wall. The massive obelisk quakes from the hit. Kirtaunta becomes furious.

"Surely the Ruler of Darkness is faster than that," says Rose. Kirtaunta grunts and roars as she provokes him to anger. Stomping his hooves he becomes inflamed with rage. Rose lands across the room and elegantly displays the beauty of her Angel wings. They radiate a magnificent violet. Blue and purple bolts of energy streak through her lustrous electric wings as the light and dark energy dances inside of her soul. Rose's face dawns a scowl of

313

hatred for Kirtaunta, who glowers back at her with equal hate.

Rose launches at Kirtaunta and he rushes at her. They both blitz at super speeds and collide! A shockwave blasts from the extreme power of the collision. Rose grasps onto Kirtaunta by the horns and flutters her wings while pushing against the tremendous Minotaur. Kirtaunta digs up the stone floor as he opposes her in the stalemate. Neither one is budging, screaming and growling as they fight with all their might!

Kirtaunta begins to frantically buck up and down. He gains momentum and drives Rose back, but she tilts to the side and sends Kirtaunta sailing through the air. Before he lands she zips over like lightening and delivers a devastating punch, hammering him into the ground.

Her power has grown immensely due to the dark energy flowing through her. Kirtaunta does not underestimate Rose any longer. He jumps to his feet, rockets a right hook at her, and she falls backward slamming into the ground. For all the power she has gained, she is still no match for the size and strength of Kirtaunta. Rose runs for the stairs to see if she can find reinforcements in the prison, and Kirtaunta chases after her.

Rose flies down the swirling staircase and Kirtaunta thrashes and bangs his way down behind her. The walls of the tower crack from the force of the storming Minotaur.

Rose makes her way down to the platform where the captives are held. She glances inside and a gruesome sight befalls her. Blood is splattered all over the entryway. A stream of thick red plasma pours from the dismembered bodies. All the imprisoned Light Warriors have been murdered.

Rose freezes; she is struck by the horrid scene. Gai and Malcore lay with their throats slit amongst a sea of corpses. They massacred the poor helpless prisoners, such a cold fate. When Kaylark came down to retrieve Layne, one by one she mutilated the captives.

Rose hears the ruckus of Kirtaunta barreling down the staircase. She has no time to mourn the loss of her friends. She fires a few shots to try to slow him down, but he's hell-bent on smashing her to pieces and charges right through. With nowhere to escape, she must continue downward.

Kirtaunta fiercely races down the steps like an avalanche down a mountain, bashing the walls as he goes. Rocks fall from above and shatter around Rose. The damage caused by the raging Minotaur is destroying the foundation of the tower. Kirtaunta blinded by pride and drunk on hate couldn't care less. Death is the only thing on his mind.

Rose comes to the bottom of the stairs outside of the dungeon where her dead mother's body rests. She looks up and can see the tower swaying from side to side. The fortress cannot withstand much more destruction.

The prior taunting from Rose echoes through his mind as Kirtaunta thrashes into view. Rose braces herself as Kirtaunta hones in on her like a hawk. She's pinned in the corner like helpless prey. He ferociously pounces at Rose and she launches herself into the air!

Kirtaunta rams into the foundation of the tower with extraordinary force. The powerful hit sends a tremor up the walls and they begin to collapse. Kirtaunta roars loudly in frustration. Rose's attention shifts as giant black stones plummet from the dismantling staircase. She dodges an enormous slab that thunders down onto Kirtaunta! The impact knocks him unconscious and more stones from the toppling tower follow, battering Kirtaunta, and entombing him in rubble.

Rose forgets about Kirtaunta and soars to the top chamber. She flies up to his throne room and spots her uncle Layne passed out on the ground in a puddle of blood. The tower fervently shakes under her feet and is beginning to crumble to the ground. Rose grabs her uncle and flies out of the giant window and off into the horizon, as the fortress of darkness collapses into a disastrous wreckage.

Support Beautiful Rose

Thank you for reading Beautiful Rose. Please submit a review on Amazon.com. Appreciate all feedback. Beautiful Rose: The Vanishing Veil coming soon! Visit us at Aurea-Publishing.com for future news. Thank you.